BLIND VOICES

BLIND VOICES

by
Tom Reamy

Published by
BERKLEY PUBLISHING CORPORATION

Distributed by
G.P. PUTNAM'S SONS, New York

SBN: 399-12240-0
Library of Congress Cataloging in Publication Data
Reamy, Tom.
    Blind voices.

    I. Title.
PZ4.R28755Bl   [PS3568.E25]   813'.5'4   78-3817

79-1556

BLIND VOICES

1.

It was a time of pause, a time between planting and harvest when the air was heavy, humming with its own slow, warm music. Amber fields of ripe wheat, level as skating rinks, stretched to the flat horizon and waited for the combines that crawled like painted-metal insects from Texas to the Dakotas. Dusty roads lined with telephone poles made, with ruled precision, right-angle turns at section lines separating the wheat from green fields of young maize.

Farmers stood at the edges of the fields, broke off fat heads of wheat and rolled the kernels between their fingers, squinting at the flat blue sky. The farmers' wives, finished with the dinner dishes, paused before going back into the hot kitchens to begin a long afternoon of cooking, doing it all again for supper. They sat on the front porches in the shade, trying to catch a nonexistent movement of air. They spread apart the collars of their dresses and fanned their necks with cardboard fans printed with a color picture of the bleeding heart of Jesus on one side and an advertisement for the Redwine Funeral Home on the other.

Then the farmers turned their attention from the sky to the road. Their wives stopped fanning and leaned forward in their chairs. Children paused in their chores and their play and shaded eyes with hands. They looked at each other and grinned, feeling excitement tightening in their chests like clock springs.

In that long-ago summer afternoon in southern Kansas, when the warm air lay like a weight, unmoving and stifling, six horse-drawn circus wagons moved ponderously on the dusty road.

A two-horse team pulled each wagon, their heads drooping slightly, their shod hoofs dragging a bit before lifting to take another plodding step. The six drivers dozed in the heavy dusty air, holding the reins lightly, letting the horses choose their own pace. The wagons creaked and groaned as they swayed; rattled and jolted when the wooden, iron-rimmed wheels bounced in chugholes.

The wagons were a little shabby, their once-bright paint doubly-dimmed from sun and dust. The sides of the wagons promised miracles with gilt curlicues and wonders with gingerbread flourishes. Shaking and rattling and squeaking, the wagons were a gallery of marvels, a panorama of astonishments.

The drivers reined in the horses and the line of caravans creaked to a halt when they met the black Model-T Ford arriving in a billow of dust from the opposite direction. The car pulled off the road into the shallow ditch filled with the red, yellow, orange, brown, black, and purple of Indian paintbrush, black-eyed Susan, and Russian thistle.

The man who stepped from the car was nattily dressed in a dark gray pin-striped double-breasted suit and a pearl-gray fedora. Louis Ortiz was thirty-two, handsome in a swarthy

8

way, carefully cultivating his more imagined than real resemblance to Rudolph Valentino. A smile hovered over his full lips, ready to alight, but his eyes were as cold as steel balls.

Louis looked into the glowing eyes painted on the lead wagon, and they looked back at him, fiercely, beneath a brow cleft almost in two by a widow's peak spearing down from varnished black hair. The mouth was thin and stern and uncompromising. Louis shifted his eyes to the second wagon, to the portrait painted there; the portrait of a pale and beautiful young boy, a gilt corona painted around his white curls, his white-robed arms uplifted, his face beatific and rapturous.

The smile almost alighted on his lips.

He walked to the rear of the first wagon and propped his foot on the step, wiping the dust from his black patent leather shoe with a white handkerchief. The caravan door opened and a man stepped out. He was an older version of his portrait. His hair was not so sleek nor so black, his face not so smooth nor firm, but his lips were just as uncompromising. He wore a black satin robe and carpet slippers, like some Oriental alchemist. He waved his hand petulantly before his face to clear away the floating dust and looked inquiringly at Louis.

Louis flipped the dust from his handkerchief and folded it into his breast pocket. "We're all set," he said with no trace of the Latin accent his appearance would suggest. "The posters are up with the merchants. I rented the vacant lot and got a permit from the sheriff."

He looked up at the older man, squinting in the sun, and the smile settled softly. "There's only one thing that might be a problem."

The other man raised an eyebrow.

"The movie house," Louis continued, "will be showing

9

their first talking picture tonight. It's the main topic of conversation in town."

The older man grimaced. "There's always one petty annoyance after another. It would be very pleasant if this movie palace were to burn to the ground."

"It needn't be that drastic."

"Perhaps you're right," he sighed. "The unpleasant bumpkins might blame us. This trip has been extremely wearisome. We should head back east where the towns are closer together."

Louis's mouth twitched slightly and the other man frowned. "I'm sure you will think of something, Louis. You're a very clever man."

Louis grinned and made a slight bow with his head.

"How much further to this prairie metropolis?"

"Hawley," Louis answered. "About ten miles. There's a little place two miles ahead called Miller's Corners. You can rest and water the horses there. Hawley's eight miles beyond that."

The man shrugged with massive indifference. Louis returned to the car, still smiling slightly. The man stood in the doorway of the caravan watching the car turn around to chug and rattle back the way it came. He grimaced at the fresh cloud of dust and went back inside, closing the door. The wagons began to move.

He opened a door in the partition dividing the wagon in half and stopped, leaning against the door frame. He looked for a moment at the pale, naked boy lying on the bunk, and then sat on the edge beside him. The boy looked much like his portrait, though he was older and perspiration wet his strained face. His white curls were matted and the pillow under them was damp. His eyes moved nervously behind his closed lids.

The man put his hand on the boy's stomach and leaned

10

over him. "Angel," he said softly. "My own beautiful angel." His hand moved up the boy's body until it lay lightly on his cheek. "Shall we begin again? There is still so much to do."

The boy's ruby eyes opened, but they did not focus.

2.

Hawley, Kansas, dozed under the warm Friday sun. The clock in the high tower of the white rococo courthouse chimed twice, lazily scattering sparrows which immediately settled back again. Old men sat in the courthouse square, on benches under the shade of sycamore trees, telling half-remembered or half-invented stories of better times, whittling sticks away to nothing, pontificating on the government, President Hoover, the Communists, the Anarchists, the Catholics, the Jews, the stock market, and other topics about which they knew little or nothing. They nodded solemnly and spit dark brown globs of tobacco juice on the dry ground, predicting doom in every conceivable form.

Cicadas screamed in the trees, shimmering the air with their voices, but it was a sound so normal, so much a part of summer, that it was scarcely noted. Lethargic dogs lay on the wooden sidewalk in pools of shadow, panting in their sleep. Hawley was suspended like a brown leaf floating on the still surface of a warm pond.

A truck came around the bend in the road at the east end of town where the pavement ends. The old men nodding under the sycamore trees looked up. The truck went through town and stopped at the depot. A woman dressed in traveling clothes, dark and much too heavy for the heat, got out. She put on her hat and pinned it, then took a straw valise from the back of the truck. She said something to the driver and went into the depot. The truck turned around and went back the way it had come.

Three girls came out of Mier's Dry Goods and squinted in the brightness. They waved at the man in the truck. All three of the girls were eighteen years old. Rose and Evelyn had been born in Hawley; Francine hadn't been but her father had, so it was practically the same thing. They had gone to school together, from the first grade to the last, had graduated together the month before, and knew practically every intimate detail about each other. They didn't have a lot in common, except Hawley, but their differences were complementary and they had been friends most of their lives.

"There goes Eula May to see her sister in Kansas City again," Rose said, looking at the woman sitting placidly on the bench at the depot. "I swear. Her sister's been at death's door as long as I can remember. Mr. Gardner's gonna go broke buying train tickets."

The other two girls didn't comment. When they reached the drugstore and started in, Francine suddenly pointed and yelped, "Look!" Evelyn and Rose stopped and looked through the fly-specked glass of the drugstore window at the poster propped there that morning by Louis Ortiz. The poster duplicated in silk screen the painting on the lead circus wagon. At the bottom, hand-written, were the dates the show would be in Hawley.

Evelyn Bradley shivered at the burning eyes which followed her everywhere she moved. Evelyn was slim and tanned; her Buster Brown haircut framed her oval face with auburn. Her eyes were hazel and smiling, but there was a seriousness to her face. Now, however, the goosebumps brought on by the poster were a curiously enjoyable sensation.

"Wouldn't you just know it!" Francine Latham snarled prettily. The braces on her teeth created a faint sibilance when she spoke. Dr. Latham was a widower and did not quite know how to cope with a grown daughter. Because her father liked it, Francine still wore her dark hair like a little girl, tied back with a bow and hanging almost to her waist.

"Wouldn't you just know it! A talking picture and a freak show, both at the same time. I don't know how I'll ever make up my mind which one to see," she said fretfully.

"Go see one tonight and the other tomorrow night," Rose Willet said with maddening logic. Rose was plump, pink, and pretty. She wore her light hair short and rippled with finger waves, a style much too old for her. She twirled her parasol, making the lace stand up, and wished Evelyn and Francine took their social positions more seriously. As the daughters of the doctor and a well-to-do farmer, they were suitable associates for the judge's youngest girl, but Francine was a mouse and Evelyn was likely to run into the street and start playing baseball with a bunch of little boys. And look at them, both of them as brown as field hands. Rose shifted the parasol to block a ray of sunlight striking her properly pale arm.

"I can't," Francine whined. "I've only got a dollar." She looked back at the poster, changing the subject quickly. "Haverstock's Traveling Curiosus and Wonder Show. What is a 'curiosus' anyway?"

"I don't know," Rose snorted. "Look what they call old beady eyes, 'Curator of the Lost Secrets of the Ancients.' Brother, they really think we're hicks," she grumbled.

14

"'Angel the Magic Boy! Mermaids! Invisible Women!' Brother!"

"A dollar's enough, Francine," Evelyn said with a slight smile, knowing full well the cause of Francine's dilemma. "The picture's a quarter and the freak show's fifty cents. That's only seventy-five."

"Well . . . " Francine looked at her Mary Jane shoes and fiddled with the tie on her sailor blouse.

"Don't tell me Billy's broke again," Rose said with indignation, pursing her lips, trying to make them look bee-stung.

Francine looked up defiantly. "Well, you always go dutch with Harold."

"But I don't have to pay his way," Rose explained with a sigh.

"I don't always have to pay for Billy, either!"

"Ha!" Rose snorted rudely and pushed into the drugstore.

Bowen's Drugs & Sundries dozed with the rest of the town that warm Friday afternoon. The ceiling fans rotated lazily, moving the air, stirring the sweet odors of chocolate and vanilla ice cream from the soda fountain with the pleasantly pungent odors of camphor and wormwood from the prescription counter. The girls sat at the soda fountain on stools covered in red leather. Phineas Bowen, Sr., waved and smiled at them from behind the prescription counter.

Sonny Redwine, who had just graduated with the three girls, put down the magazine he'd been reading and wiped the already spotless marble counter. Sonny's father and uncle owned the Redwine Funeral Home and he'd been offered a job there for the summer, but he'd decided without having to deliberate overly much that he preferred Mr. Bowen's offer to jerk sodas until it was time to go away to college in the fall. He enjoyed his work and was proud of the gleaming fountain with the rows of syrup pumps and the two water nozzles, one for carbonated and one for plain, that rose in

15

the center like the heads of graceful, long-necked birds. And he got to see his friends often; practically everyone came in at least once a week.

He grinned at the girls. "Hello, ladies. What'll it be?"

"A cherry phosphate," Rose said.

Francine echoed her.

"Make it three," Evelyn smiled.

Sonny made the drinks with a flourish, well aware of the girls' eyes on him. He was getting very good, if he did say so himself. He hadn't spilled anything in almost a week.

Francine sat thoughtfully on the stool, twisting lazily from side to side. "I think we'll go to the Majestic," she said. "That way I'll have money for popcorn. Besides, it's Ronald Coleman."

Mr. Bowen went behind the soda fountain and mixed himself a Bromo Seltzer, pouring the sudsy liquid from one glass to another and back again. "Hello, Rose, Francine, Evie," he greeted them. "What are you girls up to this afternoon? Did you see the poster in the window?"

"Yes," Evelyn laughed. "That poster's what's causing all the trouble."

"Oh?" Mr. Bowen raised his eyebrows.

"We're trying to help Francine make up her mind whether to go to the talkie or the carnival," Rose said with a sly grin.

Mr. Bowen smiled indulgently. "Yes, I can see where this will take careful consideration." He drank the Bromo Seltzer quickly, made a face and shuddered.

Sonny put the pink drinks before them and wiped the counter with more industry than necessary as Mr. Bowen returned to his prescriptions.

"I've already made up my mind," Francine said and lifted the top of the straw container. "I just *told* you I'd decided to go see the movie."

Sonny stopped wiping the counter directly in front of

16

Evelyn. He cleared his throat twice, changed his expression four times, and said, "Evie . . . " His voice cracked. He cast a wary glance at Rose and Francine.

"Yes, Sonny?"

"Uh . . . will you go with me to the picture show tonight?" he blurted.

Rose and Francine looked at each other and smothered giggles. Evelyn glanced at them with an annoyed frown and Sonny turned red.

"Of course, Sonny. I'd be happy to," Evelyn said and smiled at him.

Sonny grinned in relief, nodded at her, and frantically wiped the counter. He looked up at Rose and Francine, who were still grinning. "And it won't be Dutch," he said airily. "It's my treat." He grinned at Rose and Evelyn and went to the other end of the counter. Evelyn bent over her cherry phosphate to hide her smile. Rose and Francine gaped at Sonny's back.

The drugstore door slammed open, hitting the wire rack of magazines, making it ring tinnily. Phineas Bowen, Jr., age twelve, charged in. Mr. Bowen looked up and frowned. Finney's hair was sun bleached, his body brown as chocolate. He wore only a pair of old corduroy knickers, frayed and dusty. His bare feet slapped on the white tile floor. His eyes sparkled and danced with suppressed energy. One end of a yard-long piece of sewing thread was tied to his finger; the other end to the leg of a large metallic-green June bug. It droned loudly in a tight circle around Finney's head. He stepped beneath the revolving ceiling fan and let the cool air rush over him. The moving air grounded the June bug on his hair.

"Hi, Pop!" he sang as he began untangling the insect. "Hi, Evie. Hi, Francine. Hi, Fatty." He moved to the fountain and launched the June bug again.

Rose twisted around on the stool and fixed him with a

17

poisonous glare. The tired June bug landed on her arm. She shrieked and jumped. Finney quickly pulled the insect from danger. "Finney, you little cross-eyed ape," she hissed.

"Phineas," Mr. Bowen said reproachfully. "That's no way to talk—and you're not any better, Rose."

"Aw, Pop." Finney groaned. "My old June bug didn't hurt her. I bet Evie wouldn'ta had a fit."

Rose grinned. "You know we're only kidding, Mr. Bowen." She hopped from the stool and grabbed Finney in a bear hug. He squirmed but couldn't break her hold. "Deep down, we're very fond of each other." Unseen by Mr. Bowen, she gave Finney a hard pinch on his bare back. He yelped and broke away.

"When you go to the Wonder Show, Rosie," he said haughtily, "be sure and take a good long look at Medusa."

"Stop calling me Rosie," she snapped and sat on the stool again. "And we're not going to the freak show. We're going to the talkie."

Finney was aghast. He stared at her and climbed on another stool—well out of her reach. "You crazy or somethin'? You'd rather see a dumb old picture show than the Invisible Woman?" He groaned. "Girls?"

Rose grimaced at him in disgust. "If I remember correctly, you've been jabbering about seeing this dumb old picture show for the last solid month."

"But that was *before!*"

"Besides, you can't *see* an invisible woman," Rose said with finality.

"Oh, yes, you can," Finney said, trying to convey to her the magic of everything. "You can see her if you know how to look. You don't know how to look, Rose."

"Finney," Mr. Bowen called, holding up a small paper bag. "Take this medicine over to old Miss Sullivan."

Finney slid off the stool. "And Electro, the Lightning Man. He pulls lightning from the sky just by waving his

18

arms and he eats it and never singes a hair. And Medusa wasn't really killed by that Greek guy. She's been alive all this time still turning people to stone. And the Snake Goddess who's been hiding for a million years under an old Egyptian pyramid."

Mr. Bowen handed him the bag. "Take it right straight there and don't dawdle, then your mother wants you home."

Finney didn't break his stride. "And the Little Mermaid who's the last mermaid on earth, but that's all right 'cause she'll never die. And the Minotaur who's still mad because they destroyed his maze. And Tiny Tim . . . and Henryetta . . . and the Magic Boy who can do *anything* . . . and the Curator who was smart enough to find all these marvelous people and was smart enough to talk them into sharing their secrets with *us*! Isn't it absolutely phantasmagorical? Something's finally happening in this old town!"

He sprinted out the door, rattling the magazine rack again. "Sumbitch! Something's finally *happening*!" he yelled as he clattered across the wooden sidewalk and leaped into the street.

"Finney!" his father shouted. "What have I told you about . . . " He didn't finish; he just sighed, shook his head, and sank down behind the prescription counter.

Sonny and the three girls stared after Finney's running figure flickering in the sunlight.

Rose sighed clinically. "I think that kid's lost what few marbles he started out with. You got any insanity in the family, Mr. Bowen?"

Mr. Bowen frowned at her slightly. Just because her father is the county judge, he thought, she thinks she can say anything she wants to.

"I think I know how he feels," Evelyn said thoughtfully. "I had a little bit of the same feeling myself. Wouldn't it be . . . phantasmagorical . . . " she chuckled . . . "if

19

they were real? If it really was the Minotaur and the Medusa and a mermaid and a snake goddess, if the Magic Boy really were magic? If it all weren't just a trick of some kind?"

She looked meditatively at the floor. Her reverie was disrupted when Francine's soda straw gurgled in the bottom of her empty glass.

"I don't think I'd like it very much if it was really the Medusa," Francine said. "Put this on the charge account, Mr. Bowen." She destroyed the mood completely. "I wish I had a charge account at the picture show; then I wouldn't have to make these decisions." She sighed.

They heard the train whistle as it pulled into the depot. "Well, there goes Eula May," Rose said.

"I'll pick you up right after supper, Evie," Sonny said and smiled.

"It isn't necessary, Sonny. I can meet you at the Majestic."

"If I don't pick you up"—he grinned—"I won't have any reason to ask my father to let me use the car."

"Okay," she laughed. "I'd be happy for you to drive me to town."

3.

Jack Spain, a tow-headed twelve-year-old and Phineas Bowen's best and closest friend, sat bareback on Quicksilver, a bald-faced sorrel mare with a sweet and patient dispositon who usually occupied her afternoons pulling a plow for Jack's father. But the plowing was done and Jack's chores were completed with a speed that surprised his father—until he thought about the tent show coming to town. So, he smiled and remembered and let Jack have the old horse for the afternoon.

Jack wore a pair of faded overalls without a shirt and was as brown as Finney, though, unlike Finney, he was covered with freckles. He squinted from beneath the frazzled brim of his straw hat at the road stretched before him. He could see them coming, wavering in the afternoon heat, surrounded by dust, six magic circus wagons.

Jack yelled and waved his hat. He dug his bare heels into the horse's flanks and bounced up and down. He slapped her with his hat and clicked his tongue frantically.

"Come on, Quicksilver, you old sumbitch! Move! Go! Go! You old sumbitch, Quicksilver! Haaaw!"

Quicksilver took a last bite of buffalo grass and turned slowly. She ambled back toward town, totally indifferent to the bundle of energy exploding on her back.

4.

Evelyn, Rose, and Francine strolled across the courthouse square, listening to the cicadas screaming from the sycamores. They smiled at the old men and paused when they saw Judge Willet descending the courthouse steps. He tipped his hat and bowed slightly.

"Miss Bradley, Miss Latham, Rose," he said. "How are you girls this afternoon?"

"Just fine, Judge," Evelyn said. "How are you?"

"Prospering, Miss Bradley, prospering." He put his hat back on. "Give my regards to your folks," he said and marched away.

"Have you ever noticed," Francine asked, "that the Judge never perspires, even on a hot day like this?"

"His sweat glands wouldn't dare," Rose said, twisting her mouth. Francine giggled.

They walked on toward the Majestic. RONALD COLMAN in BULLDOG DRUMMOND, THE ONLY TALKING PICTURE HOUSE THIS SIDE OF DODGE CITY, proclaimed the marquee. The girls crossed the street and looked at the posters and tried to imagine what it would be like to hear the actors talking.

"Who do you think is handsomer," Rose mused and twirled her parasol, "Ronald Colman or Wash Peacock?"

"I don't know." Evelyn shrugged. "They're entirely different types."

Rose sighed. "I just can't picture Wash Peacock and Sister getting married."

"Grace Elizabeth? And Wash?" Evelyn raised her eyebrows. "I didn't know that."

"I did," Francine said.

"I thought everybody knew," Rose groaned. "Can you imagine it? Sister and Wash? It's like Beauty and the Beast."

"I don't think Wash is a beast," Francine protested. "He doesn't have much of a personality, but I don't think he's mean or anything."

"I meant it the other way 'round." Rose sighed.

"They don't seem to have much in common," Evelyn agreed. "Why did they decide to get married?"

"They didn't," Rose said. "Daddy didn't want an old maid in the family. Sister's twenty-six, you know, and never has had a beau. So Daddy fixed it up with Wash's daddy."

"Was it all right with Grace Elizabeth?" Evelyn frowned, well aware of Judge Willet's tyranny over his wife and three daughters.

Rose lifted her eyebrows. "Why wouldn't it be? How else could a Plain Jane like Sister get somebody as gorgeous as Wash Peacock?"

"That wasn't exactly what I meant," Evelyn said softly. She suddenly had a feeling of sadness. The thought of gentle, shy, intelligent Grace Elizabeth with Wash Peacock, who always reminded her of a big, beautiful, dumb stallion, was depressing. But there was nothing she could do about it, and it might work out. The fact that they were such opposites might be to the benefit of both. And Francine was right; Wash wasn't mean. If he would be kind to Grace Elizabeth, it might work out.

"You're just jealous, Rose," Francine smirked.

"Jealous?" Rose snorted and her parasol spun. "Wash Peacock may be about the handsomest man in the county, but he's also the dullest. When he comes to call on Sister, he just sits like a lump. When he does talk, it's always about the farm: the milo is doing poorly this year, the corn has a blight, the oats only came to four bushels an acre, the harrow broke. I wouldn't be surprised if he didn't even know the name of the President of the United States. It's enough to make you climb the wall. I wouldn't marry Wash on a bet." A sly smile crept across her lips and she twiddled the parasol handle. "Of course, I wouldn't mind being Sister on their wedding night."

Francine gasped and sniggered, putting her hands over her face to hide her blush. "Rose Willet, you're terrible!"

Rose rolled her eyes.

Suddenly Jack Spain's excited yells floated through the thick air, shaking it, quaking it, trembling and quivering it, stirring the town like sediment in the bottom of a warm pond. The girls craned their necks and hurried back toward the main street. The old men sitting in the shade of the sycamore trees looked up from their whittling and shuffled toward the sound. Mr. Bowen and Sonny stepped out of the drugstore and peered down the street. People appeared at the doors of shops and houses, shading their eyes against the sunlight.

A black Model-T Ford chugged from the alley that ran behind the Majestic and clattered past the girls. Louis Ortiz smiled and tipped his hat. Francine giggled.

"Who was that?" Evelyn asked, watching the car move away.

"I don't know," Rose frowned. "He must be with Haverstock's Traveling whatchamacallit." Her lips pursed into a smile and her eyes narrowed in Francine's direction. "He sure was good looking, though. Didn't you think so, Francine?"

Francine blushed.

Jack Spain and Quicksilver appeared around the corner where the pavement ended and the county road began. He bounced and yelled and waved his hat as if the old horse were running with the wind instead of plodding along at her normal plowing speed.

Folks left their houses and shops and stood beside the road, stretching their necks, trying to see around the corner. Women, interrupted in their chores, dried their hands on cup towels and found themselves still holding spoons damp with soup. They carried half-bathed babies and half-darned socks and grinned at each other, delighting in the unexpected break in their routine.

Finney ran to Jack, his bare feet popping as they hit the pavement. Dozens of yelling, shrieking children appeared from nooks and crannies and hidey-holes, converging on Jack. They jumped and hopped and screamed in pure physical release, some of them not even knowing what was happening, but suspecting that it must be something truly stupendous.

Jack stopped the horse, threw his leg up and forward, and slid from her back. He and Finney talked excitedly, glancing back at the bend in the road.

The wagons turned the corner abruptly. Finney and Jack ran toward them, trailing a wake of shrill children and barking dogs. Quicksilver wandered into the Whittaker yard and delicately began to nibble the petunias.

The girls strolled casually toward the painted wagons, letting it be known their interest was incredibly slight.

The children and dogs surrounded the wagons like rampaging Indians. The roustabouts driving the teams ignored them with lofty indifference and boredom.

26

Suddenly the rear of the last wagon folded open with a clatter to reveal a calliope, red and gold and shining in the sun. Steam hissed from the valves. It began to play; raucously, gloriously, with festive blasts of sound. And no one was at the keyboard.

"Oooh!" Francine breathed, her eyes round, when the first wagon passed them. "Look at those scary eyes!" The eyes seemed to focus on her even as it moved past. She quickly looked away.

"I'd hate to meet him on a dark night, all right," Rose agreed. She turned her gaze to the second wagon. "I don't know if he's magic or not, but he sure is gorgeous."

"He's even prettier than Ronald Colman," Francine said with awe. "Prettier than Ronald Colman and Wash Peacock put together."

Evelyn looked at the picture of Angel the Magic Boy speculatively, letting her eyes follow it as the wagon moved by.

"I know all about the Minotaur," Rose said complacently. "You'd better stay away from him, Francine."

"What? What?" Francine hissed, trying not to look at the picture of a heavily muscled man wearing only a brief loincloth, with the head and hoofs of a bull.

Rose winked at Evelyn and leaned over to whisper in Francine's ear. Francine's eyes grew steadily larger and her mouth formed a small circle. "Oh, Rose, you're so wicked." She blushed.

"Come on, Francine," Rose growled.

"You only have to worry if you're a virgin," Evelyn said in spite of herself.

"Evelyn Bradley! You're worse than Rose!"

"Boys, too, remember," Rose said, nodding sagely.

"Well," Francine said, blushing so hard her ears were ringing, "I suppose if only virgins have to worry, you and Evie are safe?"

"She's got us there, Rose," Evelyn laughed.

27

"I'll never tell," Rose said, trying to look worldly.

"Rose!"

"Oh, Francine!"

Evelyn was laughing so hard she staggered.

"That mermaid is probably some poor old dead fish in a jar of alcohol," Rose pronounced skeptically.

"But the poster said they're all alive," Francine protested.

"Oh, *Francine*," Rose growled.

Francine began to giggle.

"What's the matter with you?" Rose asked with faint disgust.

"A half man, half woman," Francine sputtered. "I mean . . . he . . . she . . . it . . . wouldn't have to . . . " She broke down completely.

Rose simply growled and turned back to see the picture of a beautiful woman with long silver hair. She rested in a nest of massive reptilian coils, the scales dwindling to pale flesh just below her navel. "A snake goddess! An invisible woman!" She pouted. "How gullible do they think we are, anyway? Medusa! I mean, really. If they had Medusa, they'd all have been turned to stone ages ago!"

"What difference does it make if they put on a good show?" Evelyn asked reasonably. "They don't expect anyone to really believe it. They wouldn't sell very many tickets if they advertised someone pretending to be Medusa, would they?"

The last wagon passed. Rose put her hands delicately over her ears to shut out the bellow of the calliope. They strolled leisurely in the wake of the wagons, unable to talk because of the music. Finney and Jack fell in beside them, their faces shining with wonder.

"Didn't I tell you?" Finney shouted above the noise, barely able to keep inside his skin. "Didn't I tell you? Look at that old calliope a playin' by itself! It truly is a phantasmagorical wonder show!"

28

Rose dismissed the whole thing with a shrug. "Your player piano plays by itself, doesn't it? *That* doesn't send you off in a fit."

"But this is different. This is truly different!" Finney and Jack ran on to catch up to the wagons.

"I'd better be getting home," Evelyn said and stopped at her father's '27 Buick parked in front of Mier's Dry Goods. "I'll see you tonight."

"Say hello to Harold for me." Rose grinned.

"Sure thing." Evelyn grinned back and got in the car.

When she drove by the vacant lot on the west side of town, the Wonder Show had already pulled in. She slowed the car and watched the bustle of activity with mild curiosity. Some of the roustabouts, most of them now shirtless, pulled canvas and poles and rope and iron pegs from one of the wagons. Others unhitched and unharnessed the horses, pushing the wagons in a straight row across the front of the lot. Another shooed the kids from underfoot. The calliope had stopped playing and the rear of the wagon was folded in place again. She saw the handsome Mexican-looking man who had tipped his hat to them go into one of the wagons. Then she was past it and the car bumped over the railroad tracks and rattled across the bridge over Crooked Creek, where the pavement ended and the county road began.

5.

Haverstock's wagon was partitioned into two rooms with a connecting door. The room opening to the outside was an office with a bunk against one wall where he slept. Louis had never been in the other room, but he knew that was where Angel stayed.

Haverstock looked up from the papers on his desk when Louis entered. "Did you take care of the talking pictures?"

"Sure thing. I . . . "

Haverstock waved his hand. "Don't bother me with tiresome details. I'm sure you did a commendable job. Go wherever one goes for such things and have feed delivered for the animals. You know everything that must be done before we open tonight."

"Right away, Boss." Louis grinned and left. Haverstock looked after him for a moment, wondering if he had detected a note of sarcasm in the 'Boss.' Louis was an efficient, resourceful employee, but he sometimes got a little too big for his well-tailored britches.

6.

The gray 1929 Packard hummed along the road, leaving a comet tail of dust turned gold by the setting sun. The fields of wheat on either side of the road were burnished copper, completely motionless in the warm stillness. Sonny Redwine squinted at the huge sun which seemed to be squatting on the road directly ahead. He whistled tunelessly but the sound was periodically interrupted by the pleased smile that flickered on his lips.

He slowed the car and turned into a sunflower-bordered lane at the mailbox with "Bradley" and "Star Route" lettered on it and pulled to a stop before the house at the end of the lane. The Bradley farm seemed to be prosperous. The house and barn were newly painted and the barn had a new tin roof. The outbuildings were all neat and in good repair, but he wondered; he'd been hearing some very disturbing talk in the last few months.

He got out of the car, cleared his throat a couple of times, pulled his jacket down in back, and crunched up the gravel walk. The front door opened as he stepped up on the porch.

"Come in, Sonny," Otis Bradley said. "Evelyn is just about ready." Otis was a short man in his late forties, beginning to go bald, brown and burly from working in the fields. He was in his undershirt and carpet slippers with his braces hanging down.

"Thank you, Mr. Bradley. How are you this evening?"

Otis smiled slightly at Sonny's nervousness and tried to remember if he had acted that way when he was eighteen. He wasn't sure, but he probably had. "Just fine, Sonny. How are you?"

He held the screen door open and followed the boy into the house.

"Oh, very well, thank you," Sonny said, looking around. The room was neat but comfortable, with good but not new furniture. It looked just about the same as his own parlor had looked before his mother had bought everything new last year. The only thing new in the Bradley parlor was a big Atwater-Kent softly playing gospel music.

Otis closed the screen door and returned to his chair and his newspaper. "That's good. Sit down." He motioned to another chair.

Sonny sat, a bit too quickly, and then grinned.

"Thought it might cool off a little, come evening," Otis said, "but doesn't look like it's going to." Sonny nodded and wished he hadn't worn a jacket. Otis watched him, wondering if Evelyn and he were serious. He didn't think they'd ever gone out before, but he wasn't sure. He trusted Evelyn and left it up to his wife to keep watch on her boy friends, of which there seemed to be quite a few. It wouldn't be a bad match, he thought. Sonny was a nice-looking, well-mannered boy who, as far as he knew, hadn't been in any kind of trouble. The Redwines were well thought of and seemed to have plenty of money. He glanced out the window at the Packard. It wouldn't be a bad match at all, he decided, the

32

way the price of wheat had been falling. People had to be buried, no matter what.

"Your . . . uh . . . wheat seems about ready to harvest," Sonny said suddenly.

"Yes," Otis agreed. "As a matter of fact, the advance man for the combiners was here a couple of days ago to sign a contract. They're about ninety miles north of Amarillo now. Should be here in a couple of weeks." He wondered if it was worth it, if he would make enough off the wheat to pay the combiners, if he wouldn't save money by just burning it in the fields.

"The weather is just about right."

"Just so the hail doesn't beat it down like it did six years ago. When the weather gets hot and still like this, you never know what's going to happen."

Harold Bradley came into the room, pulling down his varsity sweater. Harold was twenty-one and had just finished his third year of college. He was taller than his father, but just as brown and burly. He always spent his summers in Hawley helping with the farm, claiming he needed the exercise to keep in shape for the football team.

"Hello, Sonny." He grinned.

"Oh. Hi, Harold." Sonny stood up and then sat down again.

Harold looked in the mirror over the mantel and pressed his cowlick down with his fingers. He wondered if he should put more pomade on it.

The gospel song ended on the radio and a soft, cajoling voice came over the airwaves. "Don't let your doctor two-dollar you to death. Take advantage of our compound operation. I can cure you the same as I did Clyde Atkinson of Fort Riley, Kansas. . . . My dear, dear friends, the smoldering fires of the most dangerous disease may be just starting. Come while you're still able to get about."

Harold laughed. "Are you still listening to Dr. Brinkley

33

and his goat-glands? When are you going up to Milford and get yours put in, Pop?"

Otis grinned. "Is that what you're learning in college? To sass your father? Isn't it a little warm for that sweater?"

Harold cocked his head, still grinning. "Sure. But Rose thinks it looks sharp. Gives these small-town girls a thrill to go out with a college man." He waved and went out the door. "See you later," he said over his shoulder.

Otis shook his head. "Don't see why you kids can't all go in the same car if you're all goin' to the same place."

"Huh? Oh, yes sir." Sonny huddled in the chair then leapt to his feet when Evelyn and Mrs. Bradley came in.

"Hello, Sonny." Bess Bradley smiled and made him think of fresh bread cooling on the window sill. She was almost as tall as her husband, still pretty, getting comfortably plump, with just a hint of gray in her hair. She and Evelyn favored each other very much in the face.

"Hello, Mrs. Bradley," he said and stared at Evelyn. She stood smiling at him in a green dress of crepe de Chine with a low, loose sash. She had pinned a small nosegay of white celluloid flowers on her shoulder.

"Have a good time," Bess interrupted his reverie, "and don't stay out too late."

"Yes, ma'am." Sonny nodded and edged toward the door. Outside on the porch, he breathed an exaggerated sigh of relief that caused Evelyn to laugh.

7.

Although it wasn't quite dark, a great number of people were already in line at the Majestic. Leopold Mier arrived, jingling his keys and smiling his ever-present smile. He was a small man who looked as if he had been carved from mahogany. He was dressed as he always dressed—during the day at Mier's Dry Goods and at night at Mier's Majestic—a black cassimere suit with a tall celluloid collar and a gold chain draped across his little paunch. Leopold Mier was a contented man, happy with his life, his family, and his enterprises.

He waved to the people in line and gave the gold chain a practiced flip. A large gold watch fell into his hand. He clicked open the engraved cover. "Show starts in thirty minutes, folks."

"Just wanted to be sure we got a seat, Mr. Mier," a woman laughed.

Mr. Mier nodded. "Should be quite a crowd tonight."

"Too bad the tent show picked this weekend to come to town."

Mr. Mier sighed and muttered something about Kismet, then held up his hands. "You shouldn't worry," he said. "Everyone wants to hear Mr. Ronald Colman talk will get the chance, if we have to have him with us again next week." The people in line laughed. "And we show only talking pictures from now on. You don't get to hear Mr. Ronald Colman talk, you get to hear somebody else."

He unlocked the door and went in. After a moment the lights clicked on, one after the other, until the front of the theater was brightly lit. The people in line applauded.

Mr. Mier bustled about, getting the tickets and cash box from the safe. He looked up with a pleasant expansion of his smile when Caroline Robinson entered.

"Good evening, Caroline."

"Hello, Mr. Mier. Looks like a big crowd tonight."

He nodded with satisfaction and handed her the tickets and cash box. "That it does. That it does. Better take an extra roll of tickets. They'll really keep us jumping tomorrow when all the country people come to town. Open up as soon as you can. No point in making those folks stand outside."

"Save a seat for me during the last show," Caroline said over her shoulder. "I'll figure up the receipts after we close."

"Of course. That will be fine. Better hurry."

Mrs. Mier entered with her expression of perpetual tardiness. They smiled and nodded. She put popcorn in the machine, working slowly and carefully, but creating an impression of frantic haste.

Evan Whittaker came in, limping on his bad leg. His knee had been shattered by a German bullet in Flanders during the Great War and his leg would no longer bend. He grinned at Mr. Mier. "Well, this is the big night."

"Is all the new machinery working properly?"

"I ran the whole feature this afternoon and everything worked fine. Cross your fingers." He held up his own crossed fingers and climbed the stairs to the projection booth one step at a time.

Mr. Mier sighed and parted the black velvet curtains, going into the auditorium. He strolled down the sloping aisle, looking about him proudly. Suddenly his nose twitched like a mouse. He stopped. A look of concern crossed his face. The little smile paled and turned slowly downward like melting wax. He began moving again, walking slowly, peering down each row of seats. He crossed in front of the screen and started back up the other aisle. He stopped suddenly and stared. A little squeak escaped his throat.

The skunk pattered about under the seats, its claws making little clicks on the floor. It stopped at a bit of popcorn and munched on it. Then it sauntered to the next piece. Mr. Mier squeaked again, louder. The skunk stopped and looked at him.

Mr. Mier waved his hands in small pushing motions, squeaking with each push. The skunk turned to face him, bouncing slightly on stiff legs.

Mr. Mier backed away. His knees caught the arm of a seat and he fell backward with the clatter. The skunk tilted forward and stood on its front legs, its tail spread like a shaggy canopy.

8.

Sonny Redwine parked his father's Packard on the courthouse square across from the Majestic. He hastened around to open the door for Evelyn. Comfort had won out over fashion and he was in his shirtsleeves. Evelyn took his arm and they started across the street.

Suddenly Mr. Mier ran from the theater, a handkerchief pressed to his nose. Mrs. Mier followed him rapidly, still holding a box of salt. Evan Whittaker was right behind her. Caroline Robinson looked at them in astonishment from the cashier's booth. Then her nose wrinkled and she scrambled out, leaving the roll of tickets to unwind slowly onto the floor.

The crowd muttered and backed away and then scattered. Francine Latham and Billy Sullivan were among them, but they stopped when they reached Sonny and Evelyn standing dumbfounded in the middle of the street.

"Did you hear?" Francine shrieked. "A skunk got in. Now I won't get to see Ronald Colman."

"They'll open up again—as soon as they get the smell out," Billy assured her, but a smile lurked around his mouth. Billy was nineteen, a year older than Francine, but he looked a year younger. He was slight and barely taller than she was. He worked at his father's ice house and hated it. He'd had no desire to go to college, so he was probably stuck there.

"But that could be *weeks!*" Francine complained.

"At least you don't have to make a decision anymore." Evelyn smiled. "Looks like it's gonna be Haverstock's old Traveling Wonder Show after all."

"That's where I wanted to go in the first place," Billy confided.

Francine drew herself up and fixed him with a steely stare. "If a lady has to buy the tickets, then the lady can choose what the tickets are *to.*"

Evelyn and Sonny laughed and Billy shrugged helplessly.

"There's Rose and Harold," Francine cried, her pique disappearing. "Come on, Billy." She grabbed his arm and dragged him away. Sonny and Evelyn followed more slowly.

"Is it okay with you if we go to the tent show?" Sonny asked. "We don't have to go with them if you don't want to."

"Well," Evelyn laughed, "to tell you the truth, I'd much rather see the Minotaur than Ronald Colman. I was planning to go tomorrow night."

The warm stillness of the evening was suddenly shattered by the calliope. The metallic tones floated on the air, drawing people from their houses, pulling them in excited clumps down the street. Finney and Jack charged by, running as hard as they could toward the sound. Suppers were hurriedly finished, dishes were left unwashed, eggs were left ungathered. The sound was electricity, stirring the blood, flushing the face, a youth magic that sweetened the

39

sour and smoothed the wrinkled and softened the crusty.

They gathered and stared curiously at the painted, lined-up wagons. In the center, with three wagons on either side, was a ticket stand with the playerless calliope beside it. A large canvas tent rose behind the wagons. Electric lights were strung over them, illuminating the paintings on their sides. A banner stretched across the entrance between two tall poles. HAVERSTOCK'S TRAVELING CURIOSUS AND WONDER SHOW it read in gold on black. Torches lined the street, adding more light and festivity. Insects flocked like a snowstorm. Moths and crickets, katydids and dragonflies, big brown beetles that buzzed like airplanes and got in the hair, shiny black beetles that scurried across the ground behind huge pincers, and three dozen kinds of bugs that could only be classified as unclassifiable.

The crowd converged and laughed and pointed and bought tickets and gossiped, what little they could over the noise of the calliope, and swatted bugs. The tickets were dispensed from a lofty perch by a plump lady rapidly approaching middle age. Her face was elaborately over made-up, causing her to look like an aging saloon girl. Her orange hair was haphazardly coiffed, erratically waved, amazingly curled, sloppily piled, and appeared on the verge of toppling around her.

She wore a low-cut satin ball gown of poisonous green. It had perspiration stains at the armpits and grime around the neckline. She received money and presented tickets with grandiloquent gestures, smiling and simpering and winking at the men. Every few moments she reached behind her neck and futilely patted stray strands of hair back into place.

Harold looked at the others and rolled his eyes. Francine poked Billy and slipped him her dollar. He quickly tucked it in his pocket.

"Remember to stay away from the Minotaur, Francine."
Rose grinned.

Francine giggled. "Oh, Rose! Don't make me blush."

"What are you talking about?" Harold asked.

"Oh, nothing," Rose said airily.

They bought their tickets and moved with the crowd toward the entrance of the tent. "Boy," Harold groaned, "this better be worth fifty cents."

They gave their tickets to a young roustabout whose muscles rippled under his rolled-up sleeves as he tore tickets. Rose ogled him appreciatively and raised her eyebrows at Francine. Francine lowered her eyes. The man's eyes met Rose's and a faint smile flickered on his lips. She gave him an affronted glare and ducked under the tent flaps.

The interior was filled with rows of backless wooden benches, unpainted but polished by many backsides. Scattered on the benches were numerous cardboard fans imprinted with the Redwine Funeral Home advertisement. Many of them were already in use. Sonny picked one up, fanned himself, grinned, and tossed it back on the bench.

An aisle down the center of the tent divided the benches into two sections. A wire ran the length of the tent above the aisle with a curtain bunched at the back, as if the audience were to be divided into two parts. Half a dozen naked electric light bulbs were strung in the upper reaches in a haphazard pattern. At the front, opposite the entrance, was a small stage raised about two feet above the trampled grass floor. A curtain ran across the back of the stage, fastened with metal rings to another wire. Otherwise, the interior of the tent was featureless.

They looked around doubtfully. The benches were only about half full. They finally found room enough to sit together near the front. Finney and Jack were on the front

41

row, talking excitedly. Evelyn and the others looked a little depressed.

"This is a wonder show?" Harold asked the air and swatted a bug from his ear.

Most of the people still outside were standing around trying to make up their minds whether to go in or not. Louis Ortiz stepped onto a platform behind the calliope. He smiled and postured, letting the women get a good look at his white teeth and well-proportioned body. Then he held up his arms. The calliope fell silent. Louis waved his arms grandly and the murmur of the milling crowd died away.

"Ladies and gentlemen!" he said, relishing the rich sound of his own voice. He stood for a moment in a dramatic pose, his arms up and his legs apart. "The Wonder Show begins in five minutes. Get your tickets for the most wondrous sights your eyes have ever seen, more wondrous than your mind has ever imagined.

"Tiny Tim, a full-grown man, but only twelve inches tall.

"The Little Mermaid. She sits in her tank of water and dreams green dreams of the sea.

"The Minotaur, a man from the neck down, but a raging bull from the neck up.

"The Medusa. To look on her face means death. One glance and you turn to stone. But don't worry; you will see her only in a mirror, which makes it perfectly safe—just as the Greek hero Perseus saw her reflected in his shield and survived.

"The Invisible Woman. You won't believe your eyes. You won't believe what your eyes *don't* see.

"Electro, the Lightning Man. To him a million volts is nothing more than a firefly.

"Henry-etta. Half man, half woman. One of nature's most shocking mistakes. All of his . . . I mean, her

42

. . . well, you know what I mean." Louis grinned erotically. "All the secrets will be revealed—if you're man enough
to take it. And we promise not to embarrass the lovely ladies.

"The Snake Goddess. Is she woman or is she serpent?
She's both, my friends, she's both. This ancient creature
may be a million years old, a remnant of a forgotten race.
Who knows?

"And the most astounding of all: Angel, the Magic Boy. If
you've seen magicians before, forget them. Angel is not a
magician. He pulls no rabbits out of hats. He does not make
pink handkerchiefs out of blue ones. What Angel can do
defies description. You have to see it for yourselves. It will
shock and amaze you. It may even frighten you. They're all
inside, ladies and gentlemen. They're all alive and they're
all real."

He glanced over his shoulder at the roustabout collecting
tickets. The man gave Louis a signal. "There are only
thirty-seven seats left," he continued. "So hurry. If you
don't get in to see this show, there'll be another in one
hour. If you're skeptical, just ask your friends as they leave
the first show." He smiled and bowed eloquently. "Thank
you for your attention."

He hopped down from the platform and entered the tent.
The calliope began to play once again. The citizens of Hawley rapidly bought tickets and the allotted thirty-seven
were sold in a matter of seconds. At the sale of the thirty-
seventh ticket, the woman with the orange hair plopped a
sign over the front of the stand: "Next Show in One Hour."
She picked up the cash box, the roll of tickets, and left without a word or a backward glance, disappearing around the
side of the tent. Those who hadn't made it to her in time
murmured in disappointment.

The benches were filled. The people talked among them-

43

selves, but there was an air of tense anticipation. Louis walked up the aisle, letting his hips roll just the right amount, and stepped onto the stage. The lights dimmed slowly, leaving him in an illuminated island. Outside, the calliope stopped playing with a discordant wheeze. Louis held up his arms for silence and received it immediately.

"Good evening, ladies and gentlemen," he began with a white smile. "Welcome to Haverstock's Traveling Curiosus and Wonder Show, where you will see wonders you've hardly imagined. But I'm not going to tell you about them, I'm going to *show* them to you!"

He swept his arm to the curtains behind him. They parted, the metal rings rattling on the wire. A large doll house sat on a table. Two men rolled the table forward to the edge of the stage. The audience waited, hardly breathing.

Finney turned and whispered to Jack. "It's got to be Tiny Tim."

"I'm waiting for the Snake Goddess," Jack answered and squirmed nervously.

"Ladies and gentlemen," Louis bellowed, "Tiny Tim, the smallest man in the world!"

For a moment nothing happened, then the door of the doll house opened and Tiny Tim stepped out. A gasp fluttered through the audience. He was twelve inches tall, as promised, but the tiny figure was strangely misshapen. He was a hunchback and had a crooked leg. His face was like wax on the verge of melting. The crowd strained forward. They had known he was supposed to be twelve inches tall, but they hadn't really realized just how small that actually was. Some in the back stood up for a better look.

Finney grabbed Jack's arm and they stared, their eyes wide and their mouths open. The crowd began to murmur.

"How do they do it?" Rose hissed in amazement.

44

"Probably with mirrors . . . or something," Harold answered and wished he could take off his sweater.

"Please keep your seats, ladies and gentlemen," Louis admonished. "You'll all have an opportunity to see Tim up close." He turned to the tiny man. "Tim, would you like to sing and dance for the nice people? They've come to see you and it would be unkind to disappoint them."

Tim looked up at Louis. "Yes," he said in a small whispery voice that could hardly be heard.

There was another gasp from the audience. Finney and Jack clutched at each other in excitement that could hardly be restrained.

"Sumbitch," Finney squeaked.

Rose stared and put her hand on Harold's arm. "Is the guy a ventriloquist too?"

Louis held up his hand for quiet. "Okay, Tim. These nice people are waiting."

The air in the tent rang with silence. Tim began to sing. His voice was tiny, but it was clear and melodious, and the song he sang was slow and sad. Then he danced, slowly, awkwardly, and grotesquely, his misshapen body unable to coordinate properly.

Evelyn frowned and looked away.

After a moment Louis leaned over and put his hand palm-up on the table. Tim stopped dancing and, still singing, stepped into Louis's hand. Louis lifted him up.

The houselights brightened. Louis stepped off the stage and walked slowly down the aisle to the rear of the tent. He turned and paused, holding the tiny singing man before him. Every head was twisted around and every eye was on his hand. Even though Tim's voice was very small, the inside of the tent was so hushed he could be heard clearly by everyone. Louis returned slowly to the stage.

He mounted the stage and put his hand on the table. Tim

45

got off as the song ended and bowed to the silent faces. The silence continued for a moment and then was abruptly broken by frantic clapping from Finney and Jack. The others slowly picked it up. They laughed nervously. Then they cheered and laughed and slapped their hands together.

Tim bowed again, then turned and entered the doll house. The roustabouts came out and pushed the table to the rear of the stage, the curtains closing behind them. Louis held up his arms and grinned as the houselights dimmed. He waited a moment for the noise to die down.

"Thank you, ladies and gentlemen. Tim appreciates yo ir warm reception, but there are many more wonders to see." Shuffling and scraping sounds came from behind the curtain.

"Ladies and gentlemen," Louis continued, "there are many instruments of death used in the world to execute criminals and murderers. In France they use the guillotine. In the heathen countries of the East they use methods too terrible to describe before a good American, Christian audience. In this country several means are employed. In some states, murderers are hung, in others they are shot. The gas chamber is used and . . ." the curtains rattled open ". . . the electric chair, from which there is no escape!"

"Not too many recover from the guillotine either," Rose murmured.

Louis walked slowly behind the heavy wooden chair spotlighted on the stage. He put his hands on the back of it and paused dramatically. The audience leaned forward.

"There is no escape . . . except for one man!"

Louis turned and swung his arm toward the wings. A man stepped out. He was barefoot and shirtless, but a black hood was pulled over his head. He stood with his legs apart and his chest out. He turned his shrouded face toward the rows of people.

46

"Electro, the Lightning Man!" Louis's voice rang powerfully through the tent. Electro walked slowly to the chair. He was followed by the two men who had pushed forward the doll house. He sat stiffly, in an attitude of fearlessness, a sheen of perspiration on his chest. The roustabouts buckled heavy straps around his arms, legs, and chest and left the stage. Louis walked forward again. "Ladies and gentlemen, if Electro is ever executed in a state that uses the electric chair, there will be quite a few very surprised people."

He grinned and there was a slight laugh from the audience. "This electric chair, ladies and gentlemen, is one that was actually used to execute hundreds of criminals in one of this great country's state prisons. The electric current that will go through Electro's body when I pull this switch . . ." he placed his hand on a large knife switch mounted on a pole attached to the side of the chair ". . . will be exactly the same as used in that state prison."

The audience shifted expectantly.

"Are you ready, Electro?"

The black-covered head nodded. Louis closed his fingers slowly around the switch handle, paused to milk the last drop of suspense, and threw the switch. The chair hummed and crackled. Electro's body twitched and jerked. Louis turned off the switch and the man in the chair slumped back.

"Are you all right, Electro?"

The head under the hood nodded again. There was an almost inaudible release of breath from the audience.

"Are you ready, Electro?"

The hood dipped slightly and Louis pulled the switch again. The electric hum and crackle resumed. Electro trembled. Louis reached behind the chair and brought out an iron bar with a rubber handle. He held the bar over his head so the audience could see.

47

"As you can observe, this has a rubber handle because, unlike Electro, I am not immune to electricity."

Holding the bar by the rubber end, he reached out and touched the arm of the chair. A shower of sparks flew from the contact, filling the air with the smell of ozone. The audience inhaled loudly. He touched the chair again and again in many different places, each time producing a cascade of sparks.

Jack leaned over and whispered to Finney. "I think this is a trick."

Finney nodded. "Yes, but it's a very good trick."

Louis put the iron bar away and turned off the switch. Electro slumped in the chair again, his chest rising and falling rapidly. A drop of perspiration rolled over his stomach.

"Are you all right, Electro?"

The hooded head dipped forward. Louis turned to the audience with an expansive smile and spread his arms for applause. The two roustabouts came from the wings and unstrapped the man in the electric chair. Electro stood up, bowed to the applause, and walked from the stage as the chair was pushed behind the curtain.

"I hope the rest of it isn't as phony as that," Harold groaned.

"Tiny Tim wasn't a phony," Evelyn pointed out, arching her eyebrows.

Harold grunted. "Electro the Lightning Man certainly was."

There was once again shuffling and scraping behind the curtain. Louis walked to the edge of the stage and assumed a serious pose. The applause quickly subsided into silence.

"Many years before the fall of Troy," Louis intoned solemnly, "there were three wicked sisters called the Gorgons. They had snakes instead of hair on their heads, and anyone who gazed upon them was turned instantly into stone."

48

Behind him the curtain was slowly opening. Two panels about the size of doors, ornately decorated with fading paint and flaking gilt, stood side by side with one panel set slightly behind the other.

"Greek mythology tells us that one of these sisters, the one named Medusa, was killed by Perseus with the aid of magic sandals that let him fly and a magic cap that made him invisible. Perhaps this tale is true and perhaps it isn't. Maybe the Gorgon you are about to see isn't Medusa, but one of her sisters. I do not know, because she will not speak."

Louis stepped toward the panels. Jack grabbed Finney's arm. "Did you hear, Finney? He said it might not be Medusa."

"That's okay. It's okay if it's one of her sisters instead."

Louis put his hand on the farther panel and turned it slowly. There was a brilliant flash as the lights caught in the mirror on the reverse side. When the panel stopped moving, they could see, reflected in the mirror, the woman standing behind the forward panel. The audience hummed appreciatively.

The woman's reflection glared at them. She wore a dark robe that fell straight from her shoulders to the floor. Her arms were rigid at her sides. On her head, instead of hair, was a writhing mass of foot-long green snakes. They coiled and looped in agitation, as if trying to escape the bondage of the woman's skull.

Finney and Jack stared, transfixed.

Francine cringed. "Yaaah! Those snakes look *real!*" She shivered and put her knuckles against her mouth.

"That woman must be nuts, lettin' 'em put real snakes on her head," Rose said.

Louis looked speculatively at the audience, then turned the panel back to its original position. He walked to the

49

front of the stage as the curtain closed. The applause was polite.

Harold looked at his sister. "Well? Medusa was just as phony as Electro, but I'll admit that was a pretty good touch, using real snakes instead of rubber ones."

Francine shivered again and made a little noise through her nose.

Louis held up his hands. "We stay with Greek mythology for the next part of the Wonder Show."

Rose reached over and poked Francine. "Here he comes, Francine. Watch out."

Francine put her hands over her face to hide her blushes. "Oh, Rose, you're so *wicked!*"

"The Greek god Poseidon," Louis said scholarly, "gave a wonderfully beautiful bull to Minos, the king of Crete, for Minos to sacrifice to him, but Minos could not bear to slay the beautiful animal and, instead, kept it for himself. To punish him for his betrayal, Poseidon caused Minos' wife, Pasiphaë, to fall madly in love with the bull. Do not be shocked, ladies." Louis smiled comfortingly. "This happened many thousands of years before Christianity. The son of Pasiphaë and the bull was a monster, half bull, half human—the Minotaur!"

The curtains swept open with a rattle. There were shocked, disapproving gasps from some in the audience, a rumble of excited comments from others, and titters of embarrassment from some of the girls at the sheer masculinity standing before them.

The Minotaur's resemblance to the painting on the caravan was only superficial. He was a tall, powerfully muscled man, wearing only a loincloth. He did not have the head of a bull, but had long, bushy hair and horns sprouting from either side of his head. His face was slightly elongated, with only a suggestion of bovine features.

He stepped forward. His muscles rippled like bronze satin. His cloven hoofs clumped loudly on the wooden stage. From the knees down, his legs were shaggy with brown hair, exactly like a bull's.

Rose looked at Francine and grinned. Francine was consumed by genuine blushes.

Finney and Jack stared. "It's him," Finney breathed. "It's really and truly him."

"Sumbitch," Jack muttered.

"King Minos had a miraculous labyrinth built underneath his palace and there placed the Minotaur to live forever. Every year seven youths and seven maidens were sent into the labyrinth. What happened to them, we don't know, because none ever returned. Mythology tells us the Greek hero Theseus slew the Minotaur in the labyrinth, but there was only the word of Theseus—there were no witnesses.

"As you can see, standing before you, Theseus was prone to exaggeration." He smiled at his little joke. "You all know of the fabulous strength of the Minotaur."

A roustabout brought two straight-backed wooden chairs onto the stage. He placed one on either side of the Minotaur, who ignored him, standing placidly, seeming to ignore the whole affair.

"Haverstock's Traveling Curiosus and Wonder Show will now demonstrate that strength for you. I need two volunteers from the audience. . . ."

Finney and Jack immediately sprang up.

"Thank you, boys." Louis grinned. "But I need someone with a little more meat on their bones."

Finney and Jack sat back down, limp with disappointment.

Louis looked over the audience. They shifted this way and that, waiting for someone to volunteer. Louis suddenly pointed at a man about halfway back. "You, sir. What is your name?"

The man looked around him with embarrassment. "Uh . . . Jakey Dunlap," he said and grinned.

"What is your occupation, Mr. Dunlap?" Louis asked.

"Oh, I work at the feed store," Jakey said, warming up to being the center of attention.

"And how much do you weigh, Mr. Dunlap?"

"Oh, about two hundred and forty pounds, give or take."

"Thank you, sir. Is there anyone in the audience who weighs more?"

"Here!" a voice brayed near the rear of the tent.

"Oh, no," Sonny moaned dramatically and hunched over with his hands on the back of his head.

"The name's Baby Sis Redwine and I weigh two hundred and forty-*one* pounds," the voice bellowed. Everyone twisted around to look. There was laughter and a scattering of applause.

Louis was momentarily rattled. He had never had a woman volunteer before and he was taken by surprise, but it took only a few seconds for him to regain his rhythm. "This demonstration might be a bit too . . . strenuous for a lady, ma'am," he said smoothly and flashed his teeth.

"Oh, hell!" Sis Redwine said. "I can out drink, out shoot, and out cuss any man in this place. And I ain't scared of no hairy man wearin' drawers!" The crowd guffawed with delight. Sis was a popular character in Hawley, and Sonny's first cousin. Some said she wasn't quite right in the head, but she owned the blacksmith shop and the Sinclair station and didn't hurt for money. She was thirty-four years old and unmarried, and the pet of the Redwine family, though smiles were sometimes strained when her escapades got too rambunctious.

Louis bowed and smiled. "I bow to your wishes, ma'am.

52

Will you and the gentleman come up on the stage? You will be perfectly safe. There is no danger."

Jakey and Sis left their seats and grinned at the crowd. Sis was shorter than Jakey and almost as wide as she was tall. Her turgid body rolled with soft fat. Jakey had considerable fat on him, but it was hard and underlain with solid muscle. Even so, the Minotaur towered over him, and his chiseled muscular definition and slimmer body made Jakey look bloated.

"Give 'em what for, Sis!" someone yelled.

Sis and Jakey raised their eyes to the Minotaur critically and unconsciously edged away. The Minotaur looked at them with his big, soft bovine eyes without interest.

"Will you please be seated in the two chairs?" Louis asked politely.

Jakey and Sis looked at each other and grinned, then Sis made a belligerent face at the Minotaur and turned to the audience for approval. The audience responded with the expected laughter. They sat tentatively in the chairs. The Minotaur squatted between them, reached out his massive arms full-length and grasped one leg of each chair. After some shifting and getting into position, he stood slowly, the muscles in his arms and shoulders bulging. He held the two chairs at arm's length.

Surprised, Jakey and Sis gasped and grabbed at the chairs for support, then laughed at their own nervousness. The audience laughed with them and applauded mightily. The Minotaur squatted again and lowered the chairs lightly to the stage, then stood up. Perspiration sparkled on his chest and shoulders.

Jakey and Sis grinned in embarrassment and hurried back to their seats. Smiling broadly, Louis held up his hands. "Thank you, Mr. Dunlap and Miss Redwine. If any of you think what you have just seen is a trick, I invite you to try it when you get home tonight—with empty chairs. Is there anyone in the audience who would like a closer look at the Minotaur?"

Finney sprang to his feet like a jack-in-the-box. The Minotaur moved to the front of the stage as the houselights went up. He turned toward Finney, then stepped off the stage and went to him. He bent over so his head was level with Finney's and looked at him from brown, liquid, kindly eyes. Finney tentatively reached out his hand and touched one of the horns lightly. He ran his finger to the point, then to the base surrounded by hair. He pulled his hand back quickly and grinned at the wonder of it all. The Minotaur smiled and softly stroked Finney's hair with his large hard hand. Finney's arm prickled with goosebumps. The Minotaur straightened and moved to the front of the aisle. Finney sat down slowly. Jack grabbed his arm.

"Is there anyone else?" Louis asked.

The Minotaur walked carefully down the aisle, looking around him, smiling slightly. The silent audience watched him nervously.

Harold stood up when the Minotaur reached the bench on which he sat. "Yes, I would," he said.

"Harold," Rose hissed.

The Minotaur stopped walking and stepped toward him, leaning over slightly. Harold sat fourth from the aisle. He reached over Rose, Billy, and Francine and grasped one of the horns. He tugged at it with moderate force, then felt around the base, pushing the hair aside to examine the juncture. The Minotaur, apparently accustomed to such liberties, made no objection.

The Minotaur's leg touched Francine's knee. She jerked it away with a little gasp. The contact was like an electric shock, adding fuel to the heat already enclosing her body. The Minotaur shifted his gaze from Harold to her, looking into her eyes. He smiled. Francine quickly looked away, fleeing his eyes, pulling her head down.

Then she was looking at the protruding fabric of the Minotaur's loincloth, only a foot from her face. She could smell the odors of his body and see the fine hairs glistening on his stomach. Her throat constricted and her face began to tingle. She forced her eyes shut, but her eyelids seemed made of glass. Tears squeezed from her compressed eyes and rolled down her cheeks.

The Minotaur watched her, still smiling.

Harold finished his examination. "Uh . . . thank you," he said timorously and sat down. The Minotaur took a step backward and continued toward the rear of the tent.

Billy leaned across Rose. "Well?" he asked excitedly.

Harold shrugged. "It's a great makeup job. I couldn't tell how they were fastened. They didn't budge a bit when I pulled on 'em. If I didn't know better, I'd think they were real." He looked thoughtful for a moment. "I wish I could examine the hoofs."

Billy turned back to Francine and saw her closed eyes and pinched face. "What's the matter with you?" he asked, half-concerned and half-amused.

The others turned to look at her. None of them had noticed her reaction; they had been watching Harold and the Minotaur. Francine quickly wiped the wetness from her face with her fingers and sniffled. "Nothing," she said quietly. "Nothing's the matter."

Billy gave her his handkerchief and she daubed at her eyes with it.

"Are you sick?" Harold asked. "Do you want to leave?"

"No," Francine said tensely, twitching her head. "I'm not sick. I don't want to leave. I said nothing's the matter." She gave Billy his handkerchief and wouldn't look at them.

55

Rose watched her with a little ghost of a smile and a twinkle in her eye.

The houselights went off and applause rose around them, drawing their attention to the stage where the Minotaur bowed as the curtains slithered together and blocked him from view. There were more grating sounds as something heavy was moved behind the curtain.

Louis stepped forward. "Thank you, ladies and gentlemen." He paused until there was complete silence.

"There are many strange stories of the sea and the marvelous creatures who dwell there. One of the most awesome of these sea-creatures is the mermaid—half woman and half fish. Are they one of nature's mistakes? One of nature's experiments that didn't work? Or are they one of nature's secrets? Ladies and gentlemen, decide for yourselves."

He gestured grandly and the curtain opened on a large water-filled glass tank. A slight rustle swept the tent as the audience strained forward to get a better look.

The creature floated in the tank, her body rotating slowly with the movement of the water. She was a fish from the waist down, but barely human from the waist up. Her body was greenish-gray and leathery. Her small breasts were like deflated bladders. Her arms were small and her fingers stubby and webbed. Her head was bald and scaly; her mouth very small with horny lips; her eyes round and lidless like a fish. Her ears were tiny holes. She had the look of being half-finished.

Rose leaned across Harold, bracing herself with a hand on his thigh, and whispered to Evelyn. "What did I tell you? It's just an old dead fish."

Then the Little Mermaid moved. She swam around in a tight circle, gracefully undulating her tail fins. She stopped and put her hands against the glass, looking at the people with eyes like pearl buttons. The gasps and murmurs gradually turned to applause.

"The poor horrible thing," Evelyn said.

"There she is, ladies and gentlemen: the Little Mermaid," Louis called. "What secrets does she hold? What does she think about? We'll never know because she does not speak."

The curtain closed and the applause died.

"How did they *do* that, Hal?" Rose asked.

Harold shrugged. "I'm not sure. It's probably somebody in a costume."

"Ladies and gentlemen, our next guest is already here. She's been standing right beside me for the last five minutes." He looked around furtively and then laughed. "At least, I *think* she's standing beside me. Are you there, invisible woman?"

"Yes, I'm here." The voice was musically feminine and seemed to originate in the air beside Louis. Laughter rippled from the audience.

"Don't you think it would be a good idea if you got dressed so the people can see where you are?" Louis asked, laughing with the audience.

"Oh, very well," the voice pouted. "But it's been such a dreadfully warm day and this tent is so stuffy. It's so cool and comfortable without clothes." There was more laughter from the audience.

"Please!" Louis gasped with mock indignation that managed to be half leer. "You'll shock these nice people. There are children in the audience."

"But I don't have a thing to wear," the voice complained.

"I'll fix that," Louis said with a flourish.

A roustabout came through the curtains, disinterest on his good-looking face and a red dress over his arm. He held gloves, a hat, and a pair of shoes in the other hand.

57

"Will these do?" Louis asked with a little bow to the empty air.

"Ooh, those are lovely," the disembodied voice cooed.

The dress suddenly lifted from the man's arm, contorted through the air, and slipped down as if someone had pulled it over her head. It settled and stood there as if it were on a well-proportioned female body. The audience cheered and laughed as the dress turned and bent, the skirt swirling.

"Will you hook me please?" the voice asked sweetly. There was thunderous applause. Finney and Jack could hardly contain themselves. Louis reached over, as the dress turned its back to him, and fastened the hooks and eyes.

"Thank you," the voice said pleasantly.

The gloves went into the air and onto invisible hands; the shoes were slipped onto invisible feet; the hat went atop an invisible head. The gloves lifted the hem of the skirt slightly and the invisible woman curtsied. She turned and sashayed toward the rear of the stage, swinging her hips. A glove parted the curtain and the dress twirled through the opening.

"Boy!" Harold shook his head as he applauded. "You gotta give 'em credit. They're really good. Of course," he said complacently, "it's either done with wires or mirrors."

"I'm proud of you, Harold," Evelyn said with feigned awe. "It's amazing what three years of college can do."

"What do you mean?" he asked, looking at her with lowered brows. "You don't believe all this stuff is *real*, do you?"

"It's as easy to believe in an invisible woman as it is to believe they could do all that with wires."

"Okay." He shrugged. "They do it with mirrors. I'll explain how when we get home."

"Thank you . . . Hal," she said, smiling sweetly. He looked at her with a suspicious frown.

Louis ended the applause. "Thank you, ladies and gentlemen. You've seen some wondrous sights tonight, but what you will see next is perhaps the strangest of all. Stranger than the Minotaur, stranger than Tiny Tim, stranger than the Little Mermaid, stranger even than Medusa."

Jack grabbed Finney's arm and stared at the closed curtain with round eyes. "It's the Snake Goddess—it's finally the Snake Goddess."

"There have been many legends of a race of snake people who dwelt on Earth before the dawn of civilization. Legends of the lost continents of Mu and Lemuria where the snake people lived. How can we doubt these legends when we have the living proof before our very eyes?" He gestured dramatically and stepped to the side of the stage. "The Snake Goddess!"

The curtains rustled open, revealing a low platform on which rested the giant coils of a snake, coils as thick as the Minotaur's thigh. Propped in the nest of coils was the torso of a woman. Silver hair crested on her head like the feathers of a jungle bird. Her skin was white and mottled with patches of light brown. She had the startled face of an idiot.

Her small hands rested on the pile of coils. She looked nervously about, with quick, jerking movements of her head. A leather collar encircled her neck. A chain attached to the collar lay across the coils. A roustabout held the other end.

The audience drew in its collective breath and leaned forward tensely.

"Don't be alarmed, ladies and gentlemen," Louis said quickly, smiling and holding up his hands. "The Snake Goddess is not dangerous. She is at least a million years old and senile. The collar and chain are merely to keep her from wandering off and injuring herself."

Harold made a sour face of disbelief.

Finney looked at Jack anxiously. "How do you like her? Is she everything you wanted her to be?" he whispered.

"Sumbitch," Jack answered softly, not taking his shining eyes from the creature on the stage.

"Come along," Louis said to the snake woman. "Let the folks get a better look at you."

The roustabout gave the chain a casual jerk and stepped toward the front of the stage. The pale torso slowly rose up on its serpent body. The coils shifted, gleaming dully under the lights. The snake woman slid off the platform and undulated across the stage, her body uncoiling behind her. The audience stirred nervously, the muttering growing in volume.

The man led her off the stage as the houselights came up. The reptilian body flowed over the edge until it stretched twenty feet down the aisle. The people rose to their feet, trying to see but only managing to get in one another's way. Those on the aisle shrank back against those straining forward. The roustabout held the chain with a practiced hand, not letting her get too close to either side, but he could not control her slithering body. A woman screamed as the Goddess brushed against the bench on which she sat, then giggled in embarrassment.

The snake woman turned at the rear of the tent and drew her body around her, then flowed back toward the stage. She held her small arms out slightly as if keeping her balance. Her eyes darted from one side of the aisle to the other as she seemed to hurry back to her platform.

"Which is it, Harold? Wires or mirrors?" Evelyn asked with a wry smile. Harold gave her an annoyed glance and held Rose's hand as she huddled against him.

Francine watched the snake woman's scaly body glide by her feet with little reaction. She felt that she probably should be carrying on like the others, but it was just some sort of trick and she couldn't get excited over it. She felt numb and wished she were home.

Billy gave Francine an occasional worried glance but said nothing.

Louis had some trouble quieting the audience as the Snake Goddess gathered her coils around her on the platform. But they finally settled down as the houselights dimmed and the curtain closed.

"Thank you, ladies and gentlemen," Louis said over the fading murmurs. "Now, I would like to introduce the man who made the Wonder Show possible, the man who brought all these oddities of nature and legend together for your amusement and edification. Ladies and gentlemen, may I present: the Curator."

Haverstock stepped from between the curtains, wearing flowing black robes. He walked to the front of the stage, ignoring Louis, who ducked through the curtains. There was expectant applause.

"I was wondering when he was gonna show up," Harold said from the side of his mouth.

"Doesn't look very much like his picture, does he?" Sonny whispered.

"He looks too much like it to suit me," Rose said.

"I am not a magician," Haverstock began. "I do not do card tricks, saw ladies in half, or pull paper flowers from my sleeve."

He spoke in a perfunctory voice, using none of Louis's theatrics. He seemed confident his performance would stand on its own, without razzle-dazzle.

"Nor am I a mentalist," he continued. "I do not identify keys or pocket watches concealed by an assistant. I do not use sleight of hand nor legerdemain in any way. I am here to reveal to you the powers of the Ancients, the race that ruled the Earth before Man. The Ancients were the masters of the

61

elements, but perished because they used their powers unwisely. In a cataclysm that sank whole continents beneath the seas, they perished, leaving no trace of their great works. I, and I alone, have rediscovered a small fragment of their incredible powers.

"Before we go further, I would like to introduce my assistant. Angel the Magic Boy."

The interior of the tent went suddenly and totally dark. There was a nervous rustle in the audience as they heard the curtains parting.

A single light sprang into being over the stage near the top of the tent. A face floated there, pale and beautiful, topped by slightly unruly white hair. The light spread gradually until the entire figure was illuminated, floating six feet above the stage.

Angel wore a robe similar to Haverstock's, but white. He floated upright, his arms outstretched, his face calm and bland.

He began to move. He floated out over the wide-eyed faces, his robes billowing around him like a slow-motion wraith, like a ghost ship sailing on moonbeams. The light stayed with him as if he were radiating it himself. The startled faces looked up at him, illuminated by his warm glow.

He reached the rear of the tent and turned in a fantasy of swirling robes. He returned to the stage and turned again, facing the audience. Then he slowly lowered to the stage. The audience applauded madly. Angel's glow waned as the stage lights came up. He stood looking vaguely at the audience as Haverstock held up his hands for silence.

"The Ancients recognized only four elements: air, earth, fire, and water. They knew complete mastery of them all. Tonight I will demonstrate these powers for you." He lowered his eyebrows sternly. "I must caution you, however, to remain in your seats during this demonstration. What you see may frighten you, may even terrify you. There will be apparitions and manifestations in the air over your heads and in the ground under your feet, but there is no danger if you remain in your seats and do not panic!"

Finney and Jack trembled in anticipation and looked at each other in delicious fright.

Harold rolled his eyes. "Oh, brother," he groaned.

"Remember," Haverstock admonished, "no matter what you see, no matter what you hear, there is no danger if you remain seated. I cannot be responsible for your safety otherwise. Do not leave your seats!"

He pulled a wand from his robes as the audience sat, barely breathing. He held it above his head and the tent was again pitched into total darkness.

"Fire!" Haverstock bellowed.

The tip of the wand burst into flame, illuminating the stage and creating ruby reflections in the wide eyes of the spectators. Angel stood where he had, calmly, his arms at his sides, his eyes partially closed, his head moving faintly side to side. Haverstock reached downward with the wand and touched the flaming end to Angel's robes.

Angel burst into flame as though the robes had been soaked in gasoline. The audience screamed and jumped to its feet. Evelyn gasped and involuntarily clutched her throat. Haverstock held up a cautionary hand.

Angel was completely obliterated by the fire. No trace of him remained, only a raw flame that burned with no source. Then the flame shrank, pulled into itself, became not a fire but a ball of light, a chunk of the sun a yard across that rose from the stage and convoluted in the air. Haverstock stood beneath it, his arms outstretched, his head thrown back, staring intensely at it.

Suddenly feathery extensions of flame stretched from either side of the fireball. The flickering appendages co-

63

alesced, shaped themselves, became wings of fire. The fire-ball shifted, transmuted, shrank further, and took form.

The fiery swan flapped its wings of blazing feathers and took flight over the audience. It reached the rear of the tent, stretched its wings, banked, turned gracefully, and returned toward the stage. It repeated the maneuver, circling the tent, leaving behind it stray little flames that died in the air.

The audience followed it with reddened faces, swiveling heads and bodies. They crouched in their seats, hardly breathing.

"Water!" Haverstock shouted.

The air in the center of the tent darkened. Wisps of fog appeared from nowhere and rushed to the center of the darkness, swirling around it, and then were drawn into the cauldron of roiling air. The firebird continued to circle, now trailing feathers of steam as it flew through the damp air. The darkness grew light, became a whirlpool of mist. The walls of the tent billowed inward, though there was no wind. The mist thickened swiftly, rounding its shape.

Then a six-foot globe of clear water floated high in the tent. The surface rippled and trembled as if trying to dis-integrate. The tent walls settled back and the swirling tur-bulence in the air died away.

The people watched in amazement, craning their necks, too far into shock to make a sound.

The swan of fire plunged suddenly into the sphere. Steam hissed and billowed, obscuring the globe of water for a mo-ment. When the steam cleared, Angel was inside it, naked and unharmed. He lay curled in the center of the globe, seen as if through a fogged window, his pale, slim body gleaming although no lights were on. The air itself seemed illuminat-ed.

Then his body uncurled and he swam in the globe of wa-ter, executing graceful turns and flourishes, slow, dream-like movements which belied the limited space in which he floated.

Evelyn watched, lost in a reverie, overwhelmed by the beauty of what she saw. Only when she couldn't see any longer did she realize that her eyes had filled with tears.

"Earth!" Haverstock called, though it is doubtful if anyone heard him.

The hard-packed earth that was the floor of the tent trembled. The people looked away from the globe of water, looked at the ground, held their breaths, waiting for the next onslaught on their senses. The earth moved again and they screamed. They heard a grumbling, a grinding, a rending. They were frozen, afraid to move. Then there was a new sound, a sharp crack like gunfire and a fissure opened down the center of the aisle, exposing raw earth and stones. It started at the stage as a mere crack, then widened to about a foot and dwindled away to a crack again at the rear of the tent. Loose earth and small stones broke away from the sides and fell with small clattering sounds. The people drew back, away from the miniature chasm.

Then there was a sound above them, a huge sigh of suddenly rushing water. The globe collapsed like a punctured water-filled balloon, the water streaming into the fissure. For a moment, the audience was divided by a shimmering curtain. Then when the water had stopped falling, with a rumble and more trembling the ground closed, leaving no mark where the fissure had been.

An exhalation filled the tent and all eyes shifted upward. Angel floated where the water globe had been, his naked body still making its own light, still obscured by a haze.

"Air!" screamed Haverstock.

The haze around Angel grew heavier. His body became tenuous, out of focus, vaporous, vague, until finally it was indistinguishable. The haze darkened, became a mist that gradually spread until it filled the top of the tent. It grew darker still, thickening into a storm cloud. There was a faint rumble of thunder and heat lightning played over the surface of the darkness. The thunder grew louder and broke through the tent. The lightning grew in intensity until it singed the air.

All eyes were on the electrical display. No one saw a roustabout walk onto the stage, carrying a robe. He stood beside Haverstock and held it in readiness. Haverstock stared at the cloud intently, deep in concentration.

Suddenly a bolt of lightning lanced from the cloud. It crackled through the air and struck the stage with an ear-rattling crash. Heads twisted toward Haverstock.

Angel was standing on the stage, tying the sash of the robe around his waist. The roustabout walked away, unconcerned, and the storm cloud dissipated almost instantly.

Angel bowed to the silent audience. A whisper rustled over the benches. A babble shook the air. Laughter escaped from tense throats. The applause became deafening. Cheers and whistles added to the bedlam. Angel bowed again, his face composed and empty, then turned and went through the curtains. Haverstock bowed slightly and followed him.

Louis emerged and held up his hands for quiet. He was slow in getting it.

"The last item on the program is Henry-etta, half man, half woman," he said as if he had lost interest in the whole affair. "Because of the delicate biological nature of this performance, we must request that all children under the age of eighteen please leave the auditorium. Also, any ladies who might be offended are urged to leave also. Thank you." He departed through the curtains.

Finney and Jack looked at each other in horror, then reluctantly got up to leave. The children and a number of women, as well as a few men, rose and left, their eyes still a bit glassy.

Evelyn sat in deep contemplation. Francine was dazed. Rose still clutched at Harold's arm. The boys looked at each other and grinned at their own seriousness.

"Boy," Harold exhaled, "they really put on a show."

"How did they *do* that?" Billy Sullivan squeaked. "There was no way they could *do* that!"

"I don't know," Harold said, shifting on the bench. "It must have been mass hypnotism."

"I almost wet my drawers when he set Angel on fire." Rose shivered deliciously.

"Do we stay and see Henry-etta?" Sonny asked with a grin. "Or are you girls too refined for this delicate biological exhibition?"

"If it's as good as the rest," Rose said flatly, "I wouldn't miss it for the world."

"Evie?" Sonny asked.

"Huh?" She looked up, coming out of her reverie. "Oh. Yeah. We might as well."

Louis stepped from between the curtains and waited impatiently for the remaining audience to settle down.

"Because we have no desire to embarrass anyone," he said over the noise, "we must ask that all the ladies move to this side of the auditorium." He gestured to his right. "And all the gentlemen move to the other side. Thank you." He once more left the stage.

"Henry-etta must be a dilly," Rose grimaced as she stood up.

"Are you sure you girls want to stay for this?" Harold asked, wrinkling his forehead.

"Sure," Rose said. "Sounds like it might be the closest I'll ever get to a smoker at the Grange Hall."

"Okay." He grinned and waved his hand. "Good-bye, ladies."

The girls moved to the other side, as did the other women. The men already on that side shifted, creating a lot of confusion and conversation in the aisle. A few more people, unnerved by this latest request, left the tent.

A roustabout, the same one who had been collecting tickets, came from the stage and loosened the curtain bunched by the exit. He pulled it, stretching it down the aisle, closing off each sex from the sight of the other. He caught Rose's eye as he passed and winked at her.

"Well, *really!*" she huffed and then grinned behind her hand. "Isn't he the cutest thing?" she whispered to Evelyn. "Have you noticed? This place is absolutely crawling with gorgeous men. The ticket-taker, that Latin hot tamale . . . "

"He's not quite as gorgeous as he thinks he is," Evelyn said wryly.

" . . . Angel, all those stage hands." She leered at Francine. "The Minotaur. Hotcha!" But Francine didn't rise to the bait. Rose frowned at her and then smiled wistfully. "I wonder if I could get a job with this outfit."

"If you did, you wouldn't have any competition," Evelyn said. "There don't seem to be any women with the show."

"That woman selling tickets."

"Oh, yeah," Evelyn said frowning. "I forgot about her."

Louis stepped onto the stage so he could be seen by those on both sides of the curtain.

"Thank you, ladies and gentlemen. Now, I would like to introduce Henry-etta, as strange in his . . . I mean, her . . . " He grinned. "You know what I mean, *its* own way as anything you've seen tonight. Henry-etta!"

The curtain opened and the houselights went down. The fat lady in the poisonous green dress stepped coquettishly onto the stage.

Harold looked at Sonny and Billy and groaned.

Rose snickered. "Well, you were half right when you said

there were no women with the show," she whispered to Evelyn.

"Thank you, Louis, you darling boy," Henry-etta said in a thin, reedy voice, pursing her lips and simpering. "Ladies and gentlemen, your master of ceremonies was Louis Ortiz. Isn't he the handsomest thing you ever saw, ladies?" Her mouth twisted into a provocative smile, but her eyes remained flat. "Give him a big hand for doing a wonderful job."

Henry-etta applauded and the audience half-heartedly joined in, feeling uncomfortable but not wanting to appear unsophisticated. Louis smiled and bowed and left the stage. Henry-etta watched him leave, then turned to the audience.

"Ladies and gentlemen, my real name is Claude Duvier. I was born in Tours, France, in 1887. My parents moved to America when I was four years old. We lived in New Orleans until I was fourteen, when my poor ma-ma and pa-pa died of fever. Desperate and alone, I was placed in an orphan asylum. It was there, shortly after—" she touched her breasts "—that the female half of my body began to emerge. Up until that time I had assumed I was a normal boy. I later discovered, thanks to some older boys, that I was female as well as male in every way.

"I have been married twice—once to a man and once to a woman. I am the mother of two children and the father of three. I am at present unmarried." She touched the hair at the back of her neck.

Harold rolled his eyes and Billy put his hand over his mouth to keep from laughing out loud.

"My body has confounded the greatest doctors and scientists in the world," Henry-etta continued. "Because of the delicate and shocking nature of the rest of my performance, I must request the ladies to leave."

The young man pushed the curtain back to the rear of the

69

tent. As he passed, Rose held her head at what she imagined to be a sophisticated angle, not looking at him.

Evelyn laughed. "Rose, if the judge could see you . . . " The consequences were too dire to put into words.

The women began moving out, looking embarrassed. Several more of the men joined them.

"Thank you for attending Haverstock's Traveling Curiosus and Wonder Show," Henry-etta called over the departing conversation. "I hope you had an entertaining and enlightening evening. Thank you and good night. Don't forget to tell your friends that there will be two performances tomorrow night."

The girls stopped for a moment to talk to the boys.

"Rats!" Rose snarled.

"This is stupid." Harold stood up. "We'll leave with you."

"You'll do no such thing!" Rose put her hand against his chest. "You'll stay right here and tell me everything that happens. I want to know exactly why Henry-etta's body has confounded medical science the world over."

Harold laughed. "Hold it down. She'll hear you."

Rose *humphed*.

"We'll wait for you outside." Evelyn waved and smiled. They moved away, whispering and giggling.

Henry-etta waited patiently until everyone who wanted to leave had left. Only a very small group remained.

"Good," she said and smiled. "Now that the ladies have left, we can get down to business. My, what a handsome group you are. There will be an additional charge of ten cents for the remainder of my performance," she stated flatly.

"Is she kidding?" Harold spread his hands in disbelief.

"Come on, let's stay," Billy urged gleefully. "This ought to be good."

"You've got a dirty mind," Sonny said, grinning.

"Isn't it the truth?" Billy smirked.

A few more left as Henry-etta passed among them collecting their dimes.

"I thought you were broke," Sonny said.

"Well, I've got a dime." He shrugged. "Besides, Rose'll be mad if we don't stay so we can tell her all about it."

Henry-etta reached them and held out her hand. They placed their dimes in it and tried not to meet her eyes. She continued down the row of benches.

"Boy, is Henry-etta a phony," Harold whispered.

"Why?" Billy asked.

"I just looked down the front of *his* dress. All that frontage is pure cotton."

"Really?"

Henry-etta climbed back onto the stage with a grunt. "Would all you lovely gentlemen move up closer, please? I am about to show you exactly what it means to be half man and half woman."

Henry-etta bent over and pulled the long skirt up to her waist. She wore nothing underneath.

"Good Lord," Sonny croaked.

"I was bigger than that when I was five years old," Harold snickered.

"You can see my male sex for yourselves," Henry-etta continued, a little bored with it all. "The female part is more difficult to see—but it's easy to feel. Would any of you gentlemen like to come up and feel for yourselves?"

Henry-etta looked around questioningly, but she had no offers. Some of the men shifted nervously and others did their best not to laugh. Suddenly a man rose from the rear of the tent and walked to the stage.

"Who's that?" Sonny asked. "I never saw him around here before."

"Me neither," Billy agreed.

"Of course not," Harold said with a superior tone. "He's with the show. He's a shill."

"What's a shill?" Billy asked.

The man stepped up onto the stage. Henry-etta moved to him and he very matter-of-factly stuck his hand between her legs. "Ooooh," she moaned and squirmed. "Don't stick it in too far," she said wryly. "You might lose it. Are you satisfied? Is it the real thing?"

The man leered and nodded.

"Okay. That's enough. Don't get carried away."

The man dropped his hand, stepped off the stage, and walked back down the aisle. Harold turned and watched him leave the tent.

"As you can see, I am fully equipped as a man and as a woman. For an additional ten cents, you can watch me screw myself."

"Let's get out of here," Harold grunted. They left, as did all the others.

Henry-etta watched them leave, standing there with her skirt ridiculously around her waist before the rows of empty benches. She sighed and let her skirt drop. "We really had an adventurous crowd tonight," she said in a deeper voice. "Thank goodness." She sighed again and pulled off the orange wig, then turned and walked through the curtains at the rear of the stage.

Harold, Sonny, and Billy joined the girls outside the tent. There were more people gathered around the lined-up circus wagons than there had been earlier. Those who had seen the show were excitedly telling all about it to those who hadn't.

"What happened?" Rose asked excitedly.

"It was very tacky," Harold grimaced. "I'll tell you later."

Finney and Jack ran up to them, their bare feet pounding on the hard ground, their chests heaving in excitement.

"Did you see Henry-etta?" Finney gasped. "What did she do? Tell me. I want to know. I want to know everything."

"Oh, Finney, you can't know everything," Jack said. "There just isn't time."

"But you can try, Jack. You gotta at least try."

"Henry-etta's a phony and his act wouldn't interest you, believe me," Harold said seriously.

Finney looked at him a moment, then nodded, accepting his word. He and Jack ran to get in the rapidly growing line for tickets to the next show. The word had spread like a grass fire. Those who had missed the first show weren't about to miss the second. There was suddenly cheering and applause as Henry-etta came around the side of the tent, the cash box and roll of tickets under her arm.

Rose shook her head, staring at Finney. "I swear. That kid gets stranger by the minute."

Evelyn also looked at Finney, but she smiled and understood.

9.

Hawley, Kansas, like any small farming town on Sat ir-
day morning, began to stir. Slowly at first, gradually shrug-
ging off the lethargy of the uneventful weekdays, it prepared itself for Saturday afternoon when the farmers and
the country people would quit for the weekend and go to
town. It was a ritual, Saturday afternoon in town, a necessary vacation. It was a time to visit with neighbors on the
courthouse lawn, a time to exchange gossip, to compare the
growth of babies. It was a time to escape the kitchen, to forget cooking square meals and eat junk, hamburgers and hot
dogs and ice cream cones and all the marvelous things a
sensible person never cooked at home.

And it was a time for necessary things; the next week's
groceries, flour and coffee and cornmeal and maybe, if there
was money to spare, as a special treat, a few cans of fruits or
vegetables they hadn't been able to grow and can themselves. Other stops were often necessary: the feed store, the

dry goods store, the dime store, the auto store, but these were done first, done quickly, gotten out of the way for the holiday part of the afternoon.

Many of the merchants could count on twice as much revenue on Saturday afternoon as they had taken in all week. It was the choice part of the week for almost everyone.

The farther out they lived, the bigger the occasion. They came thirty or forty miles on dusty roads, in old cars and trucks that would barely get up to thirty-five on a downhill grade. They came with the back seat or the truck bed filled with children. The children were as well behaved as their clock-spring bodies would allow them to be, as angelic as the endless ride would permit. They were well aware that an infraction that early in the day could easily lead to a curtailment of activities later on.

Saturday afternoon was especially good for the children. No adult was capable of anticipating it with such feverish intensity. It was an afternoon free of chores, of freedom to explode—within prescribed bounds. And most important of all, it was an afternoon to go to the picture show.

Some had already heard that there would be no picture show on that particular Saturday; Mier's Majestic was still being fumigated.

But what would have been a tragedy on any other Saturday was of no consequence. The tent show was in town.

Folks usually came to town right after dinner and returned home in time for evening chores and a late supper, but not that Saturday. The tent show was in town. Chores were rearranged, schedules were shifted, plans were made to stay late that one time.

The telephone lines had been singing down the lanes and across the fields. It was the most fantastic tent show ever. It was an experience of a lifetime, a sight not to be missed. It was the Columbian Exposition and Halley's Comet rolled into one.

The events had been related over and over until everyone in the county knew exactly what they would see. Those who weren't called heard it on the party line. Most didn't believe the fantastic claims, but they would go anyway— just to see if the teller of the tale was as windy as they suspected.

Early that Saturday morning, before the heat had become uncomfortable, while Hawley was still yawning and stretching, Evelyn Bradley left Mier's Dry Goods with a bundle under her tan arm. She felt good, enjoying the relatively cool air, thinking of the night before. She felt a certain ambiguity about what she had seen at the tent show. She couldn't accept her brother's unshaken conviction that everything had been a sham—entertaining and brilliant, to be sure, but a fake nevertheless. Nor could she quite accept it at face value. She was certainly aware of the implications, the disturbing implications, if it were real. But, for some reason, she wasn't at all disturbed by it. Instead she felt only wonder and a nagging worry that Harold was probably right, after all.

Sonny had been something of a disappointment. He had driven the Packard to the picnic grounds on Crooked Creek and parked with obviously amorous intentions. He hadn't wanted to talk about the Wonder Show at all—and she hadn't been able to get her mind off it.

She put the bundle in the wire basket on her bicycle and pedaled down the quiet street toward home. She wondered if her father would make an "arrangement" for her the way Judge Willet had for Grace Elizabeth. She smiled at the thought and then felt a little depressed. She didn't know anyone she'd want to marry, and she supposed she knew every eligible boy in Hawley County.

76

She didn't know why she worried about it. She was definitely not planning marriage before she finished college—if she was able to go to college this fall. He hadn't said anything to her, but she knew her father was worried about the slump. He was afraid the crops wouldn't make much this year, the way the prices were falling.

Well, maybe Sonny Redwine wouldn't make a bad husband—if she had to settle. She liked Sonny; liked him a lot. He had been very sweet last night—and a little surprising, because he was usually so bashful. She smiled to herself.

Then her smile broadened and she laughed out loud. She had known Sonny all her life and he had never asked her for a date before yesterday. They had been friends, but he had never shown any romantic interest. Why, suddenly, had he? Unless . . . *he* had looked around and decided, if he had to settle, she was the best available. She didn't know whether she felt flattered or not, but she thought it was very funny, if true.

She waved at Elmo Whittaker loading salt blocks on his wagon at the feed and grain store, smiled at Sonny's mother leaving the bank, yelled, "Hello," to Billy Sullivan at the ice house. (Did Sonny's mother seem friendlier? Was she a part of the plot?)

She slowed when she passed the Wonder Show and looked at it curiously. It was silent and a little shabby in the bright sunlight, and no one was about. She passed the yellow depot and her bicycle tires *plocked* four times crossing the railroad tracks.

The pavement ended at the bridge over Crooked Creek. The boards rattled rhythmically as she rode across. She looked down at the water and saw Angel sitting on the bank fishing.

She stopped, leaned against the iron railing, and watched him. How pale he is, she thought, and how sweet and innocent and sad he looks. She would have had a difficult time explaining her emotions at that moment. There was awe, because of what she had seen him do, but, again, she wasn't disturbed by it. There was pity also because he was so different and exotic. A bit of erotic fascination because she had never seen a man quite so good looking, except maybe at the picture show. And there was no small amount of simple curiosity.

He suddenly looked up at her. His tousled white hair shone in the sun like silver. His first expression was wary, like a beautiful cat, she thought, uncertain of the danger but ready to flee. Then, apparently deciding that he wasn't threatened, he smiled, hesitantly and shyly. Evelyn felt a pain in her breast, an honest physical pain.

My God, she thought, and Sonny Redwine vanished from her mind. She smiled back tentatively and made a sudden decision. She rode the rest of the way across the bridge, parked the bicycle, and went down the path to the water.

He watched her approach and then stood up, again reminding her of a cat preparing for flight should the situation warrant it.

"Hello," she said a little nervously. "I saw the show last night. It was slightly overwhelming."

Angel smiled and nodded slightly. Evelyn began to feel a bit embarrassed by her forwardness and a little flustered when he said nothing. She noticed his eyes and realized the irises were red. She fidgeted and tried not to stare, although her fascination was nearly overpowering.

She cleared her throat and forged ahead. "I'm Evelyn Bradley. I live down the road a couple of miles." She indicated the direction with a nod of her head. Angel still said nothing, just looked at her with his clear ruby eyes and smiled foolishly. "Well," she said and took a step backward, "I didn't mean to disturb you. I just wanted to tell you how much I enjoyed the show last night."

Disappointment crossed Angel's face. He put his fingers to his mouth and shook his head.

"He can't talk," a small voice said near the ground. Tiny Tim stepped from behind Angel's leg. Angel smiled and nodded again.

"Oh," Evelyn said, startled, "I didn't know. If I'm bothering you, I'll leave."

"Perhaps . . . " Tim began, but Angel stopped him by reaching down and touching him on the top of his head. Tim squinted up at him and frowned. Angel put his fingertips to his mouth again, then held the hand out toward Evelyn. He looked at her questioningly.

Tim sighed a small sigh and sat on a three-inch rock. "Not at all," he said. "Pull up a rock and join us. Are there any fish in this creek?"

"I think so." She sat on a large flat stone and folded her skirt under her knees.

"They must be somewhere else this morning," Tim grumbled, a frown creasing his ugly little face. "We haven't had a nibble."

Evelyn smiled and listened to a couple of scissortails squabbling in the cottonwood leaning over the water. Angel reseated himself and picked up his fishing pole.

"It's a pleasant way to spend a little time, even if you don't catch anything," she said and felt a lethargy of contentment creeping through her.

"That's true enough, Miss Bradley." Tim nodded.

She was a little amazed at the casual way she talked with these two exotic creatures: an ugly little gnome whose head didn't reach her knee and the pale young man with the ruby eyes. And Angel was a part of the conversation, she suddenly realized. His marvelously expressive face commented on everything said. She supposed it was a normal characteristic of mutes.

"I . . . ah . . . suppose it would be tactless of me to ask

how some of the things in the show are done? My brother thinks that you, for instance, are done with mirrors. Now I can tell him you're one hundred percent real."

"I would have no objection to telling you how everything is done, but if Haverstock found out, I'd wind up as the snake woman's breakfast." He pitched a pebble the size of his fist into the water. "Miss Bradley," he said without looking at her, "it might be a good idea if you didn't mention speaking to us, not even to your brother. Haverstock doesn't like us to have anything to do with the town people. We're not even supposed to leave the wagons, but I thought Angel needed some sun. He's been a little peaked lately."

Angel frowned at him.

"Of course." She stood up. "I'd better leave before someone sees us. I wouldn't want to get you in trouble."

Angel rose to his feet and smiled at her. His sadness and loneliness and tenderness radiated against her. She felt a funny sensation in her stomach.

"Good-bye, Miss Bradley," Tim said, unable to keep the relief from his voice.

"Good-bye," she said and turned. Her foot landed on a round river rock. The rock was wet and slick with moss. Her foot slid sideways. She gasped and fell toward the water. Angel reached forward to grab her.

She stopped falling, but Angel's hand was still six inches from her. Then his fingers clasped her wrist and pulled her to her feet. He looked at her with concern as she caught her breath. She laughed in embarrassment.

"You see, Angel!" Tim shouted with excitement. "I told you! I told you!" Then he looked at Evelyn and composed himself. "Are you all right, Miss Bradley? It's a good thing Angel has quick reflexes."

"Yes, I'm fine." She looked at Angel's hand, still holding hers. He released it suddenly and wiped his hand nervously on his thigh. Evelyn touched his arm briefly. "Thank you," she said. He grinned and nodded, radiating pleasure.

She turned to Tim with a perplexed expression. "I was aware of everything that happened. Angel didn't touch me until I had already stopped falling."

She looked back at Angel. He frowned in confusion.

"You must be mistaken, Miss Bradley," Tim said and smiled. His little face twisted grotesquely. "Naturally Angel caught you. What else could have happened?"

"That's what I'm asking you. It could have been the same thing that makes Angel fly, that changes him into a flaming bird, that makes a thunderstorm in a tent, that makes an invisible woman."

Tim laughed. "But those are just tricks. Nothing but side-show tricks."

"I don't believe you."

Angel looked from one to the other with a bewildered expression on his face.

Tim spread his tiny hands and shrugged. "I'm sorry, Miss Bradley. What else can I say? In the excitement of the moment, you must have imagined it." He looked up at Evelyn with a bland expression on his face.

Evelyn frowned, feeling slightly foolish. She was positive she hadn't been imagining anything, but now she didn't know what to do. She couldn't just stand there calling him a liar. She decided the best action was a hasty retreat.

"Hello, down there," a voice called from the bridge. All three looked up. A plump, middle-aged man stood watching them. "Haverstock's awake," he said loudly. "You'd better get back. He's in a rotten mood as usual."

Tim tugged at Angel's trouser leg. "Get him down here," he commanded when Angel looked at him. Angel was puzzled but motioned for the man to join them. He looked questioningly at them for a moment and started down.

81

"What's the matter?" he asked, looking curiously at Evelyn.

"This is Evelyn Bradley, Henry. Miss Bradley, this is Henry Collins; better known as Henry-etta," Tim explained, his voice tense.

"Hello." Evelyn held out her hand. "I thought you looked familiar."

He hesitated and then shook her hand quickly. "How do you do? Angel, you'd better take Tim and get back before he misses you. You know what he's liable to do."

"Angel and I have to get back, Miss Bradley. Tell Henry what you thought happened. I'm sure he can convince you that it was your imagination."

"What happened?" Henry asked, concern edging his voice.

"It was nothing . . . " Evelyn began, deciding not to go into it again.

"Miss Bradley almost fell in the creek," Tim said. "Angel caught her just in time, but she seems to think there was something supernatural about it. I've warned her not to mention that she's talked to us. Let's go, Angel."

Angel lifted Tiny Tim from the ground and placed him on his shoulder. He smiled at Evelyn and touched his lips with his fingers. He turned and went up the path to the bridge.

Henry watched them go and then turned to Evelyn. "What's this all about?" he asked with no friendliness in his voice.

Evelyn sighed. "It's really nothing. I'm sure it was just my imagination."

Henry nodded. "Very well. Just go on home and forget the whole thing, Miss Bradley. Mr. Haverstock is very strict. We are forbidden to talk to town people. We must make sure he doesn't find out about this. Your curiosity could get some very nice people in serious trouble. Forgive me for speaking so harshly."

"No," she said, looking at her hands, "I understand. B it it isn't just curiosity; at least I don't think it is. I don't know . . . " she finished lamely.

"Oh, I see." Henry nodded ruefully. "Our beautiful, guileless Angel has smiled and captured another fluttering female heart. It happens in every town. There are usually several trying to sneak into his wagon. So far, none have succeeded." He snorted fondly. "The poor, dumb thing probably wouldn't know what to do with them if they did."

"I'm sure I don't know what you mean," Evelyn said with more heat than she had intended. She knew she was over-reacting because he had come so close to the truth. She had felt a little like some giddy girl swooning over a movie star.

"Miss Bradley. Angel is . . . well . . . don't be offend-ed; Angel's friendliness to you means nothing. Angel is . . . simple. He's like a puppy that's been mistreated. Any kindness will cause him to act in that affectionate way. Just like a puppy that wags its tail and licks your hand. It doesn't mean that he has any special interest in you; it would be the same with anyone. Don't go getting the wrong idea."

"I won't, Mr. Collins." Her face felt hot and she hoped she wasn't blushing. Why didn't he stop talking? She want-ed to run, but she wouldn't do it. She had every intention of retaining as much of her dignity as she could.

"Good," Henry said in a kindlier voice. "Now run along and don't say anything to anybody."

"I won't. Good-bye, Mr. Collins." She turned and began climbing the path back up to the bridge. She walked very carefully; she couldn't see too well through the haze of em-barrassment.

"Good-bye, Miss Bradley," he called after her. "We'll

pack up and be out of town in the morning and you'll forget all about us."

Suddenly, to Evelyn, the situation became absurd and very funny. She felt exactly as if she were a lecherous man being warned away from an innocent young girl by her father; a gentle warning, but with threats of greater severity if he persisted. She began laughing. She turned on the path and waved to Henry.

"I doubt it," she called. "I really doubt it." She continued up the path, got on her bicycle and rode away, still smiling to herself. She looked back once and saw Henry hurrying toward town.

10.

The tent show slept in the bright morning, waiting for darkness to spring to life with wonders beyond imagination. But there was activity behind the wall of wagons not seen by the curious eyes on the street. One of the six workmen carried a towsack on his shoulder, then emptied oats into a trough within easy reach of the tethered horses. Another entered a wagon with a covered bowl in one hand and a pail in the other.

Medusa sat at a small table, patiently waiting to be fed. She looked at the man and ran her gray tongue over her lips. The snakes on her head writhed and squirmed and squabbled over a captured grasshopper too big to swallow, flicked little red tongues and hissed. A tic in Medusa's cheek jerked rhythmically.

The roustabout put the covered bowl on the table. She removed the lid and ate the stew clumsily with a spoon.

He took a package wrapped in butcher paper from the pail

and dumped fish in the mermaid's tank. She grabbed them and devoured them greedily, leaving scales and bits of fish flesh to float lazily in the cloudy water.

He tipped the pail over the snake woman's cage and poured out a chunk of raw meat. It hit the floor of the cage with a bloody thud. The snake woman looked at the man with her startled bird eyes, then stirred her coils and picked up the meat with dainty hands. She nibbled at it fastidiously, swaying slightly.

The roustabout left the wagon and returned to the tent. The sides had been pulled up to let in a faint breeze. He watched the Minotaur and three other roustabouts shoot dice on a blanket for a while. The Minotaur wore a blue chambray shirt and drab moleskin trousers. His hoofs stuck grotesquely from the cuffed bottoms.

The roustabout tired of the crap game and looked at Kelsey Armstrong asleep on a bench. He knew Kelsey had been out last night with a town girl. Kelsey had been with Haverstock nearly a year, longer than any of the other roustabouts. He'd been around so long he was getting careless— or fed up. If Haverstock found out, Kelsey would have his ass in a sling, the man thought. He sighed. Well, Haverstock will find out. He always does, but not from me. I might score a few points, but I don't want Kelsey on my conscience. He can just be glad it was me who saw him last night and not one of the others.

He lay on another bench and went to sleep.

The Minotaur, finished with the crap game, stood up and stretched. His muscles strained at the fabric of his shirt until it seemed about to split. He rubbed his crotch, trying to ease the ever-increasing ache that centered there. The ache was always with him, always growing until it had to be satisfied. Even then it never went away completely, but

86

nested quietly between his thighs, beginning its growth all over again.

He left the tent and wandered to the wagons, started to enter one of them, and stopped. He saw her between the wagons, though she couldn't see him. It was the girl from last night, the one with long, silky hair. His fingers moved unconsciously, stroking her long, soft, lovely hair.

Haverstock sat by the open door of his wagon, eating mechanically, as if hunger were an unwelcome intrusion. He watched the Minotaur and knew the danger point was rapidly approaching. Louis had said he was on the trail of a likely prospect. He would have to speak to Louis and make sure. . . .

His eyes narrowed suddenly when Angel walked by with Tim on his shoulder.

"Angel!" he snapped. "Come in here."

Angel stopped and turned, apprehension in his ruby eyes. Tim whispered quickly in his ear. Angel mounted the steps and stood in the doorway of the caravan.

"Where have you been?"

"We didn't want to disturb you," Tim said hesitantly, "so we were in my wagon playing cards."

"Where's Henry?"

"I don't know. Neither he nor the Minotaur were in there."

"Angel, take Tim back to his wagon. Then come in here and have your breakfast." He looked intently at Angel. "We have some work to do."

Angel nodded and descended the steps. Tim held on to Angel's snowy hair and looked back at the dark man barely visible through the open doorway. There was worry on his small doughy face.

* * *

Tim's sleeping quarters were in a small packing crate set on the end of Henry's dressing table. After Angel left him there, he paced up and down the table among the scattered cosmetics, hobbling on his crooked leg. His reflection matched his every move in the dressing table mirror.

He stopped and released his breath when Henry came in.

"Where's Angel?" Henry asked, sitting on the stool.

"With Haverstock. Henry . . . "

"What was all that about at the creek?"

"I'm trying to tell you. That girl fell. Her foot slipped on a rock and she fell. Angel grabbed for her, but she stopped falling before he touched her. His hand was six inches from her when she stopped falling. I've always told you it was Angel who had the gift and not Haverstock. I was right! It's Angel and not Haverstock. I saw it." His tiny voice grew more excited. "Angel is really the one. Haverstock just uses him under hypnosis."

"You're sure? There's no mistake?"

"There's no mistake."

"And the girl? She saw it too? Was that what that was all about, that supernatural business?"

"Yes, didn't she tell you?"

"No." Henry gnawed on his lower lip. "She didn't say anything about it. She just said it must have been her imagination."

"Do you think she meant it?"

"I don't know."

"She told me she didn't believe me when I suggested that. I didn't know what else to say to her. That's why I called you down. Do you think she'll tell anyone?"

"I don't know, but I don't think she'll be hanging around anymore. I told her our poor Angel was simple-minded. If she had any lustful designs on him, that should cool it off."

"That should do it."

"It seemed to be doing the job, then, I don't know . . . a funny thing happened."

"What do you mean?"

"She started laughing. She was going up the path in a proper pique; then she started laughing. It was very peculiar."

11.

Evelyn leaned the bicycle against the porch railing and went into the house with the bundle from Mier's Dry Goods. She walked through the front room into her parents' bedroom. Bess looked up from her sewing machine.

Evelyn handed her the bundle. "Here's the material."

"You sure took your time," her mother scolded mildly.

"Sorry, Mama," she said and plopped into the gold overstuffed chair. "I . . . ah . . . I was talking with some-one."

"It couldn't have been Sonny Redwine, could it?" Bess teased.

"No . . . it couldn't," she said. Her mother looked dis-believing and Evelyn decided it was just as well.

Bess unwrapped the bundle and spread the yellow percale on the bed. "Rose Willet called. I told her you'd call her back."

"Thanks, Mama. Mama . . . " she hesitated " . . . do

you think it's kinda odd that Sonny asked me out last night?"

"In what way, dear?"

"Well, I've known him all my life, and he never asked me out before."

Bess smiled. "Maybe it just occurred to him how pretty you are. He's always been shy." She put pins in her mouth and spread a tissue-paper pattern on the yellow material.

"I was thinking a while ago if, well, if I had to marry somebody in Hawley, who would it be?"

"And who . . . " Bess took the pins from her mouth. "And who did you decide on?"

"Nobody. But I was thinking, what if Sonny had thought the same thing, if he had looked around to see who in Hawley he would want to marry, and . . . well . . . picked me."

Bess shook her head, pinning the pattern to the material. "Sonny's a little young to be thinking about marriage."

"He's the same age as me."

"I know, dear, but it's different for a girl. Girls are more mature at eighteen than boys." She looked up from her work. "Are you and Sonny getting serious?"

"No." Evelyn shrugged. "I mean, I'm not in love with him or anything, but I like him well enough, I guess. I've just been thinking . . . Rose told me about Grace Elizabeth and Wash Peacock and it made me feel kinda sad, and I wondered, if I couldn't find anybody I wanted to marry, if you and Daddy would make an arrangement for me like the judge did for Grace Elizabeth."

Bess chuckled. "You know we'd never do that."

"I know, but you don't want an old maid haunting the house any more than the judge does."

"Hawley's not the whole world. What's got into you today? Isn't it a little early for you to start worrying about be-

ing an old maid? Girls don't get married as young as they
did when I was your age."

"Yeah, but if I don't go to college this fall, I don't know
where I'll ever meet anyone new." Images of Angel and
Tiny Tim and Henry flicked through her mind.

Bess looked up and frowned. Evelyn thought for a moment her mind had been read by her mother.

"I could go to the big city and become a career girl," Evelyn said quickly, "but the way it sounds on the radio, everybody is out of work these days. Well . . ." she chuckled
" . . . I guess I'll have to hang around the depot and check
out all the drummers coming to town."

"Evelyn!" Bess said, then she stopped working on the pattern and sat on the edge of the bed. "Has Dad talked to you
about college this fall?"

Evelyn felt a knot forming in her stomach. "No . . . but
I know he's worried."

"Oh, Evie, darling, I didn't know how to tell you," Bess
said with a catch in her voice. "I know how much you've
been looking forward to college, but we're pretty sure there
won't be enough money. If things get as bad as your father
thinks they will, all the money we've saved will have to go
to the farm. Your father is afraid things will be bad for several years, the way it looks. What little we can spare will
have to go to your brother so he can finish his last year. We
wouldn't even have enough for that if he wasn't getting that
football money. There just won't be enough for both of you,
and it's more important for a boy to get a college education
than a girl. I'm sorry, dear."

Evelyn smiled and took her mother's hand. "I know," she
said. "Well . . . " she stood up " . . . I guess I'll have to
keep an open mind about Sonny. Aren't you going into
town this afternoon?"

Bess shook her head. "Dad has work to do, and so do I—
and so do you."

Evelyn went to the phone in the parlor, gave the crank a couple of quick turns, took down the receiver and put it to her ear. She pulled the mouthpiece down a couple of inches so she could reach it. She always had to if Harold had used the phone last.

"Hello, Reba," she said, still having to stretch her neck a little. "Would you ring the Willets, please?" She smiled. "Fine. How are you? . . . Yes, I saw it last night. It's really good. I think you'll enjoy it. . . . Thank you, Reba. . . . Hello. . . . Who's this? . . . Finney? What are you doing there? . . . Is the judge paying you enough to see both shows again tonight?" She laughed. "Is Rose there? This is Evie. . . . Yeah, it was really terrific all right. How was it the second time? . . . That's good. . . . Bye, Finney. . . . Rose, Mama said you called. . . . Probably. I'll have to ask."

She turned her head toward the bedroom and put her hand over the mouthpiece. "Mama?" she called.

"Yes, dear?"

"Rose is having a slumber party tonight. Is it okay if I go?"

"I suppose so, if you get all your chores done."

"Thanks, Mama." She turned back to the phone. "It's okay, Rose. . . . I don't know if I can make it in time for supper or not. I have quite a few chores stacked up because we goofed off so much yesterday. . . .Well, I'll make it if I can. . . . Bye, Rose."

Evelyn hung up the receiver and looked thoughtfully out the window, her mind not on Rose's slumber party.

12.

On the other side of the partition in Haverstock's wagon, on the side opposite his office, was the room where Angel slept and where he and Haverstock spent their afternoons. The four sides of the room were almost solid with books. Only a space against one wall where Angel's cot sat; the door in the partition; a small high window opposite the cot, closed against the outside heat; and a panel through which communication with the driver was possible: only those spaces in the comfortably cool room were not covered with books and locked cabinets.

Angel and Haverstock sat in facing chairs beneath the window in a little island of light. As the time neared midday, the sun's rays entered at an oblique angle, sparkling dust motes in the air, giving silver fire to Angel's hair and glistening the perspiration on his face.

Haverstock sat with his arms akimbo and his hands on his knees. He leaned forward into the shaft of sunlight and looked hard into Angel's face. Angel was in an uneasy trance, his eyes like pink agates, his hands lying limp and palm-up in his lap.

"You're fighting me, Angel," the older man said softly. "What's gotten into you? You've never behaved this way before. Stop fighting me!" he barked, then his voice softened again. "If only you could talk, my beautiful Angel."

He leaned back in the chair, his face moving into shadow. "If you could talk, we would have finished all this years ago. It's very slow with you sitting there like a dummy. If you could talk, you could tell me what the hell's the matter with you."

He leaned forward suddenly and slapped his knees. "Stop fighting me!" he said, his voice grating angrily. Angel's body trembled, his muscles contracting as if an electric current ran through them. His jaw locked and his neck corded. New perspiration popped out on his flushed face. His breath gurgled in his throat.

Then his body slumped. He closed his eyes and breathed with difficulty. Then he opened his eyes and looked at the other man with fear. He was out of the trance.

Haverstock sighed and sat back. "I'm sorry, Angel. I didn't mean to hurt you, but you do vex a body." He took a pencil and pad from a shelf and handed them to Angel. Angel hesitantly took them.

"I'm about to ask you some questions and I want you to answer them. I want you to answer them truthfully and in full." His voice smoothed into cream. "I don't like to hurt you, Angel. You're fighting me, my boy. You've never fought me before. You've always been as malleable as damp sand, as resistant as pudding. Tell me, Angel, my boy. Tell me why you are resisting me now."

Angel looked at him in confusion, not knowing. He looked helplessly at the pencil and pad he held loosely in his hands. He raised his eyes to the other man and shook his head, frowning.

95

"Angel, do not aggravate me further. I asked why you are resisting my control. I want an answer!"

Still confused, Angel wrote I DON'T KNOW on the pad and held it up for Haverstock to see. Haverstock growled. His face flushed with anger.

Angel's body jerked. His head flew back and a silent scream rattled in his throat. His elbows clamped to his sides. Then his muscles went limp. He slumped in the chair. The pencil and pad dropped from his flaccid hands.

"You see what your stubbornness has caused me to do?" Haverstock asked in martyred tones. "Angel, Angel, why do you make me do this? I am not a hard-hearted man. All I want from you is cooperation; the same cooperation you've always given me." He smiled and patted Angel's knee. "Now, we're going to try once more. Pick up the pencil and the pad and tell me what is bothering you."

Breathing heavily, Angel reached to the floor and retrieved the pencil and pad.

"We must resolve this, Angel, before we can continue with our work. I do not like this impasse. What has happened to cause this resistance? What little adventure have you had to bring this about? Have you had a tiny revelation? Have you learned something you would be better off not knowing? Where have you gotten this unexpected strength? Tell me, Angel."

Angel looked at Haverstock, then drew a line underneath the words he had already written. He held up the pad.

His fingers writhed. The pad fluttered to the floor. He doubled up in the chair, clamping his arms across his stomach. His eyes bulged in his reddening, damp face. Spittle glistened on his slack lips. A rivulet of blood ran from his nose. His body shivered uncontrollably in the shaft of golden sunlight. The clock in the courthouse tower lazily began to strike eleven o'clock.

13.

The people came to town—in automobiles, new and old, in wagons, on horseback, they came to see the Wonder Show. The shopkeepers looked out their windows and rushed to finish lunch. They quickly telephoned sons and daughters, mothers and fathers, brothers and sisters to drop what they were doing and hurry to the shop to help. The people were coming sooner than expected, in numbers not seen since the county fair.

Mr. Mier watched the crowds and then looked across the square at the closed Majestic. He sniffed.

The town geared for a busy afternoon.

They already stood in small groups on the courthouse lawn in the shade of the sycamore trees, sat on the benches in the sun. The women talked of new babies, clothes, hints of scandal, and the tent show. The men cussed the falling farm prices, cussed the Republicans, cussed Hoover, and chuckled at the tent show nonsense.

The children raced around the square like perpetual motion machines, rolled on the grass, got chiggers and scratches, explored shops to see if anything new had appeared since last Saturday, looked sadly at the closed picture show, ate ice cream and candy. But mostly they stood before the line of painted circus wagons, staring at the pictures, whispering among themselves, daring each other to sneak in right now, looking ahead with dread at the long, endless afternoon before the Wonder Show opened.

In Bowen's Drugs & Sundries, Mrs. Bowen washed dishes while Sonny Redwine waited on the counter. Mr. Bowen filled prescriptions and tried to handle the people coming and going, getting their shopping done before time to go to the tent show.

The fountain was busy every summer Saturday afternoon, but it approached bedlam on that day. Mrs. Bowen could barely keep the sundae dishes and the soda glasses and the Coke glasses washed faster than Sonny could fill them.

Louis Ortiz came in suddenly and created an instant electric silence. Spoons of ice cream stopped halfway to mouths, sweet liquids ceased flowing in paper straws. Twenty-two pairs of eyes followed him to the cigar case. Mr. Bowen hurried from behind the prescription counter. Louis bought two packages of Fatima cigarettes and left, smiling and tipping his hat to the ladies. Noise returned with a rush. Women looked at each other and grinned. Little girls sniggered behind their hands.

Finney and Jack came in sedately, being exceptionally careful to create no parental ire that might block tonight's visit to the Wonder Show. They looked back over their shoulders at Louis and stopped under the ceiling fan for a quick cool air bath. Then they leaned on the counter and looked at Sonny with shiny faces.

Sonny grinned at them, feeling good, thinking of last

night, thinking of Evelyn, humming while he put extra nuts and extra fudge on sundaes and extra large scoops of ice cream on cones.

"A triple-dip, please, Sonny. One strawberry, one chocolate, and one tutti-frutti," Finney said politely.

"The same for me," Jack said.

"Comin' right up." Sonny pulled the cones and scooped the ice cream with a flourish, giving the dipper extra little clicks.

"Are you going to the Wonder Show again tonight, Sonny?" Finney asked, wanting to talk to someone new about it. He had completely exhausted Jack's recollections and imagination.

"I don't imagine," Sonny answered, piling chocolate on strawberry.

"Me and Jack are. We wouldn't miss it for anything. It was the most phantasmagorical event in the history of the world."

Jack smiled in agreement. Mr. Bowen, finding himself in a lull, came over to help with the counter.

Sonny chuckled. "You may be right about that." He presented them with the towering cones. Jack handed him fifteen cents.

Mr. Bowen sighed happily. "He managed to talk Mrs. Bowen and me into going tonight."

"Wait'll you see . . . " Finney began with a rush.

Mr. Bowen laughed and threw up his hands. "Please! You gave me a blow-by-blow account last night. I feel like I've already seen it."

"It gives me the creeps just to think about it." Mrs. Bowen shivered.

"Finney's been so engrossed with the freak show," Mr. Bowen confided to Sonny with a grin, "he didn't even notice the new *Amazing Stories* came in yesterday."

99

"What?" Finney shrieked.

"Only got three copies and they're already sold out," he said with mock sadness.

"What?" Finney shrieked again, his eyes bulging.

"Don't bust a gusset." Mrs. Bowen smiled, taking pity on her son. "I saved you one."

Finney and Jack looked at each other, exhaling heavily. "You shouldn't do that, Pop," Finney said seriously. "It's enough to make a person drop dead."

"You boys run along and keep out of mischief." Mr. Bowen chuckled.

They left, running their tongues in circles on balls of tutti-frutti ice cream perched on top of chocolate perched on strawberry. The Bowens and Sonny looked at each other and smiled.

It was a good day.

14.

"My party is going to be a disaster!" Rose Willet shrilled petulantly. "Francine is acting like a zombie. Half the girls I invited are going to that stupid freak show."

She sat grimly on her bed, giving black looks at anything that moved. The only thing moving at the moment was her mother. She pulled an armload of bedclothes from the cedar chest.

"They can come over after the show, dear," Mrs. Willet said as she moved toward the door, taking the bedclothes outside to air on the line.

"They'll come straggling in all night. What fun will that be? Nobody'll be here to help me; Sister and Lilah, both going off. Even you won't be here to help me. What do you want to go to that stupid freak show for?"

"Yes, dear." Mrs. Willet sighed and went out. She closed the door of the bedroom and leaned against it, exhaling wearily. "I don't know which will be worse, a woman with snakes on her head or a house full of giggling girls," she muttered to herself and went on downstairs, trying to see over the heap of linens in her arms.

Rose grunted and hit the flowered comforter with both fists. Her mother had washed and marcelled her hair that morning and it shone like gold leaf. Her new frock of chiffon mull was the color of daffodils. And her bottom lip protruded like a shovel.

She suddenly stood up and flounced from the room. She was halfway down the stairs when the wave of heat hit her.

Kelsey Armstrong.

She stopped and clutched the bannister. Her knees felt wobbly, but she resisted the impulse to sit on the steps. Why did he keep popping into her mind like a hot poker? She had tried all morning to bury the memory. Sometimes she could go half an hour, sometimes nearly an hour, with the memory completely suppressed and then, suddenly, as if someone had opened a furnace door, it was there, red and hot and burning.

My God!

My God!

My God!

What if her father were to find out. She was enveloped in gelid air. Why had she been so stupid? Why had she gone back to the tent show after Harold brought her home?

She continued on down the stairs, still hanging onto the bannister, forcing the memory away. She knocked on the door of the judge's study. She heard a grumble that sounded like an invitation to enter. She willed Kelsey Armstrong from her thoughts and went in. Her father looked up from his book and smiled tolerantly. Tolerance was the closest thing to affection that he could manage.

"Daddy," Rose said in a little-girl voice, "everyone's leaving me alone tonight. How can I cope with my party without anyone to help me? You and Mama are going to the tent show, and Sister is going with Wash, and Lilah is spending

102

the night with Mavis Peevey. How can I manage all alone? Can't you make Lilah or Sister stay here and help me?"

The judge's smile had gradually shrunk smaller and smaller until it disappeared completely. "You should have thought of that when you planned the party so suddenly this morning. You knew everyone had already made plans. Your mother did her utmost to convince you to postpone it until next Saturday."

Kelsey Armstrong.

·Was the heat showing in her face? She had to have the party tonight. Kelsey Armstrong wanted her to meet him again tonight. She had invented the party out of thin air. Now she had to have it tonight.

"But you always make Sister help me," she whined.

"Grace Elizabeth and Wash Peacock are to be married this fall. If they want to see each other on Saturday night, I will not interfere. There is no more to be said."

Rose turned and walked out like a wilted buttercup. "Yes, sir," she muttered as she closed the door. She knew if the first wheedle didn't work, a second was not only useless but dangerous.

Judge Willet looked at the closed door and sighed. How could a man be saddled with three such useless daughters? Grace Elizabeth was plain and bookish, and he was damned if he would have an old maid in the family. Lilah was delicate. Not physically; physically she had the constitution of a tractor, but emotionally. She was high-strung and suffered from frequent and opportunely timed headaches and fainting spells. Rose was high-spirited and subject to fits of temper and petulance. Why couldn't he have had sons?

Rose wandered into the kitchen, her mind a muddle. If her father ever found out about last night, well, the consequences were beyond the limits of her imagination. Why had she lost control of herself?

She opened the door of the big wooden icebox and rummaged around. She ate a deviled egg left over from dinner. Her mother came in from the back yard as she poured a glass of milk from the crockery pitcher.

"Are you eating again? I just got the dinner dishes put away," her mother said.

"Why shouldn't I?" Rose grumbled. "Everything is going wrong today." She took a swallow of milk and made a face. "This milk is blinky."

Mrs. Willet frowned. "It shouldn't be. I just got it yesterday." She opened the top of the icebox and looked into the ice compartment. She groaned. "The block of ice I got yesterday is almost melted." She shut the lid. "There's something wrong with this old thing. Air's getting in somewhere. And this is Saturday. They won't deliver ice again until Monday and everything will spoil. Your father will have to go to the ice house." She sighed. "He won't like it. If I didn't have enough to do today, what with your party and going to the tent show and everything. If you're not going to help, at least get out from underfoot." She started toward the judge's study.

Rose went back to her room and flopped onto her bed and thought of Kelsey Armstrong. Oh, Lord, what if Harold were to find out? She had every intention of marrying Harold next year when he finished college. He was handsome and sexy and pliable and would come into a lot of money when he got the farm. She'd heard some talk about the farmers going broke, but she decided it was a lot of nonsense. The farm. That was the only drawback. Well, she'd do something about that after they were married.

Kelsey Armstrong was Harold's fault anyway. If Harold weren't such a damned gentleman, she wouldn't have to sneak out to see somebody else. She compressed her lips. On their next date she would do something about that too.

She was beginning to wish she hadn't planned the party after all. Last night on the pile of cottonseed in the gin, she had felt nothing but fear when he asked to meet her again tonight, but now her body was overruling her caution. It was too late now.

She twitched on the bed, remembering his hard arms around her and his naked body on hers. It had been wonderful, marvelous, fantastic, terrific, sensational. She knew it would be as soon as he smiled at her when he took the tickets at the tent show.

Oh, Lord, what if her father found out!

15.

Dr. Horace Latham lived in the same house he was born in. He had been weaned on the odor of carbolic and ether. He grew in the house, an only child, carefully nurtured on mumps, whooping cough, measles, diphtheria, chicken pox, hives, pregnant women, and a variety of broken bones and abrasions. He had never considered not becoming a doctor.

He went to Kansas City, finished college, became a doctor, got married, had a baby, and established a nice little practice.

Then his father died. He brought his wife, his baby, and his practice to Hawley, to the house he thought he had left forever. It was a fairly old house, built a block from the courthouse in 1887, just three years after the courthouse itself was built. It reared up rather grandly, but it wasn't as big as it seemed. The wide veranda on three sides gave it a deceptive appearance of size. The high peaked roof, crowned with gingerbread and lightning rods, added to the illusion.

But there was more than enough room for Dr. Latham and Francine. They were the only ones left. His mother had died within a year after his return; his wife and newborn son, both from influenza, in 1916 when Francine was four. Now the two of them rattled around in the old house, even with his office and small clinic sharing the downstairs with the kitchen, parlor, and dining room.

He stood at the front door, watching Francine through the closed screen, and wondered if she ever felt the same lack he had as a child. He hadn't really put a name to it until he was grown, but the vague uneasiness had always been there. The lack of a refuge, of a hiding place. The lack of a home where strangers didn't wander in and out all day.

Francine sat in the glider on the porch, swinging lightly, her mind a thousand miles away. The chain squeaked a little, almost like a cricket. Dr. Latham opened the screen and sat beside his daughter, putting his arm around her shoulders. She looked up at him and smiled faintly.

"What's the matter, Francine?" he asked gently.

"Nothing, Daddy." She looked back at her hands in her lap.

"Are you sure? You can tell me if there is, you know."

"I know."

"Well?"

"I don't know, Daddy. I just feel kinda sad."

"Sad? Did you have an argument with Billy Sullivan?"

"Oh, Billy," she dismissed him completely.

"Well, whatever it is, I'm sure you'll get over it when you go to Rose's party tonight."

"I don't really want to go to Rose's party."

"If you don't want to go, don't go."

"I don't know how to get out of it."

"Just tell her you don't want to go."

"I couldn't do that." Francine sighed. "She's already called twice to make sure I'd be there. She's acting like a real witch."

"Well, do whatever you want to do." He gave her shoulder a pat and went back in the house.

She looked after him without expression for a moment, and began to swing slowly again. The clock in the courthouse tower struck three.

16.

Louis Ortiz stretched his arm and shoulder from the bed and retrieved his fancy bracelet watch from where it lay on his neatly folded suit. He brought it to his face, squinted, blinked the sleep from his eyes. It was after five o'clock. He wound the watch and yawned, baring his large, even, white teeth. He put the watch back and stretched his arms over his head. His hands bumped against the brass bedstead. He looked up and watched the muscles play under his brown skin.

He let his arms drop back and scratched his chest, rubbing his fingers over his nipples. He slid his hands under the sheet, across his flat stomach, over his pelvis, down his hard thighs, and back up between his legs. He felt dry and crusty; he should have washed but he had been too sleepy.

He slid his legs from under the sheet and sat on the edge of the bed, yawning again. He stood up and stretched, then ran his hands over his buttocks, enjoying the feel of the tight muscles.

Louis looked at the woman still sleeping in the bed. He had dragged the sheet down to her waist when he stood up. She lay on her side, facing him, her large breasts drooping grotesquely sideways. She slept with her mouth open slightly. Spittle had made a damp spot on the pillow. Her marcelled brown hair had become frizzy with her squirming. Louis smiled. He could really make them squirm.

Shirley Ann Waldrop.

Tiny vertical creases appeared between his eyes. Why had he thought of Shirley Ann Waldrop? He hadn't thought of her or the farm or El Paso in years.

The beautiful, beautiful, golden Shirley Ann; Mr. Waldrop's youngest girl; nineteen years old; the daughter of *El Patron*. Her long skirts sweeping the ground; her lace parasol keeping her skin soft and pale; her corseted waist cinched so small he could, even at fourteen, almost close his hands around it.

It all came back to him, all the old bad memories, sweeping over him like tepid syrup. He remembered how she drove her buggy past the adobe shack, waving cheerfully at the dirty little brown children playing in the sand under the hot Texas sun. There was no shade in the Mexican quarter, no trees but scrubby salt cedars. The big house, the house of *El Patron*, sat in green gloom under giant poplars and cottonwoods. To the Mexican children the temperature seemed to drop twenty degrees as soon as they walked into the yard, something that was not done lightly.

Shirley Ann driving her buggy in the bright, bright sun; her golden curls shining even though she always kept the top up to protect her milky skin. He remembered her riding with her father in his automobile, the only one for miles on either side of the Rio Grande, waving at him and his father and his brothers as they worked in the sandy fields.

His younger brothers and sisters: he couldn't even remember their names or how many there were. He could

110

only remember the three older ones. Inez was sixteen, Magdalena was fifteen. They and his mother worked in the big house.

And the oldest: seventeen-year-old Raphaelo. Dark, handsome Raphaelo. Proud Raphaelo. Proud as a fighting cock. The handsome, proud, smiling, doomed Raphaelo.

Louis had heard a noise in the loft and climbed up to investigate. They were both there, both of them naked. Raphaelo's dark body covering Shirley Ann, Raphelo breathing heavily as he moved, Shirley Ann's soft ivory body moving with him. She moaned, and squirmed and turned her head from side to side—and saw Louis watching them.

She made a noise and Raphaelo jumped to his feet like a cornered tiger. Louis ran, but Raphaelo ran after him, too frightened to care that he was naked, and caught him and dragged him back to the loft and threatened to cut out his liver if he told. But Shirley Ann smiled and caressed Louis, telling him that she trusted him, rubbing her breasts against him.

She had turned back to Raphaelo, but Raphaelo was a flower wilted by fright. He sat in a black shame as Shirley Ann coaxed and fondled him. She moaned and squirmed and turned to Louis. She undressed him, touched him, complimented him, guided him, taught him.

Louis's own pride, his pride at besting Raphaelo even temporarily, overrode his fear. And the next six months were the most glorious he had ever known, better than anything he could have imagined. He had the beautiful, beautiful, golden Shirley Ann Waldrop nearly every day, sometimes twice a day, sometimes only he, sometimes only Raphaelo, but mostly both of them at the same time.

Then, one day, she didn't meet them. Louis and Raphaelo never saw her after that. She stayed in the big house all the time and suddenly married a junior clerk in Mr. Waldrop's

111

bank. The junior clerk moved into the big house and they saw him only twice a day as he rode with Mr. Waldrop to and from the bank.

When the brown baby was born, Mr. Waldrop tied Raphaelo to a wagon wheel and whipped him with a silver-studded bridle until the leather was jellied with blood. His mother had screamed and wailed and prayed to the Virgin, and his father had watched, white-lipped, but he hadn't interfered. Mr. Waldrop was *El Patron*, and Sancho Ortiz was only a peon, even on the north side of the river.

Louis hadn't waited to find out if Shirley Ann had accused him as well. He sneaked into the big house, stole thirty dollars, rode one of the plow horses to town, and caught the first train out. He hadn't been within a hundred miles of El Paso since.

Shirley Ann Waldrop. Why had he thought of her now?

He looked at the woman sleeping on the bed. She had looked a lot better with her clothes on. They were scattered on the floor, where she had flung them in her haste: a boned corset to keep her hips flat, with a tangle of straps, clamps, and hooks to keep her stockings up, a bandeau to keep her breasts flat, enough undergarments to conceal anything.

But the Minotaur didn't care. He had never turned away anyone Louis had brought him, and some of them had been recruited in desperation. Louis always waited until the second day to hunt a partner for the Minotaur, giving them a chance to get a look at him. He usually didn't have much trouble, though Haverstock might be unhappy if he knew that Louis sampled the presentable ones ahead of time. But then he might know and not care. Louis had discovered over the years that Haverstock found out about everything sooner or later.

This one had seen the Minotaur in the show last night, and when Louis had brought it up, her eyes had suddenly sparkled. But the sparkle had quickly changed to craftiness.

She demanded an extra twenty dollars. Louis was pretty sure she would have been happy to do it for nothing, but he hadn't argued. It wasn't his money.

His bladder felt on the point of bursting. He looked around and then under the bed. He pulled out the japanned slop jar and relieved himself.

The noise woke the woman and she lay watching him. He finished, put the lid back on, and slid it under the bed. He washed himself at the washbowl and felt her still looking at him. He turned. She was smiling. He posed, showing his body, washing erotically. He felt a hardening under the cloth and returned to the bed.

17.

Henry Collins stretched his upper lip down over his teeth and applied the powder puff vigorously, trying to cover his beard shadow. He looked in the mirror critically, twisting his mouth at different angles. He curled his lip and tossed the puff in the box of face powder. Rouge on his cheeks, Maybelline on his brows and lashes completed his Henryetta face.

Tiny Tim stepped from his packing crate home, smoothing his doll's suit. Henry had made it from fine batiste, but to Tim it felt as heavy as canvas. He walked across the dressing table and checked himself in the mirror.

Henry settled the orange wig on his head, tilting and tucking until it seemed secure. He stood up and tugged at the low neckline of the green satin gown, shaping the padding in the bodice. He smoothed the skirt over his ample hips, twisting around to check the back in the mirror.

"How do I look?" he asked.

Tim glanced up at him. "Not like anybody I'd take home to mother."

"Thanks." Henry grinned. He turned from the mirror and looked at the Minotaur sleeping naked on the other cot.

The Minotaur lay on his back, his hand on his genitals. His mouth was slightly open and he rasped faintly as he breathed. Henry frowned at the new hole the Minotaur's horn had torn in the pillow. He kicked the leg of the cot.

The Minotaur woke instantly. He looked at Henry with his big, soft, alert eyes. No part of his body moved except his eyelids.

"Get up, you big lummox," Henry said. "It's nearly time." He put Tim on his shoulder and left the wagon.

The Minotaur sat on the edge of the cot, scratching his massive chest. He stood up, stretched, and rubbed his crotch. He took his loincloth from a peg on the wall and slipped it on. He continued to rub himself through the fabric.

Outside, Henry squinted at the setting sun. The canvas of the tent looked like sheet copper. Bullbats circled in the sky, rising higher and higher on warm air currents, then dived like falling stones. They pulled out of their dives with musical bass *thrums*, snatching flying insects, and began their circling climbs once more.

Henry paused and looked at Haverstock's wagon with concern. The doors and windows were closed. It sat, still and silent.

"They sure are at it a long time today," Henry mused.

"Henry, I'm worried about Angel," Tim said fretfully. "I gave him strict orders not to let on about the gift, not to tell him anything about what happened this morning, but I don't know if he can keep anything from Haverstock or not."

115

"What do you suppose they do in there every day?"

"I don't know. Angel can never remember, but he's always completely worn-out."

"Well, come on. I'll put you backstage so I can open up the box office."

18.

Bess Bradley removed the kettle from the stove and poured scalding water over the dishes in the dishpan, then filled the kettle from the pump and put it back on the stove. Evelyn, Otis, and Harold finished their apple pie and brought their plates to the cabinet and put them by the dishpan.

"Do you want me to dry the dishes before I go to Rose's?" Evelyn asked.

"You go ahead, dear. I can manage. You don't want to be late," Bess said, taking a clean cup towel from the cabinet drawer.

"You're sure it's all right?"

"Yes, dear. Go ahead."

"Take the car," Otis said, checking the slop bucket before going to feed the pigs.

"I can ride my bike."

"I'd rather you didn't. It's already dark, and I'd feel better if you were in the car, what with that tent show in town."

"Oh, Daddy." Evelyn grimaced.

"He's right, Evie," Harold chimed in. "I never saw such a scurvy bunch in my life."

Evelyn wrinkled her nose at him. "All right. Whatever you say . . . Hal." She turned quickly to her mother before Harold's black look could turn into a retort. "Mama, did you see *Kindred of the Dust?*"

"What?" Bess looked up and frowned.

"*Kindred of the Dust,* by Peter B. Kyne. 'The soul-searching story of Nan, the sawdust-pile mother and a child who cries for a father he will never know. Of Donald McKay, torn between love for Nan and the love he bears for his father,' " she recited dramatically. "Francine wants to borrow it. She reads Kyne and Harold Bell Wright and bawls her head off."

"I put some books on the mantel," Bess said absently. "I don't know about any others. If you wouldn't leave them layin' around, you wouldn't lose 'em."

Evelyn kissed her mother. "Sorry, Mama," she said.

Bess grinned and shook her head. She pushed back her hair with her wrist but got soap suds on her forehead anyway. "Light the lamp while you're in there, would you?"

"Sure." Evelyn gave her brother a pat on the shoulder and picked up her overnight case. Her father followed her into the parlor and lit the lamp. She got the book from the mantel and gave him a kiss. She pushed the screen door open with her shoulder. Otis caught it before it slammed.

"Be careful," he said. "Looks like there's a cloud comin' up."

She tossed the overnight case and the book in the back seat. "I will."

"And be sure and have the car back in time for church in the morning."

"Stop fussing," she said and laughed. She started the car and waved as she backed around and started down the lane.

118

Her father leaned against the porch railing for a moment, watching the car, then went back in the house.

Evelyn made a left turn at the main road and the head-lights skimmed over the undulating wheatfield. It moved in slow rolling waves that gave her the momentary sensation of almost driving into the sea. It lapped against the barbed-wire fence like gentle breakers, crowding the sides of the narrow road. She felt a brief surge of vertigo, like a tightrope walker; one misstep and she would fall into bottomless depths. She unconsciously edged the car closer to the center of the road.

Heat lightning flickered in the south, illuminating the underside of the bank of thunderheads hanging there. But in the north she could see stars. The moon, ahead of her in the southeast, caught the leading edge of the faraway storm in silhouette. As she watched, the gap closed. The cloud began edging across the moon.

She caught a flicker of movement from the corner of her eyes.

A figure stumbled from the darkness beside the road into the pool of light preceding the car. A sound caught in her throat. Her foot hit the brake frantically. She twisted the wheel and the car swerved, the tires grinding in the gravel. The figure's arms went up as it slipped past the front fender and down the side of the car. The face of the pale apparition gaped at her as it whirled by her window.

The wheels slid in the loose gravel with a ripping sound. The car bucked and stalled. The front end bounced into the bar ditch and stopped in the high grass. Evelyn released her breath with little gasps and her knuckles were white on the steering wheel. Then her hands trembled as she relaxed them. Stillness settled over the dark road threading through the grassy sea. She could hear nothing but the crickets and the ticking of the cooling car motor.

She clutched at the handle of the door, then had to use

119

both hands because her fingers wouldn't close properly. She opened the door and looked behind her. She had recognized the face as it darted past her. Even in the darkness she could see the white hair of the man on his knees in the road behind the car.

She hesitated a moment, holding on to the car door, then went to him. He crouched in the dust, his chin against his chest and his hands clasped between his knees. He raised his head slowly and watched her approach. He smiled and sunshine flickered across his face, but his eyes were pained and haggard.

"Angel?" Evelyn said. She knelt beside him. "What . . . what are you doing here? Are you all right?"

He nodded and clasped his arms across his chest, holding himself tightly, as if he were afraid he would fall into little pieces. His smile flickered and he looked at her hesitantly.

"I didn't hit you, did I?"

He shook his head quickly.

"You nearly scared me to death. Why did you run out in front of me like that?" Her voice was sharper than she wanted it to be.

The pain increased in his eyes and his throat tightened.

She put her hand on his knee, clumsily attempting to reassure him. "Do you want me to take you somewhere! Back to the Wonder Show?"

Angel's body tensed. She felt the muscles tremble under his hand. He shook his head violently. His mouth worked and air hissed from his throat. He put his hands on her shoulders and she winced at the pressure. She caught his arms, trying to comfort the agitation and pleading in his face. He pulled his arms away and held them before him, his tight fists cording his wrists. Evelyn shrank from the anger in his face, and then realized it was directed at himself and not at her. His face crumbled in frustration and he began hitting his mouth with his fist, over and over.

"No," she said softly and caught his hand. "No," she repeated and felt his hand tremble. There was blood in the corner of his mouth.

Suddenly he freed his hand and leaned over. In the dirt of the road he wrote, "Ran away," with his finger. He turned his head sideways and looked at her, his ruby eyes begging for understanding. Then he sat back on his haunches, his body trembling as if rebelling against the rigid control he had forced upon it.

"Come on," she said suddenly and stood up. "I'm taking you to Dr. Latham. You don't look like you could take three steps without falling down." She took him under the arms and pulled him to his feet. Angel shook his head and tried to push her away, then stumbled and fell against her. She put her arms around him to keep him from toppling over.

His body was helpless against hers. She felt sensations she had never felt before pouring through her. The feel of him was exciting and comfortable and warm. She cradled him in her arms like a child, his breath ruffling the hair on her neck.

"You don't have to be afraid," she forced through her tight throat. "Dr. Latham won't tell anyone." She looked into his face, into his strange eyes like embers. "You can trust me, Angel."

He searched her face, reading it, reading her eyes, reading her soul. He nodded. She helped him into the car.

She backed the car out of the ditch and continued toward Hawley. The bank of thunderheads in the south had grown high and the heat lightning was brighter. She turned her head now and then to look at Angel, slumped against the door, his head leaning on the glass. His eyes were open, but were focused on something only he could see. Occasionally he would twist his head from side to side as if to clear it of an obstruction.

121

"What . . . " Evelyn said tentatively, "what happened? Why did you run away?"

He turned his head toward her, then put his fingers over his mouth and clinched his eyes painfully shut.

"I'm sorry," Evelyn said and put her hand on his arm. "I don't mean to ask you questions you can't answer." He touched her hand with a feathery touch. "I'm just worried about you and I don't quite know what to do about it."

He spread his hands and shook his head.

"Isn't there anyone at the Wonder Show we can trust to help us? Are you running away from all of them?"

Angel nodded and held one hand about twelve inches above the other.

"Tiny Tim? We can trust Tiny Tim?"

He nodded and smiled.

"Anyone else?"

He nodded again.

"Henry?"

He nodded quickly.

"Anyone else?"

He shook his head violently. With two fingers he drew a widow's peak on his forehead , then put his hands over his eyes.

"Especially not Haverstock?" she asked.

He nodded and let his head fall back on the car seat. His eyelids began to droop.

"We'll be there in just a minute," she said.

When Evelyn pulled up in front of Dr. Latham's house, he was standing on the porch watching Francine's unenthusiastic departure for Rose's slumber party. She walked listlessly down the unpaved street, letting her small satchel bump against her leg. She didn't notice Evelyn's arrival.

Evelyn pulled the hand brake and hurried around to the other side of the car. Dr. Latham met her as she helped Angel out. Angel took a step and began to topple. Evelyn cried

122

out, but the doctor caught him, picked him up like a small boy, and carried him into the house.

The calliope suddenly began to play at the Wonder Show, loud in the cooling air.

Dr. Latham put Angel on the examination table in his small clinic. Angel moved restlessly, not taking his eyes from Evelyn.

"What's the matter, son?" the doctor asked, taking Angel's pulse.

"He can't talk," Evelyn said.

"Oh?" Latham looked at her quizzically. "Who is he? I don't recall ever seeing him before."

"You didn't go to the tent show last night?" Evelyn asked.

Dr. Latham shook his head. "No. Is he one of those people?"

"Yes. His name is Angel."

His eyebrows rose. "Angel, huh? What did it say on the poster? The Magic Boy?"

"Yes."

"Is he magic?"

Evelyn shrugged and smiled slightly. "He seems to be."

"Well," Dr. Latham said, grinning, "I'm sorry I missed it. What's the matter with him?"

Evelyn shook her head. "I don't know. He staggered into the road and I almost ran over him."

"Did you hit him?"

"No." She hesitated a moment and then committed herself. "Dr. Latham, he's very frightened about something. He's run away from the tent show, and I promised him you wouldn't say anything to anyone if he'd let me bring him here."

The doctor looked at her with concern. "Are you sure you ought to get mixed up in this? You don't know anything about these people."

"It looks like I am mixed up in it," she said, smiling wryly.

Latham looked from Evelyn to Angel, at the hope and childlike trust in their eyes. He shrugged. "Okay," he said, "I won't say anything." He gave Evelyn a stern look. "But that promise goes out the window if I find out he's done something against the law."

She nodded once. "Okay, Dr. Latham. I don't think we have to worry about that."

Latham put his hand on her shoulder. "Why don't you wait in the parlor? I'll let you know as soon as I find out anything."

Evelyn smiled at Angel and pressed his hand. He returned her smile, but his face was pale and worried. The doctor steered her from the room.

19.

When the calliope began to play its hollow metallic song, Francine was walking along the street, aimlessly kicking stones, uncaringly messing up the toes of her slippers. She looked up at the sound and paused. She could see the lights through the trees and, farther away, the shimmer of sheet lightning across the horizon. She stood bathed in the night silence, broken only by the ghostly music of the calliope and the chirp of crickets, as if one accompanied the other.

She wouldn't have been able to explain why she turned and moved toward the music and the lights. She didn't really want to see the show again; no more than she wanted to go to Rose's party. But, somehow, the vague undefined dissatisfaction she felt seemed to decrease as the music got louder, just as it had increased as she neared the Willet house.

The street down which Francine walked was dark and empty. A few houses showed lights, but most were deserted. Those who lived in them had gone to the Wonder Show.

She felt no uneasiness. The street was as familiar in the dark as it was by day. She had walked down it nearly every day of her life, to school and to the courthouse square. If she felt anything at all, it was a slight dismay at her actions; the vague feeling that she was no longer in control of her body.

She didn't know why she was on her way to the tent show, and she didn't know why she stopped at the vacant lot where the Overstreet house had burned when she was a little girl. She turned and looked at it curiously. She had played there many times, but it held no distinction that she could recall. There was the old cistern, made of concrete and stones, boarded over to keep the careless from falling in. There had been no water in it for years, and there was occasional talk of filling it in before there was an accident, but no one had ever gone further than the talk. Stone steps led up to where the porch had been. Fireflies flickered their mating signals among the dense shrubbery and bushes that had grown back around the foundation after the fire, that had grown wild and created a secluded nook where children played.

And there was the Minotaur standing and watching her.

Francine clutched the satchel to her stomach and stared at him, feeling the blood tingling through her veins like acid. Something sucked the air from her lungs. The Minotaur did not move. He was almost naked, wearing only the loincloth he wore during his act in the tent show. Light, although there was no light, seemed to reflect from his satin skin and glisten from his horns like liquid silver.

Francine noticed she had taken a step toward him, but she couldn't remember doing it. She could see his big soft eyes clearly, as if the darkness drew away from him, leaving him in a pool of moonlight, though the low moon was concealed by inky, rolling thunderheads. He smiled and she thought, how kind he looks. His arms extended toward her, beckoning and welcoming, snaking the muscles in his smooth shoulders.

She discovered she had somehow moved closer.

She relaxed her rigid arms and let the satchel slip unnoticed to the ground. She couldn't hear the crickets anymore. The calliope sounded miles and miles away, somewhere out on the horizon with the lightning. She could no longer feel her feet touching the ground, could hardly feel her body. The Minotaur was before her, close enough to touch, close enough to feel the light and heat from his body.

Francine stood looking up at the Minotaur, like a worshiper before the bronze idol of an animal god. He smiled and put his arm gently around her shoulder, leading her through a gap in the shrubbery. They were in a moonlit bubble floating in darkness, insulated from sound. She could hear nothing but the blood running in her ears.

She reached out her hand hesitantly, tentatively touching his smooth, hard chest. His skin quivered slightly under her fingertips. She slid her hand over his breast and across his shoulder. It was a familiar sensation, like stroking a horse, the satin smoothness, the muscle tremors under her palm, the clean musky animal odor.

The Minotaur's hand left her shoulder and went up the back of her neck. He fondled her long hair, letting it flow through his big fingers like water. His hand slipped down her back, caressing her like a kitten, lingering on her hip, down the back side of her thigh, leaving a wake of gooseflesh. When his hand started back up her thigh, under her skirt, she looked down and grabbed at his hand with hers.

What she saw made her forget his hand, forget everything. The only thing in the world, the only thing in the universe, was his loincloth. The fabric arched outward, pulling completely away from his stomach, straining to the point of splitting, only an inch from her body.

127

Francine whimpered and tried to pull away, avoiding the touch as if it were molten, almost feeling the heat scorching her skin. His other hand fell softly over her mouth, covering it like a pillow, so large his fingers and thumb almost touched at the back of her neck. She screamed into his palm, but it was no more than a muffled whine. She clawed at his hand and arm, pulling and tugging desperately, feeling the darkness closing in, the island of light around the Minotaur growing dim, but his flesh was as immobile as granite.

His hand left her thigh and fumbled at his waist. The catch on the loincloth parted. The fabric flew back and settled around his hoof.

His heavy phallus fell against her stomach, searing her with its heat, knocking the breath from her with its weight. She looked over the mountains of his knuckles; she hadn't known, hadn't imagined.

Sensation rushed back over her like a thunderclap. The crickets shrieked. The calliope bellowed. A pebble in her shoe cut into her foot like broken glass. An inchworm crawled on her ankle, leaving a trail of fire.

The Minotaur's hand went back to her thigh. He pushed her skirt around her waist and tore away her step-ins like tissue paper. His touch was gentle and caressing; his large liquid eyes were soft and loving; his smile was sweet.

His huge hand cupped her buttock and lifted her to him. She screamed again into his hand when she felt his hot flesh between her legs. Then there was a pain too great for screaming.

20.

The applause broke around Louis, crashing until the tent seemed to bulge with the sound. Louis smiled broadly, opened his mouth and laughed, flashed his teeth, raised his arm like a matador. It was always better the second night, he thought, when they know what to expect, when they aren't scared out of their union suits.

Tiny Tim bowed and looked up at Louis. He snorted and re-entered the doll house. He grabbed for support as the roustabouts rolled the table to the rear of the stage and the curtain closed. They rolled the table into the wings and Tim walked out through the open backside of the doll house. He watched them roll on the electric chair and worried. He felt sure something out of the ordinary was going on, but he didn't know what it was. There was a nervous tension in the air. Louis had been in and out of Haverstock's wagon several times before the show started, something he seldom did. The roustabouts were edgy, whispering among themselves, trying to stay as inconspicuous as possible.

One of them took off his shirt and shoes and slipped the black hood over his head. He stood waiting while Louis tried to settle the audience. Louis attempted to begin his Electro the Lightning Man intro several times before they let him say the first sentence.

"Ladies and gentlemen, there are many instruments used in the world to execute criminals and murderers. In France they use the guillotine . . . " The words came through the curtain.

A hand grasped Tim and picked him up without warning. He yelled and looked up the arm. "Hey!" he squeaked in tiny fury. "Take it easy before I skin you and hang your hide in the wind."

"Haverstock wants to talk to you," the roustabout said without interest. Tim didn't know this one's name, nor most of the others' for that matter. The young men came and went so quickly, and seldom socialized with the freaks.

They went out the rear of the tent as lightning flickered on the bottoms of the clouds. Tim thought he could hear faroff thunder, but just then the night freight barreled through on its way to Wichita.

They came around the side of the tent. The rumble of the train faded and was replaced by the rumble of voices. Through the line of circus wagons Tim could see a crowd of people waiting for the second show.

The door of Haverstock's wagon opened and light spilled out, causing Tim to squint. He felt the roustabout's hand loosen and another hand take him, and heard the door close and the sound of voices quieting almost to nothing. Then he was standing on the desk. Haverstock sat in the chair, watching him, smiling. Tim felt panic growing in him like a poisonous toadstool.

"How are you this evening, Tim?" Haverstock asked softly, still smiling.

"Okay," Tim answered uncertainly.

"That's good, my son. That's very good." Haverstock nodded several times and steepled his fingers under his chin, looking reflectively at a point six inches in front of Tim.

There was silence for a few moments, only the faint sound of the train whistling at a crossing and the soft spitting of electricity from the tent. Tim fidgeted. "What do you want to see me about?" he asked finally.

"Please call me 'Father,' Tim. I would appreciate it so much."

The words stuck in Tim's throat. He'd known it was coming. As soon as Haverstock had called him 'my son,' he knew it was coming. He forced the words out. "What do you want to see me about, Father?"

Haverstock nodded and smiled. "Well, Tim, it seems we have a little problem."

"A problem, Father?" He couldn't keep the nervous edge from his voice.

"Yes." Haverstock nodded again. "Oh, yes, a very serious problem. Angel has disappeared." He cocked his eyebrow at Tim. "It looks very much like the poor boy has run away."

"Oh?" Tim felt a curious mixture of terror and elation. "That's too bad."

"Yes, too bad." Haverstock tapped the ends of his fingers together and then looked at Tim, his hands freezing in position. "You wouldn't happen to have any idea where he might have gone, would you, my son?"

"How would I know, Father?"

"How, indeed."

"I didn't even know he was gone."

Haverstock's smile flickered on, then off. "Oh, yes, I can

131

believe that. But I had the idle notion you might know where he could have gone, if you knew that he *had* gone."

"No. I wouldn't have any idea."

"It was, as I said, an idle notion." He sighed and put his hands on the arms of the chair. "As you and Angel are such chums . . . well, you can see where I might have gotten the idea."

"Yes, I can see."

"Good. Now we're beginning to understand each other." Haverstock slapped his knees and stood up. He walked around the small room, then looked out the window. The lightning danced on the horizon. "The storm seems to be moving this way. We may have to cancel the second show if there's wind in it." He shrugged. "I don't suppose it matters, though, with Angel gone."

He turned from the window and looked at Tim. "Something has happened since we arrived in this wretched little town. I don't know what it is yet, but I will. You know I will, don't you, my son?"

"Yes, Father."

"And you'll help me find out, won't you, Tim?"

"I don't know anything to tell you."

"I can't believe that, Tim. That clever little brain of yours is always ticking away, adding, subtracting, calculating. Tick, tick. Tick, tick. Like a little clock with eyes, watching and ticking. I know what all my children are doing, Tim." Haverstock sat in the chair again, leaning back. "Yes, indeed. Something has happened. This afternoon Angel wouldn't let me put him under. He fought my control, and with some success, I must admit. Oh, by the way, it has come to my attention that you and Angel left the camp this morning. I believe you told me a lie about playing cards in your wagon."

"Who told you that?" Tim whispered. Dread covered him like syrup.

132

"Never mind who told me. Where did you go?" The casualness had disappeared from his voice.

"All right." Tim licked his sandpaper lips. "We just went up to the creek and fished a little. Angel has been cooped up so much, I thought the sun and fresh air would do him good."

"Oh, and did it? Did you catch any fish, my son?"

"No, Father."

"Too bad. All that effort for nothing." Haverstock leaned forward, pinning Tim with his gaze. "Now, I want you to think very hard. Very hard. And tell me where you would go if you were looking for Angel."

"I don't have any idea," Tim said and shrugged his misshapen shoulders.

Haverstock leaned back in the chair, raising his fingers again to his chin. "Very well. I can see you plan to be obstinate. You are entirely too small and vulnerable for this much stubbornness, you know."

Tim shrieked, a thin high-pitched scream like a dying rabbit. His hunchbacked body jerked in uncontrollable spasms, then went limp and collapsed on the desk top. After a moment, he rose trembling to his knees.

Haverstock raised his brows. "Have you thought of something, my son?" he asked pleasantly.

"No, Father," Tim gasped. "I haven't thought of anything."

Haverstock sighed and looked at Tim with betrayed innocence. "Ah, Tim, you vex me almost as much as Angel. I don't know what's gotten into everyone lately." He stood up. "I haven't time to play any more games with you, Tim. I want you to tell me everything you know, everything you suspect, everything you conjecture, about where Angel might be."

He reached around the end of the desk and brought a covered birdcage into view. The cage rattled tinnily as he put it on the desk next to Tim. Something moved under the cover, something large.

"Well, Tim?"

"I don't know anything," Tim said, but his voice cracked and he could not keep his eyes off the cage.

Haverstock shrugged and delicately grasped the little celluloid ring on the top of the fabric cover. He slipped it up and off. The large brindle cat looked around in bewilderment. It shifted in the cage. Its tail fell through the bars and lay twitching on the desk.

Tim took an involuntary step backward, his face the color of putty.

The cat was an alley fighter. His coat was scruffy and dirty. One ear was notched and fleas covered his nose like freckles.

"As you can see," Haverstock explained, "I anticipated your pertinacity. Now, do you tell me what I want to know, or shall I open the door?"

The cat noticed Tim. One paw reached through the bars and swiped at him. Tim shrieked and stumbled back out of reach. He tripped and fell, then scrambled quickly to his feet. The cat watched him, the tip of his tail switching slightly.

Haverstock smiled. "There's always the chance you might succeed in getting away, that you might reach some tiny nook our friend couldn't enter. But we both know the chance is so small as to be hardly worth the taking. And, of course, since you've been so disloyal to one who's taken care of you all these years, I would have no choice but to take the cat's part."

Tim looked at the cat in speechless terror, a collar of ice constricting his throat. Haverstock reached slowly to the catch on the birdcage door and released it, diddled it, toyed with it. The door swung open an inch, but he stopped it

134

with his finger. The cat growled. Four burning eyes focused on Tim.

"Well, my son?" Haverstock said softly.

"All right!" Tim screamed.

Haverstock refastened the catch and leaned back in his chair, but left the cage uncovered. He smiled, and thunder rolled far away, as if one might have been the cause of the other.

21.

Evelyn Bradley sat on the davenport in Dr. Latham's parlor and fidgeted. Her emotions confused her. Why on earth was she making such a fuss over Angel? He seemed very nice and was in some sort of trouble, but that didn't explain it. Why did she feel such an odd, enjoyable sensation when he touched her? There in the road, when he had leaned against her, when she had put her arms around him to keep him from falling . . . well, she had been practically giddy. She squirmed and looked at the closed door of Dr. Latham's clinic.

Boys had put their arms around her before, for heaven's sake. Only last night Sonny Redwine had been very romantic. He had kissed her and . . . well . . . he would have done a lot more if she had let him. And she had enjoyed it; enjoyed it very much, but it hadn't made her toes curl and she hadn't, as they always did in books, heard bells ringing or anything. Why had Angel's arms around her been so different from Sonny's?

136

Angel was very attractive, even if he did have white hair and pale skin and funny red eyes that looked so deeply into her, but she didn't consider herself the type to flutter over a matinee idol. There were several very attractive boys in Hawley, including Sonny, but they didn't have any particular effect on her. Maybe she just knew them too well and too long. She sighed.

Was she in love with Angel? She frowned. Ridiculous. How could she be in love with someone she'd known only one day? Not that long even. As a matter of fact, she didn't know him at all. It must be just fascination because he was so exotic. And Henry had said that Angel was simple-minded. He didn't act simple-minded, though how could she really tell? She had been attributing many of his actions to his inability to speak. Could they instead be caused by his being simple-minded as well? She couldn't make herself believe it.

And the other thing, at the bridge, when he had caught her without touching her. She'd forgotten about that because it still didn't seem quite real, like something interesting she'd read but didn't believe. She did believe it, though. She had seen it. She didn't believe Tiny Tim when he said she had only imagined it, nor did she really believe him when he said everything Angel did in the Wonder Show was only tricks and illusions. She really ought to be afraid of him, but try as she might, she could arouse no fear in herself.

How could she be afraid of Angel? He was so like a . . . like a lost puppy. So vulnerable seeming, and trusting. Maybe all she felt was sympathy. That's it, she nodded to herself. All she was doing was reacting to his trust and his need.

She frowned again because it didn't seem quite right. Dr. Latham emerged from his clinic and she gratefully delayed any conclusion.

"I can't find anything physically wrong with him," Dr. Latham said and sat beside her. "He seems to be suffering from simple exhaustion, as if he had performed some strenuous exercise until he collapsed."

"Will he be all right?"

"Oh, sure. All he needs is a good night's sleep. I gave him a sedative and put him to bed on the cot in the clinic. He's sleeping like a baby. I did find out why he can't talk, though."

She looked at him with more concern than she had intended, but he didn't seem to notice.

"I was curious if it were physical or emotional."

"Emotional?"

"Some people are thinking that a severe emotional trauma can cause loss of speech—and also loss of sight and hearing and a lot of other things."

"Is that what's wrong with Angel?"

"No," the doctor sighed. "His problem is physical, very simple and nothing can be done about it. He has no vocal cords."

"Oh," she said and wanted to cry because it was so unjust.

"I could see no evidence of an accident. I assume he was born that way." He shrugged. "Albinos are usually defective in some way or other—in addition to their lack of pigmentation. Quite often they're sickly or simple-minded— or both."

"Is . . . " She started to ask Dr. Latham to confirm or deny Henry's assertion that Angel was simple-minded, but she was afraid of the answer. So she said, "Is Angel . . . sickly?"

"Doesn't seem to be. He has quite an athletic build, though it's hard to tell without a lot more thorough examination than I was able to do tonight. Well . . . " he stood

138

up " . . . he can stay here tonight. He should be fine in the morning. You'd better run on to Rose's party."

"I'm not really in the mood for one of Rose's parties." She stood up also and fidgeted with a button, hoping Dr. Latham wouldn't think she was being foolish. "Could . . . could I stay here tonight? He might . . . he might not be as frightened if I were here," she blurted, making it up as she went along. "I don't know what happened, but he was really frightened about something."

Latham looked at her, about to tease her, but he saw how serious and worried she was. "You can stay if you want to. You can sleep in Francine's room." He grinned because she was so serious and so concerned. "However, there's no telling what this may do to my reputation."

She grinned also. "Shall I hide the car up the street somewhere?"

"Alas," he sighed, "I fear the damage is done."

"I'll call Rose and tell her I won't be there."

She went to the phone on the parlor wall, gave the crank a couple of turns, and took down the receiver.

"Hello, would you ring the Willets, please? . . . Fine, Reba, how are you? . . . No, I didn't go see it again tonight. . . . Thank you. . . . Hello, who's this? . . . Oh, hello, Billie Rita. This is Evie. Is Rose able to talk? . . . Okay. . . . Rose? I'm sorry, but I won't be able to make the party tonight, after all. . . . No, I'm not sick, I— . . . No, I'm not going to the tent show. Something came up. I'll tell you about it later. . . . Yes, it's very important. . . . Okay. . . . 'Bye, Rose."

She hung up the receiver and turned to Dr. Latham smiling. "Rose is having a fit. Most of the girls are going to the tent show instead of her party. Well . . . " she clapped her hands together nervously " . . . at least I came prepared to spend the night. I'll get my case from the car."

139

She went outside and got the case and the book from the back seat. She heard a distant rumble of thunder and looked toward the south.

"The cloud's getting closer," she said when she went back in the house. "It's gonna be pouring down rain pretty soon. Oh, I brought this book that Francine wanted to borrow." She put it on the mantel.

The phone rang. Dr. Latham looked at her and shook his head. "Somebody must have a pain. Should've known since there's a cloud coming up." He grimaced and took down the receiver.

"Dr. Latham," he said, then looked at Evelyn and raised his eyebrows. "Hello, Rose. . . . Francine left here some time ago. Isn't she there yet? . . . Maybe she went by the tent show. Would you have her call me when she gets there? . . . Thank you. 'Bye, Rose."

He hung up the receiver slowly and looked at Evelyn. "Has Francine said anything to you about what's bothering her? She's been acting funny all day."

"No," Evelyn said and frowned. "She was upset about something last night at the tent show. I thought she was just embarrassed about the Minotaur."

"What happened?"

"Nothing. Rose had been teasing her about . . . well, you know, about what the Minotaur did in the story. Rose had her all worked up about it, then, when the Minotaur came out, he wasn't wearing very much and, well . . . " she felt herself blushing " . . . he was pretty sexual. I thought that was all."

The doctor didn't say anything, but his face was worried.

"Is it all right if I . . . look in on Angel?" Evelyn asked.

"Huh?" Dr. Latham's eyes focused on her. "He's asleep."

"I know. I won't disturb him."

He shrugged. "Sure. Go ahead." He took his hat and coat from the hall tree. "You know where everything is. If you're hungry, feel free to raid the icebox. I think I'll take a walk down to the tent show. Good night, Evie."

"Good night, Dr. Latham, and thank you."

He gave her a little worried smile and left. She went into the clinic, but didn't turn on the light for fear of disturbing Angel. She sat in the chair beside the cot and watched him. He looks like a baby when he sleeps, she thought. She leaned over and touched his slightly parted lips with her fingers. He stirred and turned on the cot, causing the sheet to slip off his bare shoulder. She could see the rapid movement of his eyes behind the closed lids.

She pulled the sheet back over his shoulder, then left the house and headed for the tent show.

22.

The people stood around Haverstock's Traveling Curiosus and Wonder Show and listened to the gasps and shrieks and applause that swelled periodically from the tent. They looked at each other and grinned, fidgeting in delicious anticipation of the second show. But some of them looked nervously at the lightning that moved continuously closer and listened warily to the thunder that seemed a little louder each time.

The farmers with crops in the fields worried about hail or too much wind or too much rain. They had visions of rising in the pale morning light to find the wheat bent and broken, plastered to the ground by mud and water; the young maize so tattered and torn it would never recover to produce more than small anemic heads.

Others worried that the storm might cause them to miss the show. They all worried about cyclones. It was cyclone weather, they nodded to each other. Definitely cyclone weather. The one back in '17, the one that blew away the old cotton gin, it came out of a cloud just like this one, just after dark like it was now. Those who remembered, and most did, agreed. But they always managed to forget that the same thing was said about every cloud that came up.

The ones who hadn't been worried talked themselves into worry. They drifted away, one or two at first, those who lived farther out, who thought they might be able to make it home before the storm broke, then more. Children, thwarted at life's grandest moment, begged to stay, to be left behind, abandoned, anything rather than miss the Wonder Show. Pleading turned to screams and tantrums and tears of frustration, and then to tears of pain when their fathers applied hands and belts vigorously to seats of knickers and overalls. Children whose parents had made no move to leave looked at their elders warily, searching for signs of departure.

Applause suddenly burst from the tent after an unusually lengthy silence.

Inside, the snake woman settled her coils into position on her platform and the curtain closed.

Louis stepped to the front of the stage and the applause quickly died. The rows of people shifted on the wooden benches. This was it. Angel the Magic Boy. They reviewed all the things they had heard and waited, hardly breathing.

"Thank you, ladies and gentlemen," Louis said a little nervously. "Ah . . . it is my unfortunate duty to inform you that Angel, the Magic Boy, will not be able to perform tonight. He has . . . ah . . . taken ill suddenly. Thank you."

A groan arose from the crowd. Louis began speaking rapidly, trying to quell their dissatisfaction. "The last item on our show is Henry-etta, half man, half woman. Because of the delicate nature of this performance, we must request all children under eighteen years of age to please leave the auditorium."

Phineas Bowen and Jack Spain left the tent in a daze, their faces as clouded as the southern sky.

"I don't understand it, Jack," Finney said, his voice high-pitched with disbelief. "How could Angel be sick? He's magic. He couldn't be sick."

"Maybe he's not really magic," Jack offered tentatively.

"How can you say that?" Finney squeaked in astonishment. "Sumbitch, didn't you see what he did? He turned into a flaming bird, he floated through the air, he became a bolt of lightning." He leaned against the silent calliope. His brows lowered with his voice. "Oh, he's magic all right. So it stands to reason he couldn't be sick."

He looked at Jack, certainty dark in his eyes. "Something very fishy is going on around here."

They both nodded, slowly and solemnly.

Inside the tent, the curtain opened and Henry stepped out in his Henry-etta regalia. "Thank you, Louis, you darling boy," he said, but worry dulled his voice. He spoke almost mechanically, neither flirting with the audience nor leering erotically at Louis. "Ladies and gentlemen, your master of ceremonies tonight was Louis Ortiz. Give him a big hand for doing a wonderful job."

Louis bowed tersely to the sparse applause of the handful of people still there and hurried through the curtains. Henry watched him curiously, wondering what was going on, wondering what was wrong with Angel; he'd never been sick or missed a performance before. Then he began his spiel, but his heart wasn't in it.

Louis walked quickly to Haverstock's wagon and tapped lightly on the door. "It's Louis," he said softly. He heard a muffled summons from inside and opened the door.

Haverstock sat at the desk, leaning back in the chair, smoking a cigar with clear satisfaction. Tiny Tim sat dejectedly on the desk, as far from the covered birdcage as he could get.

"Did you find out anything?" Louis asked with con-spiratorial glee barely suppressed in his voice.

"Of course," Haverstock answered expansively. Louis had never seen him in such a good mood, as if he too were enjoying an adrenaline surge at the sudden departure from normal routine. "How did the hayseeds take Angel's absence?"

"They weren't happy."

"Ah, well." Haverstock grinned. "Life is full of little dis-appointments, isn't it, Tim?"

Tim didn't look at him.

"It seems that Tim and Angel went fishing this morning and met a girl. A very pretty town girl. Her name is Evelyn Bradley and she lives a couple of miles the other side of the bridge. Angel may or may not have gone there, but Tim tells me he was very taken with her. Go out and have a look."

Louis nodded and the smile hovered over his lips. Haver-stock waved his hand negligently at the birdcage. "On your way, dump Tim's friend somewhere. We won't be needing him again, will we, Tim?"

"No," Tim said softly, fear and shame coloring his voice.

"Very well," Haverstock said crisply. "Pull yourself together. You have another show to do in a little while. Louis, take Tim back to the tent."

Louis picked up Tim and the birdcage. The smile settled on his lips like a moth.

23.

Evelyn Bradley got in the line that had formed for the second performance of the Wonder Show. It wasn't very long; people were drifting away rapidly, looking at the sky with frowning faces. Already the wind had risen, blowing little spasmodic puffs of air that died as quickly as they were born. Then more people left, men holding their hats and women clutching at their skirts.

The calliope began to play and Henry came around the side of the tent in his green dress and ridiculous orange wig, carrying the cash box and a roll of tickets. He mounted the stool at the ticket stand and began accepting half dollars. He didn't look at the faces as he handed out tickets, only the hands and the coins.

When Evelyn reached him, he tore off a ticket and pushed it toward her. She put her hand on the stand, but there was no money in it. His eyes rose and looked into hers. His expression didn't change, but his eyes grew wary.

"I have to talk to you," she said, but the calliope drowned out her words.

Henry's shoulders slumped slightly. "Miss Bradley, please . . ."

She half heard his voice and half read his lips. "I know where Angel is," she said.

"Angel?" his mouth formed the word. He looked around him quickly, then at the people in line behind her. He frowned and thought for a second, then said, "Wait for me at that house across the road." He nodded his head toward old Miss Sullivan's place. "By the trellis." Then his expression dismissed her. He reached for the half dollar in the hand of the person behind her.

Evelyn left the line and found herself looking around, as nervous as Henry had been. The only person she saw was the handsome young man taking tickets, the same one who had been there the night before, the one who had flirted with Rose. There had been a break in the line entering the tent and he had looked up. He was watching her. He nodded and then began taking tickets as the line resumed.

Evelyn watched him for a moment, but he seemed to be taking no further interest in her. She turned and crossed the street, then stood in the gloom behind old Miss Sullivan's trellis, which leaned with the weight of a massive trumpet vine. She watched Henry sell tickets until the line had disappeared. There weren't many, not nearly enough to fill the tent. Then Henry looked across at her, though he couldn't see her in the shadows. He picked up the roll of tickets and the cash box and hurried around the side of the tent.

The Wonder Show was deserted. Even the mass of flying insects was gone. The torches fluttered in the intermittent gusts of wind and the electric light bulbs bobbed spastically on the wire. The sign stretching across the entrance popped as it ballooned, then sighed as it settled back. Evelyn ner-

147

vously plucked a long red-orange bloom from the vine and twirled it absently between her fingers. She couldn't see Henry anywhere.

Then he spoke behind her and she jumped.

"Oh!" she said. "I didn't see you come across the street."

"I hope no one else did either. What do you mean, you know where Angel is? I don't understand."

She was confused. "I . . . I took him to Dr. Latham's. He said it was only exhaustion. He didn't think it . . . "

"What was Angel doing with you?" Henry's voice was bewildered and angry.

Then she understood. "You didn't know? Angel ran away."

Henry stared at her, a little moan escaping his throat. He sat on the edge of the porch. "Oh, God," he said in a soft whisper. "Oh, my God."

"Angel is all right. He's not hurt," she said quickly. "Dr. Latham said it was only exhaustion." She didn't know what else to do to ease his pain.

Henry didn't say anything for a long time. He looked at nothing, his mind far away. A gust of wind rattled the trumpet vine. Then Henry looked at her. "What happened?" he said.

"I found him on the road. I was coming into town to go to a party. He stepped out in front of the car and I almost hit him. He was very frightened. He said he had run away from the . . . "

"He *said*?"

"He wrote it in the dirt with his finger."

"Did he tell you anything else? Why he'd run away?"

"No. He just said that you and Tiny Tim were the only ones he could trust. And he seemed very afraid of Mr. Haverstock. He was so weak he could barely stand up, so I took him to the doctor. He didn't want to go, but I promised him no one would tell where he was."

148

"What about the doctor?"

"He promised not to tell. He said Angel was just exhausted and would be all right after a good night's sleep. The doctor examined him." She felt a hurting in her throat. "He has no vocal cords."

"What?"

"Angel has no vocal cords. That's why he can't talk. He was born that way."

Henry looked down at his hand, pulling at a loose thread on the green satin gown. "I didn't know," he said softly. "I guess I never really wondered why he couldn't talk." He sat staring at the thread, then looked up at her. "Miss Bradley, I don't know what to do. Honest to God, I don't know what to do."

"About what?"

"Angel." His voice was tight, as if he were about to cry. "Haverstock won't let him go, never let him get away. He'll find him no matter what he has to do. And anyone who tries to help Angel get away is in danger, but if Haverstock finds him, I don't know what he'll do to him for trying to run away. Angel is in danger, Miss Bradley, no matter what we do. We have to try to help him, but we are putting ourselves in equal danger if we do. We are damned if we do and damned if we don't."

"What kind of danger are you talking about?" she asked, her voice pinched.

"Haverstock will kill anyone who gets in his way."

She laughed nervously, unbelieving. "But that sort of thing doesn't happen. You make him sound . . . We'll go to the sheriff. He can't keep Angel if he doesn't want to stay. He can't do things like that."

"We'd just get the sheriff killed as well." Henry looked across at the tent show as applause rattled inside. Then he looked back at her. "Miss Bradley, there's so much you don't know. You live in this nice little town, with nice ordi-

149

nary people, doing nice ordinary things. You don't know the craziness in the world. You don't know what people with power are capable of, people with the kind of power Haverstock has."

She sat on the porch beside him and folded her skirt under her knees. "You mean what happens in the show? What happened at the creek this morning? It's all real?"

"Yes, it's real. All that stuff in the show is done with, what do you call it? Telekinesis, or something. Mind over matter. Think what you can do with it, how easy it would be to kill. It's not just making pretty stage-show tricks. You can stop a person's heart, rupture blood vessels in their brain, any one of two dozen things so no one would ever know it was murder. It would just be a natural thing, a heart attack, a brain hemorrhage. No one would ever know."

"And Angel can do all that too?" she whispered. Suddenly the waxy sweetness of the trumpet vine was overpowering.

Henry shrugged. "Not really. I mean, I guess he can, after what happened this morning with you, but he doesn't know how. Haverstock hypnotizes him when they do the act. He can't do it except when he's hypnotized. He can never even remember what he does in the show."

"What did Angel say about this morning? He did it this morning without being hypnotized," she said.

Henry frowned. "I don't know. I haven't seen him since then." He looked thoughtfully at the ground. "You know, Tim always thought that Angel was really the one, that Haverstock was using him to do the tricks, but that was just wishful thinking. I didn't believe it, I thought it was Haverstock. I've seen too much not to know that he has the gift." He turned to her with a puzzled expression on his face. "It looks like they both have it."

"Where did Angel come from?" she asked.

"Who knows?" He shrugged. "Haverstock found him somewhere. One morning, he was there. He was about five years old, grubby and dirty and dumb as a post. Haverstock never told us where he came from, and we weren't curious enough to risk asking. We didn't see too much of him. Haverstock kept him in his wagon most of the time. Then, when he was about fifteen or so, he started doing the act you saw last night. In the beginning it was mostly straight magician stuff, nothing as spectacular as it is now."

"What about the others? Medusa and the mermaid, and the snake woman?"

"They were all here when I came. I was about your age. I ran away from home to join the carnival." He grunted. "And look at me now." He took a deep breath and exhaled slowly, looking at the black cloud that filled the southern sky. "I guess I had things pretty good when I was your age. My family had money, not a lot, but all we needed. My father was a small-time politician, not nearly as important as he thought he was, but he was doing all right. My mother was a kind, simple soul who loved us and fussed over us. And I had a little brother who was thirteen, I think. I didn't think much of him at the time, but I guess he was all you could expect a little brother to be. I think my father was a little ashamed of my mother. She didn't really fit in with his political friends, so he sorta treated her like the housekeeper.

"But he was proud of me." He stared into space and a wistful little smile formed on his lips. Evelyn sat quietly, listening to him, feeling his hurt and regret.

"I was my father's fair-haired boy, all right," he continued. "I was the best athlete in the city, had trophies all over the house. You may not believe it, but when I was eighteen I was as good looking and as well built as any of the boys Haverstock has with him now. Too well built, I guess. That kind always seem to run to fat when they get older.

"Yeah, I guess I had it pretty good, then something happened. I got into trouble. Not with the police or anything like that. Nobody knew about it except my father and . . . one other person. It probably wouldn't be such a big thing nowadays, but that was before the war, in 1905, I think. Yeah, 1905. Women still wore long black dresses that brushed the ground." He chuckled. "They'd just barely stopped covering up piano legs.

"My father didn't exactly drive me out into the snow, but I guess it amounted to the same thing. I went back once, after the war. They were all dead. My brother had been killed in France. My mother died of influenza, and my father—" he snorted "—my father got drunk and was run over by a beer wagon. He must have hated that; a blow to his prestige almost as bad as I was."

He looked at Evelyn and grinned warily. "Here I am chewing your ear off with things you couldn't possibly be interested in."

"No . . . " she said, but he hurried on.

"You asked about the freaks. There used to be a couple of others: a harpy, an ugly, smelly, very unpleasant woman with huge bat wings; and a hydra, a gigantic seven-headed snake. But they both died. I think the snake woman is about on her last legs too. Oh, well, it'll be a blessing for the poor thing.

"No matter how human they may look, the snake woman and the mermaid are only animals. Medusa isn't much better, but she can at least go to the toilet and eat with a spoon. I'm not sure about the Minotaur. Sometimes, I think he's smarter than he acts. He can't talk either. None of the creatures can talk except Tiny Tim, but he's the only one that's truly human.

"And he's the one I really feel sorry for. He's extremely intelligent and kind. I don't know how he's kept his sanity. I think if I looked like he does, only a foot tall, I'd've gone 'round the bend a long time ago. The invisible woman is just a trick, and Electro is whichever of the men isn't busy at the time. I've even been Electro myself . . . a long time ago. The way that chair is rigged, you could do it yourself and not feel a thing."

"But hasn't anyone ever guessed? There are things in the show, especially what Angel does, that can't be explained away as sideshow tricks."

"You'd be surprised." He smiled. "People don't really want to believe it's real. It would be too disturbing. Of course, the kids believe it, but who listens to kids? But Haverstock doesn't take chances. That's why Electro and I are in the show. Didn't you wonder why those two very tired acts were included with the spectacular stuff?"

She shook her head, puzzled. "No. I really hadn't."

He shrugged. "People see a couple of obvious fakes, they assume that everything is a fake, no matter what their eyes tell them. And *nothing* could ever throw cold water on an inflamed imagination like my tawdry little act."

Evelyn felt herself getting red.

"I see you know about it," he said dryly.

"Yes. The boy I was with told me."

"That was ungentlemanly of him. Well, I've been doing it so long I've used up all my blushes."

She grinned and liked him despite everything. "Go on."

"Well, if things get out of hand, if the crowd gets out of control and wants to burn him at the stake, he has a solution for that too. When Angel is floating across the audience, there will be the sound of a wire breaking and Angel will hang there by one arm. It sorta ruins the show, but it convinces them everything is a fake and not the work of the Devil. It's only happened once. We were in this little town

153

in, I think, North Carolina, the same time as an evangelist. That preacher didn't believe it was real either, but he had to make out like he did 'cause we were pulling too much money away from his collection plate."

"Why did you stay, if Haverstock is like you say?"

He settled the orange wig more firmly on his head. "What else could I do? I've been with him nearly twenty-five years. I don't know anything else. Besides, he probably wouldn't let me leave. I know too much."

He stood up and adjusted his dress. "I've got to get back. It should be nearly time for my entrance. Haverstock is doing the show. Louis is off somewhere; probably looking for Angel. I still don't know what to do. I have to talk to Tim. Maybe Tim will know what to do." He looked at Evelyn and frowned. "There's no reason for you get mixed up in this, no point in putting yourself in danger. Why don't you just go on home and forget about us? Tim and I will think of something."

"Will you be leaving in the morning?"

"Only if Haverstock finds Angel tonight. He won't leave without Angel."

"Why is Angel so important to him?"

He raised his eyebrows. "I didn't know before, but it's obvious now. Angel has the gift too. He can't leave him running around loose. He would never feel safe again. Good night, Miss Bradley. Please go home and stay out of this."

He turned and hurried away into the darkness.

Evelyn sat there for a moment, then hurried back to Dr. Latham's. She looked in on Angel, but he was asleep, still in the same position as when she'd left. She watched him for a moment, then went upstairs to bed.

154

24.

The show went badly. The tent was hardly half full and some of those left when the thunder became sufficiently loud. Haverstock paced it rapidly, getting it over with. Everyone was nervous and unsettled. Tim fell while he danced and earned a murderous glare. The Minotaur was insolent and seemed to do his best to embarrass the women in the audience. The snake woman wouldn't cooperate, wouldn't take her customary trip down the aisle. Even the roustabouts were jittery, standing around whispering among themselves.

Haverstock watched them and hated them all.

But it was over quickly. The last few left when Henry was introduced. They had heard about Henry-etta and didn't consider him worth being caught in the storm. Henry looked at the empty tent for a moment, absurd in the soiled green gown, then went back to his wagon to talk with Tim.

The lights across the line of wagons were turned off and a

roustabout extinguished the torches. The Wonder Show was silent and still, lying like a painted corpse beneath the black sky, silhouetted by the sheet lightning in the south.

Finney and Jack watched from across the street, crouching behind a bush, feeling their hearts pounding in their chests. They strained their eyes in the darkness, trying to spy a movement among the decorated wagons, but there was nothing.

They crept across the road, hunkered down like stealthy Indians converging on a settler's cabin. Then they sucked in their breaths and ran, scooting under the nearest wagon, when headlights bounced over the railroad tracks. They huddled together, peering through the spokes of the wagon wheel as the black Model-T Ford clattered to a stop. Louis got out and went to Haverstock's wagon.

Finney and Jack backed away cautiously on their hands and knees, ready to freeze if Louis should look in their direction. Jack suddenly twitched and stopped, bumping against Finney.

"Sumbitch!" he muttered.

"What's the matter?" Finney whispered.

"I got my knee on a cuckleburr," Jack hissed through his clenched teeth.

The door of Haverstock's wagon opened, spilling light across the ground. Finney and Jack stared with wide eyes and open mouths at the apparition standing in the doorway, a black-robed figure with light flowing around him like fairy mist. Then they released their held-in breaths and looked at each other, grinning sheepishly. It was only Haverstock, still in his costume from the show.

"He wasn't there," they heard Louis say. "From what I could hear through the window, the girl is in town at an overnight party. I searched the barn but didn't find anything. If he's there, he's well hidden, and the girl apparently doesn't know anything about it."

Haverstock nodded. "We'll have a talk with her in the morning when she returns, just to be sure."

He closed the door and Louis went to the Minotaur's wagon. Henry and Tim stopped whispering and turned startled eyes on the door when Louis walked in without knocking. Louis looked at them speculatively, a smile fluttering around his lips. He went to the Minotaur's cot and watched the sleeping naked figure for a moment. Then he turned and left without a word.

Jack and Finney scooted back under the wagon when Louis came out. He paused on the steps and the smile settled on his lips. He went to his own wagon, where the woman was supposed to be waiting. The boys watched him until he was out of sight.

"Which one do you suppose Angel is in?" Jack whispered.

"I don't know," Finney answered, "but I would guess he's in the one with his picture on it."

Jack nodded in agreement. They scurried on their hands and knees under the wagons. They stopped and Finney stuck his head out, looking up at the side of the wagon. He strained his neck out and looked at the other wagons.

"It's the next one," he said as he ducked back under. They crawled on and poked their heads out, looking around carefully. They saw no movements and crept from beneath the caravan, brushing their bare feet down with great care. Finney put his hand on the door handle, his muscles tightening involuntarily. He looked back at Jack, then cautiously pulled the door open.

They peered in, Jack straining to see over Finney's shoulder. The inside of the wagon was pitch black. Jack clutched Finney's arm tightly, but Finney didn't feel it. They both jumped when it thundered suddenly and lightning flashed.

157

The lightning illuminated the interior of the wagon for an instant and they saw a figure lying on a cot.

The boys tiptoed to the cot, barely breathing. A noise reached their ears, a rustling of bedclothes, and a darker darkness rose from the cot. Jack made a little squeaking noise deep in his throat and they backed away until they bumped against the wall.

"Angel?" Finney said in an almost inaudible whisper.

There was another movement from the cot. A match struck, momentarily blinding them. They squinted and pressed against the wall. The match moved to a candle. The lighted candle was lifted and the light fell on a mass of snakes writhing over a pair of glittering eyes.

Finney and Jack shrieked and grabbed each other. They hid their eyes, turned their backs and hunkered against the wall, feeling their flesh already turning to stone. Medusa sat on the cot, watching them curiously.

Finney slowly raised his arm and peeked out with one eye. Jack's arm was only an inch away. It looked normal, not a bit like stone. Then Jack's arm lowered slightly, uncovering his round eye. They stared at each other in amazement. They turned hesitantly, ready to flee if necessary, and saw the Medusa sitting motionless on her cot watching them.

"I looked at her and I didn't turn to stone," Jack said with a slow exhalation.

"I guess that part of it was just a myth after all," Finney said with some disappointment, "but she's certainly a real Medusa all right."

"How do you know?" Jack asked doubtfully. "She didn't turn us to stone."

Finney sighed and looked at him sideways. "If she was a fake she'd take her snakes off before she went to bed, wouldn't she?"

158

Jack twisted his mouth, thinking seriously. "Yeah, you're right," he said. "She's a real Medusa, sure enough."

They looked around the wagon. The mermaid floated in her tank, possibly asleep, but appearing to be dead. Beyond her the snake woman lay coiled in her cage.

"Look, Finney!" Jack hissed in excitement. "The Snake Goddess! I want to get a closer look."

"We're supposed to be looking for Angel, Jack," Finney said impatiently, feeling slightly betrayed.

"We've got time to look at the Snake Goddess, haven't we?" Jack demanded, arching his eyebrows.

Finney rolled his eyes and nodded reluctantly.

"Excuse me, ma'am," Jack said to the Medusa, his voice cracking. "Pardon us for bustin' in. We were lookin' for Angel and we got the wrong wagon. Is it all right if we take a closer look at the Snake Goddess?"

"And could you tell us which wagon Angel is in?" Finney added.

The Medusa looked from one to the other, moving her whole head instead of just her eyes. Her face showed only curiosity. Jack and Finney looked at each other.

Jack jerked his head and they moved cautiously to the snake woman's cage, casting wary glances at the Medusa. The snake woman was asleep, but stirred at their approach, candlelight sparkling dully on her gun-metal scales. Medusa followed them with her fascinated gaze, moving nothing but her head. Finney and Jack knelt down and pressed their faces against the bars. The snake woman looked back at them, her silver hair cresting over her head like a startled cockatoo. Her coils shifted slightly and she moved closer to them, her head making quick, birdlike movements. She watched them for a moment, then reached out her little hand and placed it delicately on Jack's brown grubby fingers, grasping one of the bars.

159

"Hey!" he breathed. "She likes me."

He suddenly reached up and unfastened the latch on the cage.

"You shouldn't do that," Finney protested.

"Sssssssh!" Jack hissed and opened the cage door. The snake woman looked at him expectantly. Jack reached his hand in.

Then Medusa stood up and went to them, leaning over to see what they were doing. Finney and Jack both jerked their heads around and stared into a nest of snakes two inches from their noses. Jack slammed the cage door and they bolted. They clattered across the wagon floor and clumped down the steps and were in the street before they even slowed down.

Medusa turned and watched them go with startled eyes. She heard a squeak behind her and twisted her head around. The door of the snake woman's cage opened slowly under its own weight. One hinge made a thin, rusty protest. The snake woman watched the opening door and swayed slightly. She hesitated for a moment, then flowed from the cage, across the floor, through the wagon door and down the steps, holding her little arms before her, rushing to meet the night.

Medusa watched her leave and nothing moved but her head.

Finney and Jack pounded to a halt some distance away and gasped for breath. They looked back at the Wonder Show and thunder rolled over their heads.

"C'mon, Finney, let's go home," Jack said, his chest heaving. "We can look for Angel in the morning. Besides, it's gonna start rainin' in a minute, and if your mother tells my mother that I stayed out in the rain, I won't get to spend Saturday night with you again for a month."

Finney didn't answer, but glumly agreed with a dip of his

head. They started walking toward the Bowen house, then darted behind the loading platform of the ice house when Sheriff Dwyer's car passed. They watched it, wide-eyed, when it stopped at the Wonder Show and the sheriff and three other men got out. Finney and Jack looked at each other in bewilderment.

"I told you something fishy was going on," Finney said.

25.

Haverstock was sitting at his desk, deep in thought, still wearing the black robe from the show. He looked up with annoyance when someone knocked on his door. "Who is it?" he said with a snarl.

"The sheriff," a voice said. "I want to talk to you."

Haverstock got up, growling. He threw the door open, barely missing the sheriff, and glared at the four men. "What do you want at this time of night?"

"May I come in?" Dwyer asked with studied politeness.

Haverstock stepped back and waved his arm insolently. "Of course. Come in. Ruin my sleep."

The sheriff stepped in but the other three remained outside, watching the sky, hoping they wouldn't be caught in the rain. Sheriff Dwyer looked around and ignored Haverstock's sarcasm.

"I'm sorry to disturb you, sir, but it's important. One of

our girls was murdered tonight. Dr. Latham's girl. She was sexually molested."

"So naturally you come running straight to me," Haverstock said in a martyred voice. "It happens every time a bottle of milk goes sour. We are always to blame. The strangers."

"This is a little more serious than sour milk, sir," Dwyer said, restraining his anger and beginning to hope this loudmouthed smart aleck was somehow involved.

"Of course." Haverstock shrugged an apology. "I'm sorry. Naturally, I'm very distressed about the girl. However, statistics seem to prove that in almost every case of this sort, the killer is someone known by the girl. Have you questioned her boy friend?"

"Mr. Haverstock, the girl died as a result of the rape. She died of massive internal hemorrhaging. He threw her down an old cistern when he was finished with her and she bled to death. I doubt if Billy Sullivan is much bigger than my thumb." The sheriff saw amusement in the other man's eyes at his outburst. "As far as we can determine," he went on, trying to sound calmly official, "the attack took place about the time your first show was starting. I want to know the whereabouts of all your people at that time."

"In that event, Sheriff, there is no problem. Everyone with the show has specific duties to perform and I can personally assure you they were all performing them."

"Then you have nothing to worry about. I'll still want to talk to everyone, but it can wait till morning. Right now, I would like to have a complete list of your personnel and everything you know about them."

"Sheriff, we will be leaving very early in the morning. We have an engagement in Liberal two days from now."

"You'll leave when I'm satisfied none of your people were involved in the girl's death," Dwyer said with malice and enjoyed the black look on the other man's face. "Would you mind making that list for me?" he said mildly. "I'll be back in the morning." He turned and left without a backward glance.

Haverstock stood in the doorway, watching the sheriff and his men get in their car and drive away. His face was blacker than the clouds boiling overhead. When the car was out of sight, he went down the steps and marched down the row of wagons like a locomotive, the gusty wind catching his robe, billowing it and flaring it like death wings. He mounted the steps of the Minotaur's wagon and savagely threw open the door.

Henry and Tim had been talking since Henry got back to the wagon, whispering so they wouldn't wake the Minotaur, though they weren't sure that he would care whether Angel ran away or not, but taking no chances. They had talked it around and around, but had come to no conclusion. There seemed to be only two choices: do nothing or try to help Angel get away. Both positions seemed untenable.

They both jumped when the door slammed open. Lightning crackled behind the black spectre standing in the doorway. Thunder ripped through the sky. Haverstock stormed in, his face a study in fury.

"What's wrong?" Henry asked, too startled to keep his mouth shut.

Haverstock didn't answer him, didn't seem to even notice him. He went to the cot where the Minotaur still slept with his hand cupping his genitals. A roar of rage tore from Haverstock's throat. He kicked the Minotaur in the ribs. The Minotaur sat up slowly, rubbing his side, looking at Haverstock with big, soft, confused eyes.

Henry and Tim nervously watched the tableau. The Minotaur swung his hoofs to the floor and sat naked on the cot, looking inquiringly at the man frozen in rage over him.

164

"You damned freak!" Haverstock shrieked, finally finding his voice. "You damned animal! You couldn't wait, could you? You couldn't wait until we found some slut who was willing? You had to go and take one of the town girls! You stupid freak! Look at you!" He pointed at the Minotaur's genitals. "You filthy animal. You didn't even wash yourself. You've still got blood on you! Don't you realize the danger this puts me in? I thought I made it clear the last time, it was not to happen again. Didn't the little lesson I gave you make any impression at all? Didn't my promise to cut it off, to turn you into a steer, get through to you?"

He took a deep breath and tried to calm himself. "Well, it won't happen again," he said in a deathly quiet voice. "You don't have to worry about castration. I'm sick to death of you freaks. I never want to see your hideous faces again. You do nothing but endanger my work."

The Minotaur stood up, looking uncertainly at the shorter man.

"You couldn't think of me or my work. All you could think of was your aching flesh. It won't happen again. Never. Never, again."

The Minotaur suddenly clutched at his chest and sucked in great gasps of air. His throat rattled and his eyes bluged.

Henry and Tim stared at the stricken Minotaur, then Henry grabbed Tim and ran as hard as he could.

The Minotaur staggered. His hoofs clumped uncertainly on the wooden floor. Haverstock stared at him with gleeful, burning eyes. The Minotaur's massive body began to tremble. His satin skin became ashen. He held out a shaking, imploring hand and dropped heavily to his knees. Haverstock laughed and caused the Minotaur's blood to rush to his loins. His phallus swelled and stood erect. His eyes grew glassy and confused, as if he did not know why he was dying. Blood trickled from his flat nose. His body was again seized by tremors and he clutched his arms to his chest.

The muscles in his arms and shoulders knotted and quivered. The Minotaur was incredibly strong and took a long time to die but, finally, his eyes unfocused and filmed. He toppled forward and crashed to the floor. His breath escaped slowly in bloody froth.

Haverstock turned, his own breath coming in gasps, an insane glitter in his eyes. He looked at Henry's empty cot and a whine squeezed from his tight throat. He kicked over Tim's crate and pawed through the contents. He swept the wreckage to the floor. He grabbed the lamp and hurled it against the wall over the Minotaur's cot. The glass shattered and flaming kerosene flowed down the wall and across the floor, filling the wagon with fire.

Haverstock rushed out and went down the line of caravans. He opened a door. He raised his hand. A fireball formed around his fingers, burning like a little sun. He arched his arm and the fireball splattered in the wagon. The scattered bits clung to wood and cloth and flesh, eating and spreading with unnatural speed. The roustabouts awoke, screaming. Haverstock slammed the door but, even in his fury, did not fail to notice the wagon contained only five men. The door shivered as fists pounded on it, but it would not open even though it was not locked. The screens on the windows sang as fingers clawed at them. The frenzied, agonized screams died away. Flames ate through the supporting ropes and the window coverings slammed shut. Smoke seeped through the cracks, then flames jetted out.

The horses began to scream and pull at their hitch reins, their hoofs kicking clods from the hard-packed earth. Already nervous from the thunder and lightning, they broke loose and bolted. They swept around the tent in a drumming river. Some entangled themselves in the guy ropes and fell. One lay kicking and snorting, unable to rise again. Pegs pulled from the ground and a corner of the tent buckled, ballooned, and sagged.

166

Haverstock went to the next wagon and opened the door. Medusa raised up on her cot and looked at him, red reflections flickering in her eyes. The mermaid floated motionlessly in her tank. He saw the snake woman's empty cage and growled. With extra fury he shot the fireball into the wagon.

Medusa ran past him, her robes flaming. Her mouth was open and her eyes stared. She ran across the lot with her arms outstretched, seeking something that did not exist. She left a trail of little fires in the grass. The snakes on her head writhed insanely, biting her face and neck and shoulders. Air escaped her gaping mouth in a silent scream. Then she stumbled and fell in a fiery heap. She died without uttering a sound.

The mermaid awoke and swam in tight circles within the narrow confines of her tank, her round fish-eyes glowing red from the flames surrounding her. She pressed against the glass, but drew back because it was too hot. She swam faster, sloshing water over the top of the tank. Her lidless eyes stared and her mouth opened and closed rapidly. In her panic she battered herself against the tank until the water was cloudy with her blood.

The water began to steam. Then the heat grew too great and the glass shattered. Water gushed across the flaming floor. The wagon was filled with white steam. The mermaid lay on the bottom of the tank. Her body trembled and then was still. Only her mouth opened and closed spasmodically, and soon that stopped. She died in agony and confusion.

Haverstock sent a flaming ball at the tent. It went up as if it were soaked in gasoline. He reached Louis's wagon and found Louis standing outside, wearing a bathrobe, watching him. They looked at each for a moment, measuring, judging. Then Haverstock motioned for Louis to help him and turned back to his own wagon. Louis stepped back inside

167

and returned with an armload of clothes and the frightened woman. She was only half-dressed, her mouth a little round hole and her eyes big. Louis gave a push and she staggered away into the darkness on bare feet.

Already the end of Louis's wagon was beginning to smoke.

At Rose's party, twenty giggling, gossiping girls rushed to the window and stared bug-eyed at the flames rising above the treetops on the other side of the square. With a great deal of excitement and confusion, they began to dress.

Finney and Jack had just changed into their nightshirts, getting ready to go to bed. They looked out the window when they heard the fire bell and clambered from the house without putting their clothes back on.

The crowd gathered around the fire like moths, some dressed and some with robes over nightgowns and pajamas. The men helped roll Haverstock's wagon away from the flames. Louis drove the black Model-T Ford, his clothes beside him on the seat, a way down the street out of danger. Everything else was burning furiously. The flames rose so high from the tent they turned the bottoms of the black clouds to copper. Then they settled back as the tent was consumed.

The calliope suddenly began to play, but only for a moment. Then the fire destroyed the mechanism.

Finney and Jack ran up, their bare feet pounding on the street. They looked on sadly. "There goes the old Wonder Show," Finney said solemnly. "There'll never be another one like it."

Jack nodded grave agreement as Rose and the girls arrived, chattering and making horrified faces.

The word spread quickly through the crowd: "Everyone was killed. Everyone except those two over there by the

168

Model-T." Exactly where the information had originated no one was sure, but it was too terrible not to pass on. Rose heard it and frost seemed to form on her skin.

Kelsey Armstrong!

The images she had succeeded in banishing from her mind returned, Kelsey Armstrong's demanding mouth on hers, his hard arms around her, his naked body against hers. She felt an ache in her thighs and a hollow pit in her stomach. Then the heat of relief melted the frost and eased the ache. Now no one would ever know. The thought had nagged at her. What if Kelsey had told someone? What if he had told the other men at the tent show? What if all six of them had wanted her? What if they had crept around her house, calling her in the night? Now she was safe, now he would never tell, no one would ever find out.

Haverstock and Louis stood beside the black Model-T Ford. Haverstock watched the flames, his face complacent, the fury gone. But Louis had no eyes for the flames. Instead he watched the other man with speculation.

Across the street, behind old Miss Sullivan's trumpet vine, Henry and Tim watched also.

Then, finally, the storm broke. Wind scattered the people like brown leaves. They scurried to their homes and storm cellars, clutching robes that threatened to whip away. Thunder blasted the cooling air, making the ground tremble. Lightning ripped the sky and lanced to the ground. A bolt found the Redwines' native rock fence. A section of it disintegrated with a percussion that woke everyone who had managed to sleep through the fire bell.

Evelyn Bradley sat up in bed, not knowing what woke her. She went downstairs to check on Angel and found him sleeping soundly. She climbed the stairs and went back to bed.

* * *

The wind whipped the fire and scattered burning embers for a hundred yards to the north. Children scampered about in shrill excitement, stamping them out. Old Miss Sullivan raced around in her flannel nightgown, swinging her broom and swearing like a field hand.

Henry and Tiny Tim huddled behind the trumpet vine–covered trellis.

"We gotta find Angel and get out of here," Tim said impatiently.

"But we don't know where the doctor's *house* is," Henry said petulantly. "If we go looking for it now, somebody will see us. People are running all over the place."

"We can't just leave him there. What'll he do when he wakes up in the morning? We may never find him if he goes off on his own. But Haverstock probably will."

"I don't think we have to worry about him going off on his own. Not as long as the girl is around."

"You can't be sure. She might've done what you said and gone home."

Henry shook his head. "Not a chance. Our Miss Bradley is smitten. I know exactly where Angel will be tomorrow. Come on."

They left the trumpet vine sanctuary, circled behind the old grist mill, and waded across Crooked Creek.

The citizens of Hawley cheered sarcastically when the fire truck arrived. Harley Overcash waved his grease-stained hands and explained to anyone who would listen that he hadn't been able to get it started. Then when they got the hose going, the wind blew most of the water back on the crowd.

Rose Willet held her fluttering robe together with one hand and her hair with the other. The other girls were scattered up and down the street, some of them hurrying back to the house and others lingering at the fire.

Rose was passing the ice house when she thought she

heard her name. It was only the wind, she thought. She heard it again and turned, squinting against the wind. Kelsey Armstrong stood in the shadows, beckoning to her. Joy and terror sang duets in her blood. He wasn't dead; she wasn't safe after all. Fear and desire mingled with the memories of him.

She walked slowly to him, forgetting her robe, forgetting her hair. He pulled her into his arms.

"They said you were dead," she said dully.

"I was at the gin, waiting for you," he said, hugging her to him.

"I told you I wouldn't come."

"I know. I took a chance you might change your mind."

"They said you were dead."

"I love you, Rose."

"I'm afraid."

"I love you, Rose. Come with me tonight."

"No. No, I can't." She pulled away from him, but he still held her shoulders. "My father . . . "

"Damn your father."

"No. My father would kill us."

"Remember last night. Remember how good it was."

"I remember."

"We're right for each other, Rose. We would have a wonderful life together."

"No. My father . . . "

"Stop using your father as an excuse."

Her face twisted "There's no future with you."

"There's love and happiness."

"I want more than that."

"What more is there? Love and happiness is everything."

"That's not enough."

"I'm young, Rose. I'm only twenty-two. I'm strong and I'm not stupid. I can be anything you want me to be. Please, Rose, come with me."

171

"You're too strong, Kelsey," she said, her throat so tight she could hardly speak. "I'm afraid. Please. Go away." She backed away from him. "Go away, Kelsey. I'm afraid." She turned and ran down the street. She ignored the wind, did not notice that it ruined her carefully marcelled hair, did not mind that it billowed her robe and pasted her nightgown to her legs.

Kelsey watched her until she was out of sight. He felt a great hollow in his body and a weakness in his limbs. Then he went to the railroad tracks, intending to hop the next freight.

Baby Sis Redwine watched the fire from her upstairs bedroom window and wondered if she should go help. But there already seemed to be a hundred people running around down there. She decided she could contribute little but more confusion and, besides, the fire truck had finally arrived. Then she heard something above the crackle of the thunder and the roar of the wind.

Muttering, she put a pair of overalls on over her nightgown and got the shotgun from the closet.

"What's the matter?" her mother asked. She had come into Sis's room to watch the fire; her room was on the other side of the house.

"Something's in the chicken house."

She rushed from the room, her nightgown hanging out the sides of her overalls. Her mother tottered after her.

The wind caught the screen door and slammed it back against the wall. The lightning left white streaks floating before Sis's eyes. She waddled across the porch and down the steps, listening to the panicky chickens cackle and squawk and flap.

Her mother ran after her, frantically holding her robe down with one hand as it threatened to blow over her head, and clutching the bannister with the other to keep from being blown off her feet.

Sis opened the chicken house door and looked in, holding the shotgun in readiness. The wind filled the air with feathers. The cacophony hurt her ears, but she could see a dark shape moving the storm of flapping, screeching chickens.

She raised the shotgun and fired. The tin roof rang like a bell and an unearthly squawk filled the chicken house. Lightning flashed and Sis stepped back, holding the gun in numb fingers.

The snake woman clutched at her bloody breast with her tiny hands and rose up on her serpent body. She smashed against the roof, then slumped against the wall. Blood and feathers surrounded her open mouth. Her coils threshed madly, wrecking roosts and overturning nests. Cackling chickens flew out around Sis, but she hardly noticed them. The snake woman slid slowly down the wall, her coils looping and constricting. Then she lay still. The only movement was a slight tremor in her coils and then they too were still.

Sis's mother grabbed her arm. "Did you get it? What was it?" she shouted above the wind.

"Look," Sis said and held out a shaking hand.

Her mother squinted into the darkness. It was only a second before lightning flashed. "Oh, my goodness," she gasped. "It's that thing from the tent show. Maybe you shouldn't have killed it. It must be worth a lot of money."

Indignation immediately overrode Sis's feelings of guilt. "It was killing my chickens, wasn't it? Let's see 'em try to make something out of it."

Then the rain came. Those fighting the fires heard it coming, a hissing roar that approached like the night freight to Wichita, growing louder by the second. They breathed sighs of relief as the wall of water hit, then ran under shelters to escape the pea-sized hail that came with the rain.

Harley Overcash rolled the hose back onto the fire truck, the hail rattling on his helmet. He wished the rain had come just a little earlier.

The flaming wagons steamed and sizzled under the downpour. Soon they were only piles of wet charcoal, emitting an occasional hiss of steam as the rain soaked in and found a few still-glowing embers.

The rain eased quickly. People emerged from storm cellars and went back to bed. Soon stars were visible in the south, but there was no one to see them. The only light in town burned in Haverstock's wagon, where he and Louis had taken shelter.

26.

Angel awoke slowly, stretching his arms and yawning. For a moment he didn't remember where he was, then he tensed and his eyes darted from side to side. His beginning panic was eased when he looked into Evelyn's smiling face. His body relaxed and he lay back on the cot in Dr. Latham's clinic. He smiled at her tentatively, feeling a strange sensation in his throat. He sat up.

"How do you feel?" she asked softly.

His smile widened and the room seemed sunnier.

"Good," she said and felt warm. "I don't know where Dr. Latham is. Nobody was around when I got up. He said all you needed was a good night's sleep."

They contemplated each other for a moment.

"Well, what do we do with you now?"

He looked doubtful and apologetic at being a problem.

"I talked to Henry last night."

Angel's eyebrows rose inquiringly.

She shrugged. "He didn't seem to know what to do either. He was very worried about you."

Angel's expression became apologetic again.

"He said he had to talk to Tim, that between the two of them they would know what to do. I told him where you were. I thought they might come here." She frowned when the thought flickered through her mind that maybe they had decided not to help Angel, that they were too worried about their own safety. But she dismissed the thought quickly, not able to believe it. There obviously was some other reason. She thought for a moment, then reached a nervous decision. "There's only one thing we can do. You'll have to come home with me and I'll get word to Henry where you are." She looked at him quickly. "I mean, you can't stay here. Haverstock and that Mexican are looking for you, and this is a little too close for comfort. Our place is out in the country; they'd never think about looking for you there."

He watched her with an expression she couldn't read, but she felt again that sensation she'd had on the road the night before when he had seemed to survey her soul. Then he nodded and looked at his clothes draped over a chair. He grinned and motioned for her to turn around.

She did so and smiled wryly, thinking about his act in the tent show, when he floated over the audience stark naked. Of course, with the globe of water and the clouds and the lightning, he might as well have been fully clothed for all you could see. She almost said something, but remembered what Henry had said, that Angel never remembered what he did in the show.

Angel turned back the sheet and slipped his pants on over his undershorts. He rapped on the chair with his knuckles and she turned back. His eyes twinkled like little red stars as he put on his shirt and shoes.

"The bathroom's back there," she said, tilting her head in its direction, "if you need to wash your face."

* * *

Evelyn slowed the car and looked at the burned-out Wonder Show in amazement. The sheriff and a bunch of others poked through the soggy rubble, searching for the charred bodies. She reached behind her and touched Angel, crouched in the back seat. He eased up enough to see. Worry clouded his face. "What do we do now?" Evelyn whispered.

He sank back in the seat and shrugged in bewilderment.

Just then Louis stepped from Haverstock's wagon and looked at her. She quickly shifted into second and sped away. Louis watched the car bobble over the railroad tracks and cross the bridge. His lips twitched into a smile.

Evelyn drove slowly on the wet road, splashing through still standing puddles, and looked at the wheat. It was bowed and damply motionless, but didn't appear damaged. A few days of hot sun would dry it out and stand it back up again. She knew what a heavy rain with hail could do; how the wheat could be battered to the ground in a matted carpet, impossible to harvest.

Angel leaned on the back of the seat, his chin on his crossed forearms, looking at everything as if he had never really seen it before. She turned her head and smiled at him. He smiled back like a little kid on Christmas morning. She explained to him about the wheat and the rain and the hail, not because she thought he was really interested, but because she liked to talk to him. He watched her face as she talked, a contented little smile on his lips.

The car skidded briefly in the mud as she turned into the lane too quickly. "Duck down," she said. He dropped behind the seat. She parked the car near the barn and spoke to Angel without turning her head.

"Wait until I get in the house and then scoot into the barn. I think I'd better see which way the wind blows before I tell my parents about you. I'm not sure what they'll think about all this." She laughed nervously.

177

Her parents and Harold met her on the porch, their faces flickering from anger to relief and back again.

"Where have you been?" Bess demanded, her voice strained. "We've been worried sick all morning."

"Young lady," Otis said sternly, "you'd better have a good explanation."

"This isn't like you at all," Bess said, her hands fluttering on her apron.

Evelyn looked at them in complete bewilderment. "What's the matter?" she asked, wide-eyed.

"Where have you been all night?" Otis's hand shook slightly from released tension. "Rose said you weren't at her house."

"Then we heard about poor Francine. . . . " Bess sniffled and twisted her apron into a knot.

"I was just about to take the truck and come look for you," Otis interrupted his wife.

"We called central and even Reba didn't know where you were." Bess was working herself into a state. "Reba said you called Rose. . . . "

"What happened to Francine?" Evelyn demanded, wishing they would quit fussing and explain.

"You haven't heard?" Harold asked and raised his eyebrows.

"No!"

"She was . . . killed, dear," Bess said quietly.

"Killed?" Evelyn felt as if she had started a book in the middle. "What happened to her?"

"She was murdered," Harold said flatly.

"She was also . . . molested," Otis said tightly.

"That's why we were so worried about you, dear," Bess said, whimpering.

"Molested?"

"Raped," Harold snapped impatiently.

"Harold, don't use that word," Bess whispered and put her hand to her throat.

178

"They found her down in the old cistern where the Overstreet house burned," Otis explained quietly. "Dr. Latham went looking for her when he found out she hadn't gotten to the Willets'. He found her overnight case near the old foundation. When he looked around, some of the boards had been taken off the cistern. . . . Then the tent show burned down."

"I knew about that. I saw it on my way home."

"All those people killed." Bess shivered. "Everyone there was killed except that Haverstock person and the Mexican."

Evelyn looked at her in horror. If Henry and Tim were dead, what would Angel do?

"I'm still waiting to hear where you were last night," Otis brought them back to the subject.

"Oh, that. . . . " She fidgeted.

"Yes, that. I'm waiting."

Evelyn glanced at the car. Harold looked at her suspiciously and followed her gaze. Evelyn moved toward the house, trying to get them inside. "I spent the night at Francine's," she said lamely.

"Francine's?" Bess gasped.

"Why did you put the car out by the barn?" Harold asked and narrowed his eyes at her.

Evelyn ignored him. "Francine wasn't there. I didn't know anything about . . . I thought she was at Rose's."

"Then what were you doing there?" Otis demanded.

"There was an accident. I . . . "

"An accident?" Bess fluttered her hands. "Were you hurt? Is that why you were at the doctor's?"

Evelyn went through the door, followed by her anxious parents. Harold paused and looked at the car speculatively, then went in after them.

"No, I wasn't hurt. I just didn't feel like going to Rose's party."

"Why didn't you call us?"

179

"I'm sorry. I guess I didn't think about it. I didn't know you'd be worried."

Angel watched them go into the house, then slipped from the car on the opposite side and ran crouching into the barn. He looked around for a place to hide. "Angel!" A voice hissed at him from above. He jerked his head up and saw Henry peering down at him. "I thought you'd show up here sooner or later," Henry said.

A grin of delight and relief split Angel's face. He rubbed his damp palms on the seat of his pants and shifted from one foot to the other.

"Come on up," Henry said, smiling. "We have some serious decisions to make."

A little later Otis and Bess left for church, but Evelyn begged off. "I really don't feel like going," she said as they stood on the porch.

Bess brushed a speck of lint from Otis's sleeve. "All right, dear. I don't know what people will think, with you and Harold both not showing up."

Otis tugged at his tight collar. "Harold is a grown man. If he doesn't want to go to church today, we should respect his wishes."

Bess sighed and pulled on her golves. "Everything is such a muddle this morning. I don't know whether I'm coming or going."

They got into the car and drove off. Evelyn watched the car go down the lane and turn onto the main road. Then she looked around for Harold and wondered why he had so mysteriously stayed home. She didn't see him anywhere and walked furtively to the barn.

A dozen blackbirds pecked and quarreled in the feedlot, then flew away with a flutter of wings when she approached. They settled back as if nothing had disturbed them as she went inside. The interior was silent and warmly pungent with the odors of hay and alfalfa and the still lingering cow smells where her father and Harold had milked early that morning.

She looked around and didn't see Angel. She felt a momentary panic that he hadn't waited.

"Angel," she called softly and heard a movement above her. Angel's grinning face and Henry's dour visage looked down at her.

"We're up here," Henry said.

She gasped. "Henry!" she cried with delight. "I thought . . . Everyone thinks you were killed in the fire."

"It would be fine with me if everyone *did* think so," he said sourly, "but there are a couple who *know* I wasn't."

Evelyn scrambled up the ladder to the loft and climbed into the cotton-seed bin with them.

"Tim! You're all right, too," she said, beaming.

"For the moment." He grimaced.

"What happened?" She sat on the soft cottonseed beside Angel, feeling a warmth from his nearness.

Henry leaned morosely against the wall of the bin. "Things went completely to hell last night. The Minotaur raped and killed one of the town girls. . . . "

"Francine!" Evelyn cried and felt the strangest sensation in her thighs.

"I don't know what her name was."

"The Minotaur?" She remembered him standing in the aisle, leaning across Francine so Harold could examine his horns. She remembered his massive body and satin skin and the straining loincloth. She also remembered Francine's peculiar tears and strained reaction, which she had thought was only embarrassment. Francine was so easily embarrassed. And the doctor said she had been acting strangely all day Saturday. Thoughts tangled in her head and she shivered. But she looked up and saw Angel reading

181

her soul again. He took her hand and warmth drove away the chill.

"It wasn't the first time," Henry continued, not noticing. "Haverstock's always managed to cover it up before, but last night he went berserk. He killed the Minotaur, then set fire to the place and killed everyone else. Tim and I managed to escape. Haverstock was in such a blind rage he didn't see us."

"My mother said the Mexican . . . "

"Louis!" Tim spat.

"Yeah," Henry snorted. "I guess he thought Louis was still useful. That's a matched set if I ever saw one." He looked at Evelyn seriously. "Listen, Miss Bradley, we appreciate all you've done to help Angel, but we can't stay here. He knows about you and he's bound to come here looking for us. Our only chance is to stay out of his way. If he ever finds us, we're dead. There's nothing we can do to defend ourselves."

"How does he know about me?"

"I told him," Tim said softly, shame in his voice and pain on his ugly little face.

"You told him? Why?" Evelyn asked incredulously.

"Don't blame Tim, Miss Bradley," Henry assured her. "No one could resist Haverstock's questions for very long."

"There's one thing I didn't tell him," Tim said. "I didn't tell him we know Angel has the gift too, that Angel used it yesterday morning when he kept you from falling into the water. But the only reason I didn't tell him is that he didn't ask me." His voice trembled, remembering. "Most important he doesn't know that Angel is aware he has the gift. I think that is the last thing Haverstock wants, for Angel to know."

"If Angel has the same power, can't we fight back?" Evelyn asked.

"He doesn't know how to use it," Henry sighed. "And

182

Haverstock isn't about to let him live long enough to find out."

"Then the only thing we can do is keep out of his way until Angel *does* learn how," Evelyn said logically.

"Miss Bradley," Henry said firmly, "it would be very dangerous for you to get mixed up in this."

"Dr. Latham said nearly the same thing last night, but I think it's too late."

"She's right, Henry," Tim said. "He won't like her helping us. There's no telling what he might do."

"No," Henry said and frowned. "If we go away from here right now, there'll be no way he can find out she had anything to do with us."

"He'll find out," Tim said with a chill in his voice. "You know he'll find out."

"It's all settled, then," Evelyn said with finality.

"Well, this is a cozy little group," Harold said brightly. They whirled in fright and saw him standing on the top of the ladder watching them, smiling smugly, his leg hooked casually around a beam. "I thought you were up to something, Evie."

"Harold," she groaned, "why do you have to be so damned clever? Come on and sit down before you fall and break your neck."

So they told him everything.

"You don't expect me to believe all this nonsense, do you?" he said incredulously.

"I don't care if you believe it or not," Evelyn snapped. "Just don't interfere." She sighed and shook her head. "Please, Harold."

"If this guy is trying to kill you, why don't you go to Sheriff Dwyer?" He spread his hands, solving the problem.

For the sheriff's sake, we don't dare," Henry explained patiently. "Haverstock is completely ruthless. The sheriff wouldn't have a chance. We endanger the lives of everyone

183

we tell, and I think this group right here had better be the limit."

He frowned. "The trouble is, we don't know how strong his powers are. We don't know how much of what he does in the show is him and how much is Angel."

"Doesn't Angel know?"

"No," Henry sighed. "He's hypnotized before he goes on. He didn't know he had the gift at all until yesterday."

"I still don't believe in these magic powers of yours," Harold grunted and looked at Angel. He frowned slightly at Angel's pale hand holding Evelyn's. Angel shook his head and shrugged helplessly.

"There's nothing magic about them," Henry said. "The human mind, my boy, is as mysterious as the bottom of the sea or the mountains of the moon."

Harold shifted on the cottonseed and looked at their tense faces. "Okay. I believe you when you say what's his name is trying to kill you, and I'll help you get away, but I won't let Evie go with you."

"Her life is in as much danger as ours," Tim said quietly. "And so is yours, if he finds out."

"He's right," Henry agreed. Angel nodded and looked intently at Harold.

"What would I tell Mother and Dad?" Harold threw his hands in the air. "You can't just disappear. They'd have half the county out looking for you. I'm sure Haverstock would appreciate the help."

"I know," Evelyn said softly.

The five of them sat glumly until Harold looked up.

"You could go to the old Hindley place. Nobody would find you there."

"Where's that?" Henry asked, hoping for a solution.

"It's about three miles from here." Evelyn brightened. "It's been empty over ten years, but there's water. And the road's been fenced off and plowed over. There's no way to get to it unless you walk, or by horseback. And you can't see it from the main road." She frowned. "I guess it's still standing. I haven't been out there in years."

"Dad and I rode out that way a few weeks ago. It still looks like it always did." He chuckled. "We all thought it was haunted when I was a kid. I guess they still do."

"It sounds good," Henry said, "but I'm not sure Haverstock needs a road."

"What does he do," Harold snorted, "fly?"

"Well, I've never seen him fly. But you all saw Angel do it."

Harold looked at him sourly and then at Evelyn. "I guess we could tell Mother we're going on a picnic, but that only solves the problem for this afternoon."

"Maybe I could pretend I'm staying a few days with a friend. Only I can't think of a reason why I'd be doing it."

Suddenly Angel tensed. He held up his hand and listened, a frown on his face. He stood up and scrambled to the front of the barn, looking out. He motioned frantically to the others and they hurried to him.

The black Model-T Ford clattered up the lane toward the Bradley farmhouse.

Louis pulled to a stop and looked around. "Doesn't seem to be anyone at home."

"On the contrary," Haverstock said mildly and lifted his hand in the direction of the barn. Harold stepped out, paused, then walked toward them. He put his hands on the car door and leaned down to look into Haverstock's face. His heart was pounding and his throat was dry.

"Hello. Sorry to hear about your show burning," he said and was surprised that his voice sounded normal. "What can I do for you?"

"Yes, most unfortunate accident," Haverstock said pleasantly. "We were wondering if you could help us. There's a young man with the show—Angel, the Magic Boy?"

Harold nodded.

"Very nice boy, completely harmless, of course, but a little off in the head; mentally retarded, a mute. He was frightened by the fire and seems to have run away."

"Oh?" Harold raised his eyebrows. "I thought everyone was killed in the fire."

"Yes, very sad affair. We thought so too, but it seems Angel was fortuitously spared. A sweet, harmless boy; we were so relieved."

"Is he supposed to be out this way?"

"We have no idea. He was seen with your sister yesterday morning." He smiled. "Your sister is a very lovely girl. Evelyn? Is that her name?"

"Yes."

"Pretty name. No, we are merely exploring every avenue and we thought there was a possibility he might have come here."

"No." Harold shrugged, keeping his face blank. "He hasn't been around here, that I know of."

"Well, it was just a chance." He pursed his lips petulantly. "We want very much to find him. He really isn't capable of taking care of himself." He smiled again. "Is your sister around, perhaps?"

Harold's heart did a flip-flop. "No, I'm sorry. She and my parents went to Liberal for the day . . . to visit my . . . grandmother."

"How nice." Haverstock's smile vanished. "But, then, she probably hasn't seen him either or she would have surely mentioned it to you." He turned to Louis.

"Check the house and barn, Louis," he snapped. Louis got out of the car and trotted into the house. Haverstock turned back to Harold and smiled.

Harold looked back at him, an expression of polite interest on his face, but his eyes didn't blink. Haverstock put his fingers slowly on Harold's hand resting on the car door. He slid his hand up Harold's arm to his face. It lingered there for a moment, then moved down his chest.

Louis searched through every room in the house and then went to the barn. He checked around, looked in all the stalls, climbed the ladder to the loft, but found nothing. He looked out the rear loft doors, across the rolling pasture land dotted with cattle.

Crouched in a wash, Evelyn, Angel, Henry, and Tim watched him through tall buffalo grass and released their breaths when he turned away.

Louis got back in the car. "Didn't see anything."

"Yes, I'm sure she would," Harold said.

"Well, thank you very much, young man. Sorry to have bothered you. You will let us know if you should see or hear anything about Angel?" Haverstock smiled pleasantly.

"Of course," Harold said and stepped back from the car as Louis started it.

"Good-bye," Haverstock called and waggled his hand out the window. The car chugged back down the lane.

Harold watched them leave with a perplexed expression on his face. He felt peculiar and a bit lightheaded. He shivered and went back to the barn.

27.

The Reverend Pomeroy, before his sermon that Sunday at the First Methodist Church of Hawley, announced that Francine Latham's funeral would be Tuesday morning at 10:00 A.M. at the First Christian Church. She would be at the Redwine Funeral Home for those who wished to pay their respects. He then preached a blood-and-thunder sermon about Godly retribution and the demons of Satan. Though he made great use of circumlocution, allegory, and parable, with especially heavy emphasis on fallen angels and the serpent in the Garden of Eden, no one in the congregation had any doubt that he was talking about the tent show and the fire that destroyed it. They knew their pastor and were expecting something along those lines. Some of the more worldly in Reverend Pomeroy's flock commented that they were indeed fortunate that God was keeping such a close watch on Hawley, Kansas.

When services were over, Rose Willet went ahead, leaving the judge, her mother, Lilah, Grace Elizabeth, and Wash

Peacock to their weekly after-services chat with the pastor. Wash was a new addition to the group. He wouldn't say anything unless asked a direct question, but would motionlessly fidget to get it over with, then get Sunday dinner at the Willets' over with and get back to Miller's Corners and chores that had to be done. The judge would invite the pastor to Sunday dinner, as the pastor expected; the pastor would gracefully decline, as the judge expected, and it would be over.

Rose was almost the only one to leave the church. There was far too much to talk about that Sunday morning. The tent show was the major topic, but the performance itself had been eclipsed by the fire and the deaths of all those people. The number varied from conversation to conversation. And there was also the storm and, of course, poor Francine.

Rose had been deep in her own thoughts and hadn't heard much of the sermon, but what she had heard only stirred up memories she was trying to forget. She had never had trouble pushing unpleasant memories into dark corners where they could be successfully ignored, but this was different. The memories were not unpleasant. They burned with a clear, hot fire that made her ache with pleasure. But the terrible consequences of discovery canceled the enjoyment of the memory. If only she could rid herself of the thought of the consequences and continue to bathe in the flame of the memory, but she couldn't. They were inexorably linked. The only solution was to banish them both, rid herself of both the pleasure and the pain.

She walked down the shaded street, her Bible and gloves clutched in her hand, not really seeing where she was going, aware of her movements just enough to avoid stepping in the shrinking puddles. She sensed him before he spoke; his presence tingled along her spne.

"Rose," he said.

She stopped, frozen. A roar began in her head, growing

189

louder until she could hear nothing else. She looked up. A whimper caught in her throat. She wanted to say a thousand things, scream at him to leave her alone, beg him to touch her, but nothing she could say would be heard over the roar.

"Rose," he said again. She was surprised that she could hear with the noise in her head. He stood behind a clump of lilac bushes, looking tired and needing a shave.

She could feel people in the street behind her, coming from the church. She forced her legs to move. He stepped back, farther behind the bushes.

"The same place," he said. "I'll wait for you."

She took a step, then another, forcing one foot in front of the other until she was home. She changed clothes and sat on the bottom step of the stairs while Grace Elizabeth and Lilah helped her mother put the food on the table. When her mother called her, she went into the dining room, but she couldn't eat. The judge grumbled at her and her mother fidgeted around her and she excused herself, mumbling that she wasn't hungry and was going for a walk. She went in the opposite direction of the gin, but found herself standing outside it anyway. She went inside and he put his arms around her and kissed her and led her into the room piled with soft cottonseed. She clutched at him, running her hands roughly over his chest and shoulders. He kissed her again and unfastened her clothes. Her dress slipped to her feet and she kept touching him. When all her clothes were off, scattered around them, he undressed himself. She touched each new part of his body as he uncovered it. When he was naked, she tried to touch all of him at once and wanted to scream because she couldn't.

She lay on the cottonseed, her body half-buried by her movements. He sat beside her, grinning at her and smoking a cigarette. He arrogantly blew a smoke ring at her, then

190

leaned over and kissed her, putting his hand on her breast. She put her arms around his neck and held him to her until he laughed and pulled away.

She trembled and shrank from his power.

Kelsey stretched his arms over his head, then rolled his shoulders and made a lazy noise in his throat. He stood up and went to the door, brushing off cottonseed that clung to his buttocks, as unconcerned with his nakedness as a lion. He opened the door a few inches, squinting at the sudden light, and flicked the cigarette butt outside. He looked out for a moment, then pulled the door shut. He came back to her and dropped to his knees beside her.

"What're we gonna do, Rose?" he said.

She looked away from him and followed a thin ray of sunlight coming through a nail hole in the tin wall. Finally she said, "Why didn't you go?"

He sighed and let his shoulders slump. "I almost did. After I talked to you last night, I went to the tracks intending to hop the first freight. I sat there in the ditch two hours waiting." He snorted and grinned. "When it finally came, it was going so damn fast I woulda broke my neck if I'd tried it. So I came back here. Oh, Rose," he said, putting his hand on her stomach, "I love you and I think you love me. We're right together. After the other night and just now, you can't deny we're right together."

She turned her head toward him. "I'm not running off with you, so don't go on about it."

"Well, then," he said, "I'll stay here."

Suddenly his hand weighed a ton; it crushed the breath from her body. She sat up, brushing his hand away. "I don't want you to stay. I won't run off with you and I don't want you to stay here." She lurched unsteadily to her feet.

He looked down at his hands. "Don't say that, Rose."

She began gathering her clothes. "Go away, Kelsey. Go away and leave me alone." She dressed quickly, as if his

191

power over her body would vanish if he could no longer see it. Her words tumbled from her mouth with matter-of-fact precision. "I have plans for my life, Kelsey. My life will be secure and comfortable and respectable. I will marry a man who has a place in this town, who will give me all the things I want. I'm not going to marry some fiddle-foot who'll have to get a job as a field hand or loading sacks at the feed store. I won't live in some two-room shack, taking in washing so I can have a new dress once a year. There's too many poor people around here, and I won't be one of them, not for you, not for anybody. I don't want to see you anymore, Kelsey. Go away and leave me alone." She looked away from him, adjusting her dress.

"If that's true, Rose," he said softly, "why did you come to me today?"

She paused, then looked at him. "That has nothing to do with it."

"It has everything to do with it. Don't you see? Those things you want are not important if you're with someone you love, if you're happy. Besides, who says I can't get all those things for you?"

"Kelsey, go away and leave me alone."

"No," he said and grinned. "You don't really believe all that stuff, or you wouldn't have come. I'll stay here and make you change your mind."

She looked at him, sitting there naked and grinning at her. She knew he was right. Already she could feel his power tugging at her flesh. Soon it would grow too strong and she would go to him, completely in his control.

She sighed. "And do what? Live in the gin the rest of your life?"

"I'll get a job, maybe carrying sacks at the feed store, it doesn't matter. I'll get a place to live, make some money, come calling like any respectable young man and, after a decent length of time, so you don't have to worry about your father anymore, ask for your hand all proper and fittin'."

"You've got it all figured out, haven't you? What if my father throws you out of the house?"

"He won't. I'll be so hard-working and respectable he'll welcome me with open arms." He grinned again.

"What will you do in the meantime, until you get this job and make all this money?"

"Oh," he said airily, "I've got money already. Haverstock paid pretty good and I didn't blow mine on bootleggers and loose women. As soon as Haverstock and Louis leave, I'll get me a place and start looking for a job."

She looked at him curiously. "What have they got to do with it?" She frowned. "You've been hiding in here, from them, haven't you?"

"Who did you think?"

"I don't know. I guess I thought you were hiding from my . . . Why did you run off after the fire?"

"I wasn't taking any chances."

"What chances?"

"Chances of winding up fried to a crisp like the rest of them."

She frowned again. "What does that mean?"

"I guess he's got everybody convinced it was an accident or something."

"Wasn't it?"

He snorted. "I've been with Haverstock quite a while, longer than any of them except the freaks, and I keep my eyes and ears open. I know a lot more about him than he thinks. He's a real loony from the word go. And mean as a snake. Felt real sorry for some of the freaks sometimes. Never did anything to me, though. I learned quick that a little 'cooperation' goes a long way." He shrugged. "It was about time to be moving on anyway. Haverstock gets bored. Last night, after the Minotaur killed that girl . . . "

"Francine?" Rose said, feeling a peculiar sensation in the pit of her stomach.

"Don't know what her name was. It's happened before. After that, I figure Haverstock went out of his head and wiped out the whole outfit, except for good old Louis."

"He set the fire and killed all those people on purpose?"

"Yeah."

"You can't be sure."

"I'm sure enough that I'm gonna stay outta sight until he's gone for good."

"He'd kill you too? Why? What did you do?"

"I didn't do anything. Loonies don't need reasons." He lay back and crossed his arms under his head. "Come back tonight. I'll be here waiting for you."

"No. I can't."

"And bring me something to eat. I'm starving." He closed his eyes and squirmed around, getting comfortable.

Rose pushed open the door, then turned and watched him for a moment, but didn't say anything. Kelsey lay sprawled on the cottonseed, clothed only in the pride of his flesh, comfortable and content and secure in his power. Then she looked around carefully to see if anyone was in sight, and left, pushing the door shut behind her.

Rose stepped into the shade of the circus wagon because the sun was hot and she had come out without her parasol. Several other people were there, wandering around, looking, poking in the blackened debris. Rose didn't remember walking from the gin to the burned-out tent show. She hadn't intended to go there; she was sure she hadn't intended to go there. She frowned, unable to understand why she was there.

She had only been standing there a moment, worrying the thought in her mind, when the door of the caravan opened. She jumped and looked up. Haverstock stood in the

doorway, Louis just behind him. A smile flashed on Haverstock's mouth.

"Good afternoon, young lady," he said.

"Oh," she said. "Hello."

He came down the steps, Louis following behind. "Have
you come to view the last remains?"

She shook her head. "No . . . I mean, I was just walking
by and stopped. I'm sorry about the fire. It was a good
show."

He smiled sadly. "Alas, all gone. The wonders of the ages
up in smoke. But one must be philosophical. Life goes on,
as they say. When one door is closed, you have but to open
another."

"Yes," she said slowly. She suddenly felt a wind rising,
but nothing stirred. "It's certainly lucky everyone wasn't
killed."

"Indeed. Louis and I were smiled on by Fate. And we also
learned this morning that Angel was not among the unfortunate. But the poor boy became frightened and ran away.
You haven't by any chance seen him?"

"Oh," she said, slightly startled. "No. No, I haven't."

"You will let us know if you should happen to do so?"

"Oh, yes, of course. I'm glad Angel is all right. But I
meant the other man." The wind in her head blew stronger
and suddenly chill.

Haverstock's face hardened for an instant, then his smile
returned. "What man is that, my dear?"

"Well, I don't know his name. He worked at the show. He
was taking tickets Friday night when I was there, I believe."

"Kelsey," Louis said mildly.

"And how do you know he's still among the living?" Haverstock asked, still smiling.

"I saw him. Going into the gin."

"And when was this?"

"Just a few minutes ago. I was out for a walk."

"Fortune does indeed seem to smile on us more and more by the hour."

"Well," she said, "I have to be getting back home. Good-bye."

"Good-bye, my dear."

She walked away, the wind swirling around her. It whistled through her head, chill and damp.

And safe.

28.

Will Hindley built the house when Hawley was a collection of saloons on the trail from Texas to Dodge City. He raised fine Hereford cattle and married a schoolteacher from St. Louis. He was nineteen when he started the herd, thirty when he built the house, and thirty-five when he married. He was forty when his first and only child was born, forty-three when he made his first million, and forty-seven when he was shot and killed by a drunken ranch hand.

With her seven-year-old son firmly in tow, his widow took the stage to Dodge City the same day they hanged the ranch hand. From Dodge City she took the train back to St. Louis and never saw Kansas again. She left the ranch in the hands of bankers and built a grand mansion where she lived like a duchess until she died of diphtheria when her son was fifteen. Over half the million was gone.

The bankers, to do them credit, did the best they could. They sold the cattle, leased the land, and rented the house.

But by the time the son was thirty, he had spent the other half million. He had debts he could never hope to pay, and ordered the bankers to sell everything. The St. Louis mansion had already been put on the auction block.

The ranch was too big for one person to buy in one piece, so it was parceled out, a thousand acres here and a hundred acres there, sold both to ranchers and dirt farmers. The man who bought the parcel containing the house had a fine home in Wichita and had no use for it. So it was stripped and abandoned, left like a Victorian tombstone in the middle of nowhere.

Now cattle, but not Hindley cattle, grazed around it and watered in Crooked Creek a hundred yards behind the house.

"It isn't the Savoy," Henry said as he plucked needle grass from his socks and surveyed the empty room festooned with peeling wallpaper, "but it will do very nicely."

Evelyn chuckled. "From what I've heard about this place, fifty years ago it probably would've stacked up pretty good against the Savoy. But it's not quite as big as I remembered it."

They wandered around for a bit, going from room to room, looking at the gutted elegance of the old house. There were gaping holes in the walls where stained-glass windows had been, empty doorways where elaborate mahogany doors had hung, and exposed lathing where rich paneling had been stripped away. Even the bannisters on the stairway had been taken.

"Oh, look," Evelyn moaned as she peered into a room stacked high with baled hay. "They're storing hay in the . . . what did they call it, the conservatory?"

"Looks like a sun porch to me," Harold said.

"I'm sure Mrs. Hindley called it the conservatory," Evelyn said.

They finally settled in a small room off the kitchen

198

which still had doors and windows and was reasonably free of trash and wasps. Henry rubbed his hands together. "All right, children, there is absolutely no time to lose. Angel's training begins this very minute. I do not imagine it will take Haverstock any great length of time to find us. If Angel does not prove to be an apt and ready pupil, I fear our future is rather bleak."

So they began. They sat in a circle on the faded linoleum and coaxed Angel, tested him, bullied him, loved him, but nothing worked. Angel tried, eagerly pursuing any procedure suggested, but nothing worked.

Then it was late afternoon. Evelyn fed them from the picnic hamper they had brought, and they worked while they ate.

A blade of dry grass lay on the linoleum before Angel's crossed legs. He gnawed a chicken thigh and looked at the bit of grass. He concentrated on it, willed it to move, demanded, cajoled it to only twitch. He looked out the open door, across the pasture land, listening to the brittle buzz of grasshoppers, the trill of meadowlarks, the metallic screech of cicadas, ignored the blade of grass. He willed it to move without thinking about it.

But it lay as if pasted to the floor. Angel released his breath and slumped back, easing the ache in his spine. He looked up hopelessly.

"I know it's difficult, Angel," Henry said quietly. "Your problem is you've never used the gift consciously. You're like the famous centipede who walked very well until he was asked by a beetle how he could possibly manage all those legs. The centipede started thinking about it and was never again able to do anything but lie in the ditch twitching.

"Think about the time at the river when Evie almost fell in. Do you remember what you did?"

Angel shook his head in bewilderment.

199

"Close your eyes and picture it," Evelyn said and took his hand. He closed his eyes and lowered his head in concentration, holding her hand firmly. "We were sitting on the bank," she said slowly, watching a furrow appear on his brow. "Tim was beside you. He said something about how you weren't supposed to leave the wagons, but he thought you needed some sun and fresh air because you looked a little peaked."

A smile flickered on Angel's lips.

"I got up to leave," Evelyn continued. "You stood up also. I started to go, but my foot slipped on a slick rock. I started to fall. You reached for me. . . . "

Angel concentrated. His face was placid for a moment, then a tiny wrinkle appeared between his eyes and spread across his forehead. His lips compressed and a drop of perspiration rolled down his temple. He began breathing heavily and his face twisted. Air hissed raggedly in his throat. Suddenly he pounded his knees with his fists. Evelyn grabbed his hands and held them in hers, feeling the same pain he felt.

"We're going about this the wrong way," Henry sighed.

"What other way is there?" Tim grouched.

"You're trying too hard, Angel. I'm beginning to doubt you'll ever be able to evoke the gift consciously. If one of us were a hypnotist, that would solve the problem."

They took a breather and sat with their own thoughts. Angel slumped against the wall in dejection. Evelyn sat beside him, touching him, feeling his warmth envelop her in spite of his mood.

Suddenly Harold looked up with a deepening of the perplexed frown that had been hovering about his face since they left home. "You're absolutely *sure* that Mexican guy was in the barn?" he said.

They all turned toward him, trying to hide the amusement they felt. "Yes, Mr. Bradley," Henry said. "We told you everything that happened."

"But I was looking in the car the whole time. I swear he never left."

"As soon as you went out the front door," Evelyn said, "we went out the back door. We were hiding in the wash and we all saw him in the barn."

Harold shook his head. "He never left the car."

"It may be fortunate that it happened," Henry said. "Maybe it convinces you that Haverstock's powers are as great as we said they were, that the danger we're all in is as great as we said, that secrecy is as important as we said, that every precaution must be taken. . . . "

Harold raised his hand. "All right. I'm convinced. At least, I think I'm convinced. I still haven't seen anything with my own eyes." He stood up and stretched. "Well, it's time for me to be heading back."

Evelyn walked with him to the porch. "What will you tell Mama and Daddy?" she asked.

"I'll think of something." Suddenly he grinned. "How about: you were kidnapped by painted savages wearing nothing but banana leaves and bones in their noses to be sacrificed to their volcano god?"

"They might put you away." She grinned in spite of herself.

"They certainly would if I told them the truth," he said and grunted.

"Yeah, I guess the truth is to be avoided. There's always the chance they might believe you. Then they'd be in danger too."

He gnawed on his bottom lip for a moment, then raised his eyes. "Be careful, huh?" He took her hand and looked at her with such big-brotherly concern and love her eyes began to sting.

201

"Sure." She squeezed his big strong hand. "Harold, thank you. I take back all the hateful things I ever thought about you."

"Yeah," he grunted. " 'Bye, Evie. I'll sneak some more food to you tomorrow."

"Good-bye, Harold."

He released her hand and walked away through the dry grass, sending grasshoppers buzzing away in panic. She watched him until he topped the rise. He turned once and waved, then went down the other side. She went back in the house and joined the others.

The Hindley house at night seemed to deserve its reputation among the small boys of Hawley. It looked haunted, and perhaps it was. What house had a better right to contain spirits that could not rest? Will Hindley had dreamed and worked for greatness, even empire, only to have the dream demolished on the verge of fulfillment by a drunken ranch hand. Even that wouldn't have ended the dream; the dream would have continued through his son. But what the drunken ranch hand had begun, Hindley's feckless wife and wastrel son had finished. What spirit had a better excuse for eternal unrest, seeing the center of his empire become a weather-beaten, termite-nibbled pile of lumber used to store hay?

Had the boys of Hawley seen the house that night, even the most doubting realist would have been convinced that it was haunted. It reared up from the flat prairie in a black Gothic pile silvered by the moon. Ghost clouds streaked the sky. The air sparkled and glittered with fireflies, entwining the house like wandering souls.

Inside the house, immune to the spell, all of them slept except Angel. Henry and Tim slept uncomfortably on the hard floor, resting fitfully, having worried dreams. Tim slept close by Henry, touching him, fearful because they had seen evidence that owls roosted in the house and, worse, gnawed bones where four-legged predators had visited the ruined rooms.

Angel lay drowsily on his back, his arm around Evelyn who was sleeping at his side. Her head was on his shoulder, her short hair tickling his neck. Her hair smelled of sunshine and her arm was a pleasant weight across his chest. He had never been this close to a girl before, had never even touched one that he could remember, never felt breath on his neck as she slept.

He moved slightly, shifting her head because his shoulder was going to sleep. She stirred and sighed nasally, but did not awaken. Her leg shifted and pressed against his. He felt again that delicious pain in his genitals. He had felt it many times before, but never so strongly. Always it had been there vaguely in the morning, growing pleasantly stronger as the day progressed, but it was always absent after his lost, blank afternoons with Haverstock. Often he had wished it to continue, to grow to greater heights of pleasure/pain, but always, in the afternoon, it receded to begin building again.

The movement near the ceiling had caught his eye some time earlier. He had been watching it without really seeing it. He floated halfway between sleep and wakefulness, confusing dream with reality. Images passed through his mind and vanished, brilliant images that he could no longer remember after they had passed. But the movement near the ceiling was a constant, a movement that did not flicker out of existence as soon as he thought about it. Gradually it drew his attention, dimming the random images.

A net of spun glass, spun thinner than the finest hair, suspended in space, glistening in a shaft of moonlight. The movement was black and quick. It scurried around the silvery net, increasing it geometrically, disappearing into the shadows at the top of the web, then appearing again like a

203

drop of pitch with legs as it rounded the bottom side of the circle.

Angel's drooping eyelids raised slightly, bringing the spider into focus, giving the movement a name. He watched it go its busy rounds. Around and around and around.

Then it tired, or perhaps thought of something better to do. It descended, dropping toward the floor on a shiny thread. Halting and dropping, halting and dropping, as if unsure of its purpose. A movement of air caught it, swinging it to one side a few inches. It rotated dizzily at the end of the thread.

Angel watched it as it turned and scrambled back up the thread a couple of inches and stopped. Had the movement frightened it? he wondered. The spider swayed again in a longer arc. Are you confused? Angel thought. The spider swung in a circle, its legs motionless, as if it hoped to go unnoticed.

The circular motion stopped. The spider continued to hang motionless, waiting to discover the source of possible danger. Then it cautiously turned, preparing to scurry back up the thread.

Suddenly the spider began bobbing like a weight on an elastic band.

Angel's drowsy eyelids opened all the way and a frown puckered the bridge of his nose.

The spider bounced violently, its legs scrabbling at the air.

The frown faded from Angel's face and a smile crept across his lips.

The bobbing spider began to swing in increasing circles.

Angel's smile flowered into a wide grin.

The spider sailed across the room and was suspended a foot above Angel's nose, squirming in frustration.

Angel grinned at it.

The spider careened back up toward the ceiling and

plopped into the web. It sat for a second without moving, then scrambled upward into the darkness.

Angel eased his arm from beneath Evelyn's head without waking her and moved quietly from the house. He stood on the edge of the porch and stretched out his arms to the night. His mouth opened in a silent shout.

It was all inside him. It had always been there, but Haverstock had closed the door on it, made him forget how to work the latch. Now he had the door open again, and it was all there. Everything. Flowing in his blood, oozing from his pores, bursting to get out.

Electricity.

Force.

Power.

He ran across the grass, hardly able to contain himself. The fireflies sparkled around him like energy escaping from his own body. He fell to his knees in the snowstorm of light. He plucked a dry grass blade and held it in his cupped hands. He looked at it with eyes like flame. The blade of grass rose from his hands, hovered in the air, and circled him like a minnow swimming in moonlight. He twisted around to watch it, sitting flat on the ground, leaning back on his hands, rotating his thrown-back head. Faster and faster it went, making a thin, dry hum, until it disintegrated from its own vibrations.

Angel plucked another grass blade, without touching it with his hands, and shot it straight up, higher and higher, and then abandoned it. It caught in the upper air currents and fell to the ground three days later near Jefferson City, Missouri, unnoticed by anyone.

Angel scrambled to his feet and ran in sheer joy. He carried the wind with him, writhing the tall grass around him, scattering the fireflies in swirls and eddies of light motes. He stopped and hugged himself, his arms wrapped tightly across his chest to keep him from exploding with exhilara-

205

tion. He threw back his head and yelled silently at the moon.

He flopped on the ground and rolled through the brittle grass and pungent weeds, sprawling on his back, arms and legs spread, smiling and breathing heavily. Then he raised his arms and brought them together, gathering an armful of moonlight. The fireflies swept toward him from all directions, in streams and rivers and currents of light, a vortex a hundred yards across, spiraling in to the brighter center. They met over his supine body like ocean breakers, cascading, fountaining into the air.

He waved his arms like a symphony conductor. The fireflies obeyed every movement, every gesture, swirling and dancing in a fantastic display. Then the expression of wild exuberance left Angel's face to be replaced by studious concentration. The fireflies ceased their abandoned gyrations and began to coalesce, to take form.

A gigantic shimmering nude image of Evelyn stood over him. It was a spectral image, unreal and idealized, sculpted of fairy light, suspended in the air, dwindling below the knees to merge with the night. The image bent over him, seemed to look at him, and reached down sparkling arms. He held his hands up to her. Her large hands closed over his and his arms turned black with crawling, confused insects.

He expelled them and the image of Evelyn shifted. She grew giant butterfly wings that moved and lifted her. The image flew around him and dissolved in a glittering cloud that settled to the ground.

Angel jumped to his feet and ran to the top of the rise. He stood silhouetted against the moon, his legs apart and his head thrown back. He lifted his arms and brought a warm wind that screamed around him, whipping his cotton hair, plastering his clothes to his body.

He closed his fingers into fists. The muscles swelled in his outstretched arms. The wind died and his taut body trembled. His face froze in icy purpose. Concentration wrinkled his forehead. The earth at his feet shuddered and sighed, then split with a grinding rumble. A gout of flame shot up between his arms. His eyes shone as clear and hard as garnets. The flame encircled him, spun around him in a ring, spread wider and wider, spinning faster and faster, singeing the air with sound, and then vanished.

Angel's body relaxed slowly. His arms returned to his sides and the hard light left his eyes. He sat on the ground and went to work.

A shaft of sunlight crept across the floor and awakened Evelyn. She felt Angel's absence before she saw the vacant spot beside her. She drew in her breath and turned her head in the other direction. Henry and Tim still slept. And Angel sat cross-legged on the floor, smiling at her.

She started to speak, but he put his finger to his lips. He stood with a movement as fluid as a cat and held his hand out to her. Puzzled, she took it. He pulled her to her feet and led her from the house, smiling enigmatically.

He took her in a run across the grass, his happiness so great she began to suspect what had happened. He stopped and positioned her in one spot, holding up his hand for her to stay. She looked at him in smiling bewilderment, feeling a tingling in her throat. He ran about ten feet from her and turned to face her. Grinning, he held out his arms toward her. She watched him expectantly.

The grass between them suddenly began moving as if blown by a wind, but there was no wind. The grass rustled and sighed. Evelyn looked from the ground to Angel, her eyes glistening with excitement. The rustling in the grass changed subtly. It sighed and whispered dusty words.

"Evie. Evie," it said.

Evelyn stared at him in wonderment. He smiled proudly and shyly. He walked slowly to her, the vagueness and vulnerability missing from his eyes. He bent and plucked a blade of grass and held it between their faces. The blade began to vibrate rapidly, to make a whispery buzzing sound. The sound became words, dry sibilant words.

"Evie. Evie. I love you, Evie," the blade sighed. His ruby eyes searched her face hesitantly, hopefully.

She couldn't help herself; tears rose in her eyes and she sobbed happily. He looked startled and concerned. He dropped the blade of grass and put his arms around her. She fell into them, sobbing and laughing against his chest. He hugged her tightly to him, electricity in his veins.

"Evie," the voice said, not the papery voice of the blade of grass, but a normal voice against her ear.

She jerked her head and put her hand to her ear. She looked at him in confusion.

"What did you do?"

He removed her hand from her ear and held it. "I'm talking, Evie, I'm talking." But his lips did not move.

She cocked her head as if puzzled by the source of the sound. "I hear a voice in my ear. What are you doing?" she whispered.

"I'm vibrating your eardrum, as if it were being struck by sound waves," the voice said. She knew his voice would sound that way: soft and gentle and loving.

"Angel!" she said, laughing and rubbing her damp face. "That's wonderful!"

"Does it sound right?" he asked, a worried look on his face. "I practiced on myself, but I can't be sure it sounds right on other people. I think if I worked at it some more, I could do both eardrums at the same time and make it sound like it was coming from me instead of someone sitting in your ear."

"It sounds marvelous," she said. She threw her arms around his neck and gave him a joyful kiss. Then they looked at each other soberly.

208

"Did you mean it?" she asked softly.

"Evie, Evie, I love you, I love you," the voice sang in her ear. But she didn't need the voice because his eyes spoke.

"I love you too, Angel," she said in a whisper, surprising herself a little, but knowing it was true.

Angel looked into her face for a moment, his eyes as big as moons. Then he leaned his head forward and kissed her, his mouth as light as thistledown against hers. She felt his lips tremble. Then his arms tightened. His hunger devoured her. He wanted to merge their bodies into one, to envelop her with his skin.

He threw back his head and shook his hair like a horse. Evelyn gasped for breath and then laughed. The laugh became a startled shriek, quick and high. She clutched at him as they rose slowly into the air. He put his hands on either side of her face and brushed his lips against hers.

"Don't be afraid, Evie. Never be afraid of me or what I can do," the voice said softly and solemnly in her ear.

His eyes were reading her soul again. She nodded. He grinned broadly. He put his hands on her waist and tossed her higher. She shrieked again and then laughed.

"Give me a little warning!" she wailed and looked at the ground thirty feet below where she floated.

Angel laughed with her and at her and for her. He did a back flip and a loop-the-loop. He swam in the sunshine, circling her, loving her. He stood on his head above her and kissed her upside down. He took her hand and they sailed up and around and down like two swallows.

They heard Henry yelling at them and saw him frantically waving his arms. They floated down to him.

"I feel like Peter Pan," Evelyn laughed.

"Angel!" Henry clapped his hands. "Angel!" Henry jumped up and down. "Angel!" Henry laughed. "You did it! You remembered! This is wonderful!"

Tim rode on Henry's shoulder and desperately clutched

his hair to keep from falling off, but a grin split his ugly little face.

"Once I managed to do one thing, it was all there."

Henry looked bewildered and put his hand to his ear. "What happened?" he said.

"Angel can talk by vibrating your eardrum," Evelyn explained with delight. "What did he say?"

"I think I can do two at once," the voice said in both their ears.

"I'm sorry, Tim," the voice said in all three ears.

Tim clapped his hand over his ear and grimaced. "Not so loud," he complained.

They all laughed in a happy delirium. Henry hugged Angel, then hugged Evelyn, then hugged the post supporting the porch.

Angel took Evelyn's hand and they ran toward the creek.

Henry started to run after them. "Angel!" he called. "Wait."

"No, Henry," Tim cautioned. "Let them be alone."

Henry stopped and turned his face to the tiny man on his shoulder and frowned. "But what about Haverstock! He could find us at any minute. We have to be prepared for him."

"It can wait a little while. I've never seen Angel like this. I've never seen him actually happy. I think Evie has more to do with it than learning how to use the gift. Let them enjoy each other for a while. Let him be happy before he has to battle for our lives."

Tim watched the boy and girl bounding happily for a moment. "He might not win," he said softly.

Angel flopped onto the sand in the shade of a cottonwood tree and lay sprawled on his back. Evelyn dropped beside him and grinned. He breathed heavily, his chest rising and falling rapidly, and squinted at the bright sky. His face was completely at peace. He ran his hand under his shirt and lazily scratched his stomach.

"I'm tired," he said. "I just want to lie here and burrow in the sand and not move."

"If you're so exhausted from all that running, we could have flown," she pointed out.

"That's why I'm exhausted." He cocked his eyes at her. "It may have seemed easy enough for you—you weren't doing anything; I was doing all the work. That showy razz-matazz takes a lot out of you."

"Well, quit showing off then." She made a face and he grinned impudently at her.

"You sure have gotten cocky this morning," she said, lifting her eyebrow. "I'm not sure I didn't like you better before, when you were kinda lost and helpless and I could take care of you. I'm not sure you need me anymore. I'm not sure you need anybody anymore."

He sat up and looked at her, his face serious and his eyes worried. "I need you," the voice said in her ear. "The gift is just something I can do. I don't know how I do it, or why I can do it. I don't know why some people can sing and others can't, or why some people can paint or write or compose music and other people can't. I'm a very ignorant man; there are so many things I don't know. I'm still lost and helpless and I want you to take care of me, and I want to take care of you. I need you to make sure I don't get cocky, that I don't let the gift take control of me. Last night when it came to me, I realized how easy it would be, how easy it would be to become like Haverstock, to feel that the gift made me special, above other people. You don't know the exhilaration, the freedom of being able to do almost anything you want to do. You don't know how easy it would be to feel like a god."

Evelyn looked at him, wanting to cry because he was so solemn and so serious, his face that of a little boy trying to explain something important to an adult and not sure of being understood. She leaned over and kissed him lightly on the mouth and said, "I still don't know if I'm ever gonna get used to hearing you talk when your lips don't move."

He put his arms around her and kissed her soundly. "This way I can kiss you and tell you funny stories at the same time. Did you hear the one about the traveling freak show and the farmer's daughter?"

She pushed him away, grimacing and laughing at the same time. He sat very still and frowned in concentration.

"Evelyn Bradley," the voice said in her ear and his lips formed the words. "You are the most beautiful thing in the world, and I love you." He smiled with satisfaction. Then he fell back on the sand with a groan. "That's too much trouble."

She growled and fell on him, knocking the wind out of him. He grabbed her and rolled. She yipped. When they stopped, his face was over hers. He kissed her and said, his mouth forming the words, "How was it?"

"The kiss?"

"No. My moving mouth."

"Oh. Pretty good. But your voice is still in my ear."

He nodded, then concentrated. "Evelyn Bradley, you are the most beautiful thing in the world, and I love you." He cocked his head. "Well?"

She grinned. "Not bad. Only, your voice seemed to be coming from everywhere at once."

He returned her grin. "I told you I'd have to practice." He rolled off her and lay beside her, snuggling against her. "I'll have to get it right. I can't go around talking in everybody's ear. It might make 'em a little nervous. I need to get it so I can do it without thinking about it."

She turned her face against his hair. "You can do it," she said.

212

They lay like that for a while, enjoying the feel of exhilaration turning to contentment.

"Angel," she asked softly after a time, "is your name really Angel?"

"It's the only one I ever heard." She felt him shrug.

"Where were you before you joined the show?"

"I've always been with the show."

"No you weren't. Henry said you were about five years old when Haverstock found you."

"I don't remember it."

"You can't remember anything before he found you?"

"No."

"You ought to be able to. I can remember when I was three. I can remember a dog we had that died. She was black with a white throat and her name was Lady. I don't really remember her name. Mama told me it was Lady. But I remember her dying and Daddy burying her behind the barn. How far back can you remember?"

She felt him shrug again. "I don't know. All the days were alike. We were either traveling in the wagons or set up in some small town for a show. In the winter Haverstock would get a house somewhere away from things and we would stay there. All the days were alike. How can you tell one from the other?"

She turned on her side to face him and put her hand on the back of his neck, running her fingers up into his hair. They lay like that for a while in drowsy peace.

Evelyn said, "Your real name is probably Horatio Prendergast, or something like that." She felt him smile against her neck.

"I'm really the lost heir to the Vanderbilt millions, kidnapped by gypsies as a mere tad." He sat up suddenly and grinned down at her. "Someday, someone will notice the Vanderbilt birthmark on my shoulder and I will be united

213

with my family and my millions and live happily ever after. Let's go for a swim."

"I thought you didn't want to move."

"I have tremendous recuperative powers." He stood up and reached his hand down to her. She took it and he pulled her up.

"We can't swim here," she said. "The water isn't deep enough."

"Is there a place?"

She pointed. "Down there a couple of miles closer to town, but there may be somebody there. The kids swim there all the time."

"Let's go see," he said, trying to make his voice sound as if it were coming from his mouth. "Let me know when I get it right."

"Better. That time it came from about three feet behind you. You'd make a good ventriloquist," she said and grinned. "Do you really want to go swimming? It's a long walk."

He grinned at her and raised his eyebrows.

She laughed. "Okay. I told you I needed time to get used to it."

He took her hand and they skimmed over the water like dragonflies.

About two miles southwest of Hawley, Crooked Creek made a sharp bend to the north. The eddying movement of the water had scooped deeply into the soft bottom and it had been a favorite swimming hole for as long as most people around could remember. A large old cottonwood clung tenaciously to the bank, giving shade and a jumping-in place to the swimmers. Two ropes hung from a branch paralleling the edge of the water, one short and gray and frazzled at the end where it had broken years before, and the other new, hanging almost to the ground with several knots tied in it.

214

Angel looked around appreciatively, then took off his shirt. Evelyn watched the muscles flow under his ivory skin as he removed his shoes and pants. He stood there in his undershorts, looking at her with a slight smile, his eyes sending a ruby challenge.

She kicked off her shoes. Her mouth was defiant, but her eyes were laughing. She rolled off her lisle stockings, never breaking eye contact with him. She stepped out of her dress, pulled her chemise over her head, and made a dainty pirouette in her step-ins and bandeau. Then she broke for the water in a dead run and jumped in.

Angel watched her, grinning, then went to the rope hanging from the tree. He grasped it just above his head and gave it an experimental tug. Evelyn watched him from the water, which was now up to her chin. With the rope in his hand he climbed higher up the bank. He turned, grabbed the rope with both hands, lifted his feet, and swung out across the water. He swung higher and higher, until he was almost upside down. Then he stopped and hung there, grinning down at her. She laughed and made a face. Suddenly he plummeted straight down in a flurry of arms and legs, sending the water over her in a wave.

She turned her head to keep from taking the wave in her face. When she looked back, he had bobbed to the surface, spluttering.

"I just thought of something," his voice said in her ear. "Do I know how to swim?"

"It doesn't make much difference, does it?" she said and laughed.

He grinned and shrugged. Then he got a woebegone, pitiful expression on his face and began to sink. He raised one hand, gave her a sorrowful wave, and slipped slowly beneath the water. The next thing she knew, he had her by the ankles, pulling her under.

They laughed and splashed and played in the water like

215

two otters until they were tired. Then they lay on the sand, dozing, letting the sun dry their bodies.

After a while, Evelyn raised up on her elbow and looked at Angel's face, memorizing every surface. His eyes were closed as if he were asleep. She scooped up a handful of sand and dribbled it on his chest, but the sand stopped an inch from his skin and lay suspended in the air. She looked at his face with narrowed eyes, but he still seemed to be asleep. She looked at the sand and then back at his face. Then she slapped him on the stomach.

"Stop that!" she said.

He half sat up, his eyes and mouth gaping as if she had knocked the breath out of him. The sand settled on his chest and trickled down to his stomach. He looked at the sand and then at her. She began to edge away.

He grabbed her suddenly and they rolled over a couple of times, laughing. When they stopped rolling, they were side by side, their faces a few inches apart, looking at each other in childish adoration. She put her finger on his forehead, moved it slowly down his nose, across his lips, over his smooth cheek, realizing for the first time that he didn't have to shave. She traced the contours of his face with her finger, sculpting it in her mind.

He raised up on his elbow and leaned over her slowly. He gave her a feather-light kiss on her lips and felt again the delightful pain in his genitals, spreading down his thighs and up his stomach.

He put his hand on her cheek and she turned her face to it, nuzzling his palm. He moved his hand to her neck, then slid it slowly over her smooth, warm shoulder and down her arm. He slipped his fingers through hers and lifted her hand, their forearms together. He looked at the contrast between her brown arm and the paleness of his own skin, suddenly feeling the old way again. She seemed to know and squeezed his hand, her eyes deep as wells.

216

Then it was all right again. He knew it wasn't important, but wondered if he had enough control over his own body to change his pigmentation. He leaned over and kissed her, letting her know everything was all right.

He lay again on the sand, facing her, and disengaged his fingers from hers. He ran his hand down her side and felt her still-damp underwear. His hand slid across her firm hip and his palm felt hot. She inhaled when his fingers moved up her back and under her bandeau. He unfastened it clumsily and slipped it over her shoulder, freeing her breasts.

She turned her face away, afraid she was blushing. She had never liked her breasts; they were too large for her to look fashionably flat.

Angel took them in his hands and kissed her on the side of her neck. She made a little sound in her nose. He bent his head and kissed her breast, touching the nipple with his tongue. The muscles in her stomach and thighs contracted and she couldn't seem to breathe properly. Her mouth was dry and her stomach felt as if she were falling. She put the palms of her hands against his chest and closed her eyes.

His hand went down her side again and slid under the waistband of her pants. When he pushed them down, she raised her hips slightly to make it easier for him. She drowned in electricity when his hand and fingers explored her. Her hands moved restlessly over his shoulders and sides and back.

The pressure in Angel's genitals became painful. He escaped her arms and rose to his knees, pulling off his shorts. Evelyn watched with fascination and curiosity and a little fear, because she had never seen before.

He lay back beside her, put his arms around her, and pressed her to him. "Forgive me," his voice whispered in her ear. "I don't know the right way."

Angel went slowly and tenderly. They explored, touched, investigated, examined their bodies, making marvelous and

217

wonderful discoveries. He was hesitant in the beginning and awkward, but she had no basis for comparison. She helped him when she could, forgiving his clumsiness, loving his innocence.

She whimpered at the first pain and he stopped and loved her. When he started again, slowly, it was easier for them both. But the pressure had built too high and his release came too soon.

He lay drowsily against her, knowing her restless dissatisfaction, feeling her hunger. Then the pressure was in him again, but not so fierce, not so demanding.

He moved with more assurance the second time, savoring slowly, making it last, and they were both satisfied.

Evelyn smiled luxuriously and snuggled in the sand. Angel bent over her and gave her a light kiss. He grinned at her shyly, but with a certain measure of pride. She reached up and caught her fingers in his tousled white hair and pulled his head down for another kiss.

29.

Harold Bradley made cold roast beef sandwiches and wondered just how long he could keep his parents' questions answered. If it weren't for the telephone, the damned telephone, he could have Evelyn in any number of logical places. He had finally settled on Miller's Corners. Evelyn had gone with Grace Elizabeth Willet to help her with Wash Peacock's father who had been struck down suddenly by some non-fatal, but decidedly debilitating illness.

The Peacocks had no telephone, so that part of it was all right. If his parents didn't run into Wash or his father or Grace Elizabeth or Rose or Lilah or Judge Willet or Mrs. Willet in town and ask how the patient was doing, it might work. They hadn't liked it at all that Evelyn had gone without asking, and he'd had a heart-stopping moment when his father had wanted to drive out there and check on her.

All he had to worry about now was: where would Evelyn be tonight? Would Mr. Peacock's mythical illness work again? He felt sure that if he left her there another night, his father would most certainly drive to Miller's Corners and check on her. In all probability, though, they would run into someone at the funeral home who knew Mr. Peacock wasn't sick.

Harold's head was spinning and he knew he wasn't intended to be a secret agent. He might as well face up to it; when he returned from the Hindley place tonight, he would have to tell them the truth. He had completely run out of invention. He pushed the whole thing from his mind and packed the sandwiches in a pasteboard box.

"Good afternoon, Mr. Bradley." The smooth voice spoke behind him. He whirled and knocked the box to the floor, spilling sandwiches in every direction. Haverstock and Louis walked into the kitchen.

Haverstock smiled at him. "I was talking to your parents in town a little while ago." He raised his forefinger and waggled it back and forth. "It seems you told me a naughty lie, Mr. Bradley. And a foolish lie—so easily checked. Your sister didn't go to visit your grandmother yesterday, after all. Why did you do that, Mr. Bradley?"

Harold's mouth was dry and he swallowed. "It was none of your business where my sister was."

Haverstock shook his head . "My interests are very wide ranging, Mr. Bradley. I believe you have quite a lot of information for me."

Harold's teeth clenched. Blood spread on his lips from his bitten tongue. His muscles knotted painfully. He couldn't get his breath, but when he did, he screamed.

Louis watched him. A smile hovered over his lips.

30.

The sun hung low in the west, turning the prairie grass to bronze. Angel and Evelyn sat side by side on the sand, watching the movement of the water in Crooked Creek. A killdeer trotted along the edge of the water, poking among the river rocks for snails and insects. The lonely cry of a whippoorwill floated through the still air, making Evelyn feel pensive.

She leaned her head against Angel's shoulder. "What's to become of us, Angel?" she asked wistfully. "Evelyn Bradley of Hawley, Kansas and Angel, the Magic Boy. It's a very unlikely match."

"I'm not magic, Evie," he said softly. He had his voice and lip movements so nearly right that she sometimes forgot what he was really doing. He shifted around and sat cross-legged, facing her. "Look," he said. He cupped his hands between them. The air misted above his hands, growing thicker and more concentrated until, after a moment, a small globe of water the size of a tennis ball floated there, quivering like jelly.

"I know it looks like magic, but it isn't. All I did was pull the moisture from the ground and the air and form it into a sphere." He lowered his hands. The water ball turned to mist and floated away in a dissipating fog.

"I guess it still frightens me a little bit."

He looked at her with a sad helplessness. She smiled and took his hands. "Give me a chance to get used to it. It's a lot to throw at a person all in one day, you know."

He raised her hands and touched them briefly to his forehead. "We'd better be getting back," he said and forgot to move his lips. "Henry's probably had fifteen fits already."

"I just thought of something else," she said, laughing. "We haven't eaten all day. I'm starving. I hope Harold brought lots of good stuff."

They got to their feet. Angel stopped and looked at her, then put his hands on either side of her face and kissed her. When he pulled his head back, his face was very serious.

"Thank you," he said quietly.

Evelyn grinned uncertainly. "You're welcome," she said.

Angel grabbed her in a hug and threw his head back with a yell. They shot into the air, spinning like a top.

31.

Henry and Tim sat on the floor, eating the last of the chicken. Henry was fidgety and kept pulling out his watch and checking the time.

"Take it easy," Tim said with his mouth full. "They'll be back."

Henry tossed a half-eaten drumstick back in the basket. "They've been gone all day," he grumbled. "Where are they? They went down to the river and then disappeared. For all we know Haverstock may have them."

"If he had them, he'd have us too," Tim said mildly.

"It's almost sundown," Henry continued to grumble. "We should have been making plans, getting so far away Haverstock would never find us." He slumped back against the wall. "What have they been doing all day!"

There was a footfall in the other room. Henry lurched clumsily to his feet. "Angel," he called.

Haverstock and Louis stepped into the room. A look of

desolation crossed Henry's face. Tim got to his feet and nervously wiped his greasy hands on his pants.

"Well," Haverstock said and smiled, "this is certainly a picturesque hideaway you've chosen. Where is Angel, and the girl?"

Henry swallowed. "I don't know."

"Henry, please don't be difficult," Haverstock said and sighed. "I've had a very demanding day. Where are they?"

"They're not here," Henry said, a pleading whine creeping into his voice. "I don't know where they are."

Haverstock turned his attention to Tim. "Is that right?"

Tim shifted from one foot to the other. "Yes. They went off somewhere this morning and haven't come back. We don't know where they are."

"Very well." His smile flicked on, then off. "I believe you. If they had fled, they wouldn't have left you two behind, now would they? Since you're still here, they must be coming back." He turned to Louis. "Keep an eye on them. I'm going out and look around."

Louis nodded and pulled a revolver from his pocket, pointing it at Henry. Haverstock looked at the gun and raised an eyebrow. "Louis," he said mildly, "you have hidden depths." He gave Henry and Tim a glance and left.

Louis leaned his shoulder against the door frame and smiled his almost-smile, keeping the revolver pointed at Henry. Henry and Tim stood frozen, staring at the gun. Henry swallowed and licked his lips.

"Louis," he said, his voice hoarse, "why are you doing this? When he's gotten rid of all of us, you'll be the only one left. He won't need you anymore, don't you know that? Don't you know that?"

Louis raised his eyebrows, but said nothing.

Henry swallowed again and rubbed his damp palms on his pants.

"Don't waste your breath, Henry," Tim said. "He's Haverstock's trained dog."

Louis frowned and straightened. He looked at them for a moment, then his shadow-smile returned. "Don't try anything, Henry," he said softly.

"What?" Henry said.

"Don't try it."

"I'm not doing anything," Henry said. He suddenly felt as if his body would no longer function.

"I warned you."

"I'm not . . . "

Louis fired twice into Henry's chest and stomach. Henry cried out in rage and indignation. The molten hatred he felt for Louis almost nullified the fire in his belly. He flopped like a rag doll, gracelessly spilling his blood on the faded linoleum. His heavy body seemed to deflate. He crumpled at an impossible angle against the baseboard.

Louis fired three times at Tim's running form, but all three missed the small target. Two gouged the floor, throwing splinters and dust. The third dislodged a chunk of wood from the door frame as Tim ducked behind it.

Tim surveyed the empty room frantically and found no place to hide. It must have been the dining room, he thought for no good reason. There were three other doors. He had no choice; two of them were closed. He ran toward the door that stood ajar, ran across a plain of faded pink roses that seemed as large as a baseball field. His twisted body lurched clumsily.

Louis stepped into the room, reloading his gun. He smiled when he saw Tim dart into the closet. He walked slowly and confidently toward it, enjoying himself and remembering when he was a kid in El Paso, shooting rats in Mr. Waldrop's barn.

He pushed back the partially open closet door and aimed

225

the revolver at the floor. A wrinkle appeared over his nose. The closet was empty. Then he saw light coming through the split board in the back wall. He hurried around to the other side.

Tim squirmed behind the kitchen cabinet, stumbling over the trash that had fallen back there, almost falling over the chunks of petrified crud. His skin crawled as he brushed through spider webs in the half darkness. He looked up and froze, a scream blocking his throat. A black widow as big as his head moved hesitantly toward him. She stopped when Tim stopped, testing the web with her forelegs, waiting for a telltale vibration.

Tim slowly eased to the floor and felt around for a weapon. The black widow scuttled forward an inch and stopped. Tim's hand touched something that moved. He jerked his hand away and looked down, but it was only a sow bug. It began to crawl away on its fourteen legs. Tim put his foot on it and it curled into an armor-plated ball. Tim reached down carefully, keeping his eyes on the spider, trying not to move the web. He felt around for the sow bug, then had to look down to locate it. It had uncurled and was about to crawl away. Tim whacked it with his fist and it curled again. He picked it up like a baseball, judged his distance carefully, and threw it. It bounced off the spider and caught in the web. The black widow scurried protectively back up to her egg sac.

Tim sidled past the web and looked back. The sow bug cautiously unrolled and began to squirm. The spider hurried to it and touched it with her forelegs. Then she turned her back. With graceful movements of her rear legs, she began entangling it.

Louis entered the kitchen and grimaced. Three walls were lined with dusty, sagging cabinets offering far too many places for Tim to hide. He went to the first cabinet and examined the space behind it. He grabbed the end and dragged it away from the wall. Nothing was behind it but filth and a black widow spider. He crushed her with his shoe.

Tim ran beneath a cabinet that stood on legs, moving quickly but as quietly as possible. The spider webs and insects brought involuntary whimpers to his throat. He heard the rumble and felt the floor vibrate when Louis pulled the other cabinet out. He stopped and listened, heard Louis swear under his breath.

Tim hunched over to keep his head out of the webs that carpeted the underside of the cabinet. He took a step backward, still watching Louis's feet worry around the other cabinet. Suddenly he caught his heel and sat down hard, rattling his vertebrae. He felt a metal rod across his back. He twisted his head and shoulders around and began to tremble. He sat on a rat trap nearly as big as he was. Then he felt giddy with relief. The trap had been sprung long ago. The metal was rusty and cushioned with dust. He scrambled away and his stomach turned over when he stumbled into the mummified remains of the rat. Loose bones scattered under his feet and the dry skin was as hard as sheet metal.

Louis searched the cabinet carefully. He pulled out the drawers and examined the cavities. He dragged the next one away from the wall, watching carefully that Tim didn't double back. He kicked the dead rat out of the way and took the cabinet apart.

Tim reached the last cabinet before the door that led into the room filled with hay. The door had been removed and hay spilled out onto the kitchen floor. Tim looked into the room but knew he didn't dare go in there. Rats would be nesting in the hay.

He looked back at Louis. He waited until Louis's head

227

went behind the cabinet, then awkwardly ran across the five-foot space to the next cabinet.

The gunshot made him wince and scrunch his head into his shoulders. The wall exploded over him. Splinters and chunks of wood pelted him. He was behind the cabinet on the other side before the second shot brought a haze of dust sifting from the ceiling. He rubbed at the blood oozing from his arm where a splinter had broken the skin.

He stumbled over something that rolled noisily.

Louis grinned with satisfaction and trotted past the hay-filled door. He shoved the cabinet away from the wall. He held the gun ready and got on his knees to look underneath. He hissed a curse when he didn't see Tim anywhere.

But Tim was behind the cabinet, clinging to a cross brace two feet above Louis's bent head. He grasped the object he had found, his arms wrapped around it, hugging it to him. The ice pick was rusty and half the wooden handle had split off. He held it point down and leaped toward the back of Louis's neck. He wrapped his legs around it as he fell, hoping Louis wouldn't move or the point wouldn't turn.

It wasn't very sharp, but it had Tim's weight on it and it fell two feet. It was enough. It plunged into the back of Louis's neck. Tim lost his grip at the impact and scrambled for a handhold. He caught Louis's collar and hung on.

Louis stiffened and began rising slowly. A low moan gurgled deep in his throat. He stood up carefully, holding his arms akimbo. The gun dropped from his loose fingers. He kept his head, neck, and shoulders perfectly rigid as if, even in his shock, he knew that any movement against the ice pick would be fatal.

The moan rose in pitch, continuing to rise, became a shrill keening, and ended when his lungs were empty of air. Louis took one, two steps, his head, neck, and shoulders welded solid. Tim clung to the back of his collar, hanging almost vertically.

228

Louis's face was pale, his open lips almost white. His eyes stared and began to film. He fell, as rigid as a statue, slowly at first, then faster. He hit the floor and the side of his face was filled with shattered bone.

Tim's teeth slammed together when Louis hit. He lay on Louis's back for a moment, getting his breath, then slid off onto the floor. He went around Louis's sprawled arm and looked at his face. One bulging eye stared at him but saw nothing.

Tim hawked and spat in it.

He looked up quickly when he heard someone in the other room and ran once more behind the kitchen cabinets.

Angel and Evelyn stood on the porch of the old house for a moment, watching the sun sink behind the horizon. Evelyn leaned her head against Angel's shoulder, feeling incredibly happy and contented, all thoughts of Haverstock gone from her mind. Angel put his arm around her and they went inside.

"Henry," Evelyn called. "Harold. Is anybody here?" There was no answer. The house was still, except for a couple of sparrows squabbling sleepily somewhere upstairs. They looked at each other and hurried to the room they had made their own.

Evelyn stopped suddenly when she saw Henry lying in his own blood. A whine rattled in her throat. Angel hurried to him and knelt, putting his hand on Henry's neck.

"He's still alive," Angel said.

Evelyn knelt beside them. Henry's face was the color of old ashes and his breath gurgled softly. "He's been shot," she said incredulously.

Angel nodded and straightened out Henry's twisted body.

"Can you help him?" she asked.

Angel looked at her helplessly. "I don't know what to do."

"Repair his wounds; heal him; do something," she said, hearing an hysterical edge on her words. "Can't you do that?"

"I think I could if I knew what I was doing. I'm not a doctor. I don't know the right things to do."

She started to say something else, but stopped when she saw the concentration on his face. After a moment his body relaxed. He looked at her. "I stopped the bleeding, but I think it's too late."

Henry moaned softly and began to cough. Angel put his hand on Henry's face and the coughing stopped. Henry opened his eyes weakly, but his eyes didn't focus.

"Angel?" he said, his voice whispery like the dry blade of grass.

"Yes, Henry. We're here."

"Angel? Where have you been all day?" Henry's voice drifted away for a moment and then came back. "Why did you leave us all alone? We need to make plans."

Evelyn looked at Angel's stricken face and felt an unbearable pain in her heart.

"Angel?" Henry said, his eyes closing. "Why didn't you save us?" His breath escaped slowly and he was still.

Angel twisted his hands together between his knees. His eyes clenched shut and tears rolled down his face. His shoulders heaved and his mouth gaped as if he could not get enough air.

"No," Evelyn whispered. "No." She grabbed him in her arms, but he twisted away and staggered to his feet. Then he froze, blinking the tears from his eyes. Haverstock leaned against the door frame, smiling pleasantly at them.

"Hello, children," he said. "Having a nice holiday?" He waved his hand negligently. Evelyn saw Angel stiffen, heard his breath wheeze in his throat.

She jumped to her feet. "Angel?" she cried and grabbed his arm.

Haverstock repeated the wave of his hand. "The gesture isn't necessary of course, but I fear I am a slave to theatricals. Don't worry about him, Miss Bradley." He walked casually to them. "He's perfectly all right. I don't know what little tricks he's learned since he's been out of my care. Whatever they may be, Angel, my boy, don't try any of them or the young lady will suffer for it." His eyes turned to agates. "Do I make myself absolutely clear?" he asked in a black voice.

Then his smile returned. "Did I interrupt at a dramatic moment?"

"Why are you doing this to us?" Evelyn said, her voice raspy.

"Now, now, my dear," he tut-tutted, "don't get upset." He looked around impatiently. "Louis!" he called, but there was no answer. He looked at Henry and sighed. "Louis is so impatient, and so untidy. No finesse at all," he clucked. "Louis! Where are you?" Dissatisfaction was sharp in his voice.

He motioned impatiently for Angel and Evelyn to move. She took Angel's arm and glanced at him with worry. He had a vague, confused expression on his face and tears dried on his cheeks. He moved like a marionette. Haverstock followed them, guiding them through the large house, looking for Louis.

"Angel, are you all right?" Evelyn whispered.

His voice formed in her ear, garbled and indistinct. "He's done something to my head. I can't . . . " His voice faded to noise and was gone.

When they reached the kitchen, Evelyn stopped suddenly. Haverstock stepped around them and walked to Louis, lying face down on the floor, the rusty ice pick in the back of his neck. Haverstock nudged him with his toe.

Tim ran from behind the cabinet while Haverstock's back was turned. He went to Angel's foot and climbed his

231

shoe. He ducked under the leg of Angel's trousers and climbed his sock. Evelyn saw the movement and her eyes widened. Tim lowered himself to his waist inside Angel's sock. He permitted himself a sigh of relief and a little smile of satisfaction.

Haverstock looked down at Louis and shook his head tragically. "Louis. I'm so very disappointed in you." He turned to Angel and Evelyn, spreading his hands magnanimously. "It appears that Tim has managed to elude Louis and defend himself rather cleverly. I shall miss Louis. Such a handsome young man, and so randy. It's true what they say about hot-blooded Latins." He began to applaud slowly. "Bravo, Tim, bravo!" he called. "Splendidly done!"

He stopped applauding and his voice became unpleasant. "However, I fear it has only postponed the inevitable. I'm taking Angel and Miss Bradley back to town now. I suggest you don't go outside, Tim. There are wild animals: wolves, foxes, coyotes, skunks, badgers, weasels, snakes, oh, and owls. I know they're out there because I'm gathering them right now. A solid ring, Tim. A solid ring of appetites around the house. I'm sure any of them would be delighted to see you step outside. You would make a very tasty morsel.

"I'll be back momentarily. I may even bring some friends with me. How would you like me to bring a hundred cats, Tim?" He laughed and ushered Angel and Evelyn from the house.

Outside, he turned to Evelyn. "I hope you aren't easily panicked, Miss Bradley. What you are about to experience is really quite startling to the uninitiated."

The three of them rose slowly from the ground. Evelyn gasped. "Don't be alarmed, Miss Bradley. I'm taking the two of you back to my wagon, where we will have a few of the creature comforts. I suggest you make the journey si-

232

lently. If you should see anyone and call out to them, you are forfeiting their lives. Is that quite clear?"

"Yes," she said.

"Very well. This will be quite breathtaking, but perfectly safe. Please remain calm." They began to move, drifting across the countryside, keeping low and away from signs of habitation. They followed Crooked Creek the last mile or so, staying between the trees and brush that lined the banks. They went under the bridge and circled around the depot, coming to the burned-out Wonder Show from behind. Evelyn saw no one on the street. Everything was closed but the café, and it would be soon. They settled to the ground behind the single remaining wagon. Haverstock opened the door and motioned them in. Angel went in first, still moving mechanically, his face blank. Haverstock bolted the door behind them.

He lit a hanging kerosene lamp. He adjusted the wick and sat in the chair at his desk. He breathed heavily and wiped perspiration from his forehead. Evelyn realized that he, like Angel, was physically tired after using the gift. He smiled, playing the host, and indicated the cot. Evelyn and Angel sat, but she wasn't sure if Angel was in control of his movements.

"Rather spectacular way to travel, don't you think?" Haverstock said, smiling. "Almost like magic."

Evelyn shrugged and he looked at her suspiciously.

"My," he said, laughing, "you are a spunky girl." He narrowed his eyes. "One would almost think you were experienced at this sort of thing." He opened one of the desk drawers and took out a bottle of brandy. He held it up and raised his eyebrows inquiringly.

Evelyn shook her head.

"It's the real thing," Haverstock said proudly. "Pre-Prohibition."

233

"No, thank you," Evelyn said.

Haverstock shrugged and poured some in a glass. "No point in offering it to Angel. He, too, is a teetotaler." He put the bottle back in the desk drawer. "Now, Miss Bradley, you must tell me all about the little adventures Angel has had since he left my company for yours. What sort of mischief has the dear boy gotten into?"

Tim crept from Angel's trouser leg and moved back under the cot against the wall. His mind was a whirling mass of fear and confusion. He had to do something to save Angel and Evelyn, but he didn't know what it could be. He put the thought aside and concentrated on his first objective: how to get out of the wagon. The door was closed and bolted. He had seen that from behind Angel's foot. The only other way was the small high window.

He moved to the end of the cot and behind a carton. He looked up. The window was open. But how to get up there? Haverstock sat almost directly below it. He studied a route. If he climbed the bookcases, he could crawl along the top and be within two inches of the window.

"How did you find us?" Evelyn asked, changing the subject.

"Oh, dear, I was hoping to spare you this."

"Spare me what?" she asked nervously.

"This is so distressing, so distressing. Your brother told me where you were." He frowned regretfully.

"I don't believe you," she said flatly, but then she remembered that Harold had not brought the food.

"Oh, rest assured that he didn't do it voluntarily. No, no, my child. Don't think harshly of your brother. He resisted for quite a long time. But, in the end, of course . . . " He spread his hands.

She felt dizzy. His voice echoed in her ears. "What did you do to him?"

234

"You really wouldn't want to know."

"Is he . . . all right?" But she knew.

"I'm afraid not, my dear," he said sadly, but his eyes twinkled. "There was no choice, you see."

"You killed him?" She could barely force the words through her tight throat.

Haverstock shrugged. "One of life's unfortunate necessities, I'm afraid. Such a shame, too. He was such a good-looking boy." He smiled wistfully and his eyes unfocused for a moment.

Evelyn began to sob quietly. Angel put his arms around her and held her to him. Haverstock watched them and smiled.

Tim inched along the top of the bookcase on his hands and knees. He reached the window and tried to decide the best way to get out.

"When your parents get home . . . " Haverstock shifted around in the chair and looked up at the high window. Tim ducked and rolled tightly against the trailer wall, his heart almost stopping. Haverstock stood and looked out the window, his head only inches from Tim. Only a bare afterglow of the sunset remained. He turned to face the two on the cot.

"Your parents must have gone home long ago, if they are like most farmer folk and have to be there to put the chickens to bed." He sat again in the chair. "They found your brother dead of a simple heart attack. No fuss. No alarms."

As Haverstock sat, Tim jumped onto the windowsill, swung his arms for balance, then dropped from sight. But Haverstock caught the movement from the corner of his eye. He jerked his head up but saw nothing. The window was empty and dark. He frowned in puzzlement, then got out of the chair. He unbolted the door and went outside. He looked around the wagon, then up at the window. A sleepy

235

sparrow, perched on the scrollwork above the window, looked back at him. Haverstock smiled and stopped the bird's heart. It fell to the ground like a stone.

"Can you do anything?" Evelyn whispered to Angel. He shook his head, the agony of Henry's death still on his face. "Tim will bring help," she whispered. Angel looked doubtful.

Haverstock came back in and rebolted the door.

Tim crawled from behind the wagon wheel and looked at the dead sparrow. He wished he had the gift and spent a few seconds on pleasant images of Haverstock taking months to die. But he had killed Louis; that he had done. A smile of grim pleasure twitched on his lips.

Then he looked around. Louis's black Model-T was parked beside the caravan. The burned-out Wonder Show lay in black, untidy heaps. Tim was undecided about what to do. He knew he had to get help, but he had no idea where to go for it. The logical place was the sheriff's office, but he didn't know where it was, unless it was in the courthouse at the other end of town. He began running in that direction.

"Will you tell me something?" Evelyn asked.

"Of course, my dear. Anything you want to know. There's no harm in it. Not now." Haverstock looked at her expectantly.

"Tell me about Angel, who he is, what his real name is. Tell me about his life before he joined the show."

Haverstock raised his eyebrows and then smiled at her expression and the way the two of them had never stopped touching since he found them. He leaned back in the chair and locked his fingers behind his head.

"Actually, I know practically nothing about him, but I'll

236

tell you what I can. But let me start back farther than that. You don't mind? I get so few opportunities to talk of my accomplishments. And they are quite remarkable, my dear, really quite remarkable."

Evelyn shook her head and kept her voice even. Their only chance was to stall until Tim could bring help. "No. I'd like to hear everything."

Tim ran down the street, looking for someone, anyone. But the street was deserted. The stores were closed and dark. Lights burned in a few houses. That might be better than going all the way to the courthouse. The sheriff's office was probably closed anyway. He changed directions and headed for the nearest light.

He stopped when the dog began to bark.

He looked around frantically and saw it, standing on the other side of the street, barking and looking at him. The dog launched itself suddenly and tore across the street, its claws clicking on the pavement. Tim ran in the opposite direction, not looking, not caring, only fleeing. He found himself in an alley, barrels and crates piled against the buildings. He dived behind a wooden crate as the dog skidded to a halt. Tim wormed his way into the narrow space until he could go no further.

The dog sniffed, its nose stuck in the opening. It began pawing at the crate and whining. Then it stopped and barked again. Tim held his ears against the sound and didn't hear the voice call the dog. It looked up at the voice, then back at the crate, tilting its head and perking its ears. It left reluctantly, glancing back occasionally.

Tim waited where he was for a while, getting his breath back and letting his heart slow down. Then he inched his way out and looked around. The dog was not in sight. He sneaked back to the street. The dog sat on its haunches on the other side, watching him. It stood up, whining, but didn't move toward him. Tim edged backward into the alley, then turned to look behind him. The alley went as far as the rear of the buildings and made a left turn at a solid wooden fence. He ran to the fence and looked. The alley ran behind the buildings the length of town. Strange shapes loomed all along the dark passage. Tim's tiny heart pounded with terrors a normal man could never know. He began to walk.

Haverstock pontificated.

"This will all be new to Angel, also, Miss Bradley. I thought it best not to clutter his mind with such things.

"First of all, I believe everyone has the gift. Don't look surprised, Miss Bradley. Even you have it, but it's so vestigial, so underdeveloped and untrainable you could never use it. It's a part of the evolutionary process." He smiled. "Though I don't suppose any of you in this little backwater community would know anything of that. Or accept it if you did. It's against your good Christian upbringing. In another million years, or thereabouts, I think everyone will have it. Fully developed. Of course, there will be those few born without it, just as some are now born deaf or blind or mute, as Angel was.

"There have been hundreds, thousands of recorded instances of people with unusual abilities. They could only have been those able to use a tiny fraction of the gift. I imagine those, like myself, able to develop it to any degree of perfection kept it to themselves.

"My own abilities were, unfortunately, fairly limited. I did what I could to develop them, but there were no guidelines. It's a little like trying to teach yourself to play the piano when you are tone deaf and can't read music." He smiled at his analogy.

238

* * *

Tim moved cautiously down the alley, looking around him nervously. The night's only sounds were the crickets and the faroff barking of a dog. Suddenly there was a new sound, a terrible, unbelievable sound that made him pale and his blood chill: the sound of a cat fight farther down the alley.

"There seem to be few limits to what can be done with the gift," Haverstock continued, "but specific knowledge is absolutely essential. I can, for instance, remove an appendix far more efficiently than a surgeon with a scalpel but, without medical knowledge, the gift would be as useless for the task as the scalpel would be without the same knowledge. I must confess that my study of medicine and biology was in part motivated by self-preservation."

He cocked his head at Evelyn. "How old do you think I am, Miss Bradley?"

"I don't know. About forty-five or fifty."

He smiled. "I'm eighty-two, almost eighty-three. I expect I could make myself look your age, but there's no point in it. Youth has certain disadvantages. I believe, with proper knowledge and care of the body, the gift can produce immortality." He smiled again. "Time will tell."

He shifted in the chair, making himself more comfortable. "That's where I centered my first experiments. I manipulated the cellular structure, the genes and chromosomes. It was incredibly easy to do. I could do with selection what nature occasionally does at random. I created new life forms.

"Oh, my successes didn't come right away," he deprecated. "It was almost a year before I could even sustain life. My experimental animals gave birth to dead things, some of them quite disgusting.

239

"My first unqualified success was a giant seven-headed snake. It was with the show for a while before it died. I created a lot of others. You saw two of them: the mermaid and the snake woman. They were the last," he sighed. "Now they're all gone. The snake woman was my last experiment with animals. She was so perfect I felt there was no point in exploring that avenue further. I could create any kind of creature I wanted. There was no longer a challenge.

"The next step was, naturally, to work with humans. So, I took a mistress." He grimaced. "Abysmal girl, but she served her purpose. It was all so very easy, no different really than working with animals. I did only four experiments before I realized that, too, was pointless.

"How did you like my children? They were my children, you know, conceived in the . . . ah . . . time-tested way. I merely manipulated their embryonic growth. Their mother, I'm afraid, went quite mad when the harpy was born. You never saw her. She was my first child. I had to perform a lobotomy on her mother. Improved her usefulness considerably. I only wish I had thought of it sooner.

"Medusa worked out rather well, though mentally she was an imbecile. The Minotaur was a splendid fellow. I was really proud of him, but he was too limited in intelligence and had nothing on his mind but sex." A smile flickered on his lips.

"I suppose my favorite is Tim. He's really quite brainy, but physically very limited, of course."

Tim stayed close to the buildings, creeping around clutter, staying hidden as much as possible, and looking for a passage back to the street. He felt helpless. He had taken so much time. It could already be too late. And what good would it do, anyway? If he brought the sheriff, Haverstock could kill him with a look. His feeling of helplessness quickly changed to hopelessness. He should have stayed in the wagon and tried to kill Haverstock the way he had killed Louis. But that had been a lucky fluke. It couldn't have happened twice. And Louis didn't have the gift.

The cat stepped from behind the garbage barrel and looked at Tim curiously. It was yellow and mangy and had lost half its tail in some forgotten fight. Tim's frayed nerves snapped. His brain no longer controlled his body. He screamed and ran.

The cat trotted after him and pinned him to the ground with its paw. It sat over him and nudged at him playfully. But Tim was not aware. He was lost in a red fog of mindless hysteria. The cat hopped about, rolling the small shrieking thing from side to side, its paw soft as velvet.

Another cat loped toward them, looking at Tim with interest. It was gray and dusty and blind in one eye. It reached out a paw and gave Tim a couple of quick swipes. The yellow cat snarled. The gray cat hissed and slapped at the other one. They tore into each other with claws and teeth and squalls of fury.

Tim staggered to his feet, his body still operating unconsciously. He ran a few steps and sprawled on his face. The gray disengaged and pounced on him. It picked him up in its mouth and faced the yellow, growling deep in its throat.

The yellow jumped the gray. They rolled in a tangle, their rear legs pumping like pistons, trying to disembowel each other. Tim was thrown sprawling, his clothes ripped and blood dripping from a dozen cuts and scratches. He got to his knees and began crawling, too weak to stand.

He bumped into something. It moved and made a faint rattling sound. He looked at it, trying to see through the fog. It was a tin can, a large one, probably from the café. It had been opened with a can opener and the jagged-edged top bent back. The surge of relief almost made him faint. He

241

looked over his shoulder at the squalling cats. They were still tearing at each other. He crawled to the can and worked himself inside it. It was sticky and smelled terrible, but he didn't care. He grabbed the jagged edge of the lid with both hands and pulled. It half closed and then sprang back. He felt new blood on his hands. He braced himself more securely and grabbed the lid again. The metal popped and bent so quickly he hit the bottom of the can, the breath knocked out of him. He shifted around and grabbed the lid again, pulling it in far enough that the cats couldn't hook it with their claws. Then he braced his feet against it so they couldn't push it in. Suddenly he started to laugh, and couldn't stop.

"Naturally, after that, I found it prudent to leave town rather hurriedly," Haverstock continued. "But I didn't want to destroy my children and my creatures. Then I chanced upon Mr. Carl Haverstock and his ratty little collection of dwarfs, Mongoloids, pinheads, and other mistakes of nature." He smiled. "My name, of course, isn't really Haverstock. I showed him my children and we became partners. Not only could I keep my creatures, but they would make money for me. I could continue my studies and would never be in one town long enough to arouse undue interest. It was an ideal situation.

"Mr. Haverstock, of course, quickly became a nuisance and I . . . ah . . . bought him out." He smiled.

"This is the part you've been waiting to hear, Miss Bradley. We were playing some hick town in Ohio or Indiana or somewhere. I don't even remember now, and it doesn't matter. In those days, my part of the show was a rather conventional magician act. Of course, with my ability, as limited as it was, I could do quite a few things to astound the audiences, things they had never seen done before.

242

"Then, one night while I was doing my act, some peculiar things began to happen. Things I wasn't causing to happen. I'm sure you will recognize my bewilderment. Then I saw him, sitting in the front row. He was smiling at me with his dirty, grubby, angelic little face, watching me with his little red eyes. Couldn't have been more than five years old.

"I knew right away he was doing it. After the show I asked about him. Everyone in town seemed to know him. He was quite a local character and the only albino most of them had ever seen. He was from the county orphan's asylum. He had run away to see the show.

"In a little while, an austere-looking woman in black came to take him back. I talked to her. She was only too glad to discuss him. It seems he had been nothing but a vexation to them, a thorn in her side, as she put it, since he was left on the asylum doorstep when he was about two. By parents who probably thought they had hatched a changeling. Small wonder if he was making use of the gift at that age.

"The people at the asylum couldn't keep track of him. Locking him up did no good. He always got out. Beating him did no good. He hardly seemed to feel it. He was mute, of course, and they couldn't communicate with him, couldn't make him say his catechisms. He was always running away if there was something interesting to see. But he always came back."

He shrugged. "If they'd left him alone there would have been no problem, but like all bureaucratic types, they saw their authority being frustrated. Angel and I were kindred spirits from the very beginning. As a result, I fear I have spoiled him beyond redemption.

"When I offered to take him, they were only too glad to be rid of him. I discovered later that Angel's ability was almost fully developed. He didn't know how to use it, and didn't really know he had it. Imagine, Miss Bradley, that you are the only person with power of speech. Everyone else is like Angel, mute. You wouldn't be able to use your ability because there would be no way to learn. You could make inarticulate noises that would astound and confuse and frighten those silent ones around you, but you could never actually speak.

"That's what Angel was doing, making inarticulate noises. So I began to teach him how to use his ability and, at the same time, develop my own. You realize, for my own security, I had to keep his ability a secret from him. That's why I always worked with him under hypnosis. It was slower—but safer. And of course, I had to teach him to read and write in order to communicate with him at all. He's very clever. Too clever by half, I fear.

"Now, Miss Bradley, thanks to your interference, that phase is over. I'm sure there is still more I could learn from Angel, but it's no longer worth the risk. He refused to go under the other day, and I don't know what mischief you've caused."

He sat on the edge of the chair and rubbed his hands together. "Well, I think I've told you everything you wanted to know, haven't I?"

"No," she answered him. "What are you planning to do now?"

He looked at her with a slightly startled expression on his face, as if he had not considered that question. 'Why, anything I want to do. Anything at all, Miss Bradley, anything at all. Perhaps I shall rule the world—if I should wake up one morning and *feel* like ruling the world. I have all of time ahead of me; there's no hurry, no hurry at all. I shall simply enjoy myself."

"Will you?"

"Most assuredly I will. Ah, you look at me with such bourgeois disapproval, Miss Bradley. What would you do, if you had the gift? Become a great healer of the sick, mender of the lame? Fill the world with more small-minded people who do nothing but take up space? They would hate you for it, Miss Bradley, hate, despise, and fear you. They would not rest until they had destroyed you."

He stood up. "Now I've entertained you long enough. There's no point in delaying this unpleasantness any longer; no point in your stalling. Help will not come. I'm really rather sorry this must happen. I've grown very fond of Angel, very fond. We spent many pleasant afternoons. However," he sighed, "I knew it must be done someday. It's only that the time has come sooner than expected. I just want you to understand, Miss Bailey. I'm doing this with no malice. It's strictly a matter of survival.

"Well, I have no more time to waste. I must get back out to your little retreat and dispose of Louis and Henry. I shall miss Louis. He was a comfort. But the world is full of young men. And, then, there's the matter of Tim.

"But you, Miss Bradley. I can't have you simply disappear like the others. It would cause inquiries and bothersome complications. A heart attack?" He frowned. "No. Too unimaginative. I told you I am a slave to theatricals. We need something more dramatic. I know—you will be found drowned in the river. A most tragic accident, but hardly a mystery."

He smiled at them with pursed lips. "Ah, but you look so nice together. It touches the poet in me. If you like, you may drown together. You'll be found floating in each other's arms. Very lyrical, don't you think? Just like Tristan and Isolde, Romeo and Juliet. There won't be a dry eye in the house. Shall we go?"

Haverstock looked at the water in Crooked Creek and smiled. "This will do nicely." He turned to Angel and Evelyn.

Evelyn tried to bury herself in Angel's chest. His arms

245

were tightly around her. Her brain was numb, anesthetized. It was unfair, so desperately unfair.

Angel's mind was packed in cotton batting. He poked at it, tore at it, tried to break through, tried to free his muffled senses. But each rent closed as fast as he opened it, and he fell back helplessly.

"You should make it into town by tomorrow noon," Haverstock continued. "The current is rather sluggish."

An involuntary whimper escaped Evelyn's throat.

"Now, Miss Bradley," he admonished. "You've been very brave. Don't break down now. It would only cause distress for us all. Think how badly poor Angel will feel, knowing he can do nothing to protect you."

A damp fog began forming around Angel and Evelyn. Then it was a mist, growing thicker until it coalesced into a globe of water like the one Angel had made as they sat in the sand. But this was larger; it enclosed their heads and shoulders. Evelyn fought at it with her hands, but they passed through it, scattering only a few drops. She put her hands flat on her face and tried to push it away, but nothing would dislodge it. She was drowning. She wouldn't be able to hold her breath much longer.

Angel ripped at the insulation around his mind. At first nothing happened. The rips resealed as quickly as he made them. Then a fury of desperation, fear, and hatred rose in him. He split the damping field and held it open. A cold wind of icy loathing swept away the last shreds.

The water exploded away from them, drenching Haverstock. Evelyn coughed and gasped for breath. Angel released her and stepped away.

"Don't move," his voice whispered in her ear.

Haverstock wiped the water from his face and looked at Angel in confusion. He met garnet eyes that seemed to strip away his skin. He felt a lump of ice in his stomach for a moment, but it went away.

246

"My, you have gotten into a lot of mischief, haven't you?" His voice was insolent with confidence. He sent a bolt of blue energy at Angel. It crackled and sizzled in the air. Angel flopped backward and rolled head over heels. He lay gasping for breath.

Haverstock hurled an identical bolt at Evelyn, but it spattered on the shield Angel had put around her. Evelyn screamed and trembled. She wanted desperately to run, but Angel had told her not to move. Haverstock's eyebrows rose. He looked at them speculatively. Angel rose groggily to his feet.

"Bravo," Haverstock sang. "Well done."

Angel sent a stream of flame at Haverstock, but he diverted it easily.

Haverstock smiled. "This will do you no good."

Angel concentrated. He had to make it just right. He had to make Haverstock think he was really talking, not using the gift in any way. "We'll see," he said, matching the vibration of Haverstock's eardrum to his lip movements, making the sound appear to come from his mouth.

Haverstock's eyes widened in consternation, then he smiled. "You have been a busy little bee, haven't you? How have you managed that? You must tell me."

"Why should I?" Angel asked.

Haverstock looked offended. "Dear boy! Didn't I tell you all my secrets?"

Angel smiled. "It's magic," he said.

Haverstock sent another bolt of energy, but Angel was prepared and swept it aside. It struck the ground and the dry buffalo grass ignited. Suddenly the earth split between Angel's feet. He toppled in and the earth closed with a crash like thunder.

Haverstock turned to Evelyn and smiled. He shrugged, dismissing Angel as a minor inconvenience. Evelyn watched through panic as he walked toward her.

247

She screamed when a shaft of flame erupted at his feet. He staggered backward, his hair singed. Angel stood in the center of the flame. It flickered out and the two men faced each other. A little frown of concern crossed Haverstock's face.

The sky above them darkened. The stars dimmed slowly and vanished behind black, boiling clouds laced by lightning. Angel looked up, feeling a little unsure, wondering what the other had in mind.

He sent a bolt of energy at Haverstock, but only started another grass fire. He launched a volley of bolts in rapid succession, but the older man diverted them all. Fires burned all around them. Smoke drifted across them, stinging Angel's eyes and burning his nose. He extinguished the fires and blew away the smoke. He watched Haverstock warily.

The clouds continued to thicken and lightning played across them almost continuously. Angel was ready when the first bolt speared down. It shied off him and blasted a smoking crater in the earth.

They watched each other.

"Theatricals again?" Angel asked.

Haverstock shrugged, but his face held a slightly strained expression. "I fear I have become a creature of habit. Well, my boy, it begins to look as if we are at an impasse. We accomplish nothing by throwing stones at each other, so to speak. We are both, pardon me, all three, shielded so that no outside force can reach us. You may be a bit stronger than I; oh, yes, I freely admit it, but you've forgotten what I said earlier. The gift is useless without the knowledge to use it properly. You see, your shield is perfectly adequate to keep out physical objects and force, but it can't keep out my mind."

Angel felt a terrible pain in his chest and knew that his

heart had stopped. He fought the pain and the creeping darkness and willed his heart into motion. He felt it tremble and, hesitantly, began beating. He was stronger than Haverstock, but the pain was almost more than he could bear. Haverstock was right; he could destroy Angel's body bit by bit, faster than he could repair it, if he could summon the knowledge to repair it at all. Soon he would grow too weak to resist and it would be over.

There had to be another kind of shield, one that would keep out another's mind. He had been able to do other things simply by willing it, not really knowing how he did it, pulling the knowledge from his subconscious without understanding what he was doing.

He willed it, visualizing an encasing mirror that reflected everything from him. He built it, strengthened it, shored it where it faltered. And the pressure on his heart ceased. It beat strongly again and he gulped air. But he couldn't get enough; he couldn't see and his ears rang. He had shut out everything, even light and sound and air.

Quickly, he opened the shield, enlarged it, included Evelyn within it, and closed it. She gasped and whimpered at the sudden darkness. He took her in his arms.

"Don't be frightened," he said. He felt her nod against his chest.

He experimented with the shield, carefully, letting in air and light, but only air and light. He felt Haverstock's mind nudging at him, but he shut it out. Then he probed, but couldn't get through the shield himself. He adjusted it, made it reflective on the outside and absorbent on the inside.

He probed Haverstock again and met his own reflection.

Haverstock smiled. "It seems you've picked up more over the years than I thought," he said. "And we are again at an impasse."

Angel pressed against Haverstock's shield. If he was stronger, he had to use that strength soon, before Haverstock came up with something he couldn't handle. He willed the other's shield away, but it remained. He willed it again, with as much strength as he could summon. Nothing happened, but he felt as if something had changed. He explored the shield and found it, a thinning. He pushed his way through, carefully, very carefully, to prevent Haverstock's detecting him. He didn't need much, just a tiny amount of himself. Slowly, he threaded his way through a mirror maze, backing up when he came to dead ends, carefully not touching anything.

Then he was through. He touched Haverstock's eardrum.

"You may be right," he said, "but I don't think so. . . . "

Angel's voice rose in pitch, became a piercing high-frequency shriek. Haverstock's eardrum shattered. He screamed and clamped his hands over his ears, but the noise was originating inside his head, not outside. Angel increased the pitch. Blood vessels ruptured. Nerves short-circuited from the overload.

Haverstock's shield faltered. Angel shattered it, brushed it aside. He didn't need special knowledge to rip and tear.

Haverstock's eyes bulged. His scream gurgled in his throat. Blood spattered from his mouth. The scream continued without sound.

Angel stepped away from Evelyn, dropping his own shield. He looked at the electricity-filled clouds above him and raised his hands over his head, fists clenched. Fiercely, he brought his arms down. Lightning dropped from the clouds and struck Haverstock. He flopped like a broken marionette and lay in a pile. His clothes smoldered and his flesh was seared.

Angel brought his arms down repeatedly. Lightning ripped at the other man, one crashing bolt after the other.

His flesh was blackened, roasted, riven, and pulverized. Angel brought his arms down again and didn't raise them. There was no reason for the movement of his arms except the muscular release it gave him. The last bolt of lightning cauterized the crater, leaving nothing but smoking raw earth.

Evelyn had covered her eyes. She could watch neither Haverstock's destruction nor Angel's fury. A cold fear seeped through her, but she remembered what Angel had said: "Never be afraid of me or what I can do." His voice had been tender and loving, but it didn't make any difference. Already her flesh was aching for his.

She looked up at the sudden silence. Angel dropped to his knees with exhaustion. His head fell back; his eyes closed, his mouth open, drawing in air.

It rained. The black clouds had swollen beyond containment. Evelyn walked toward Angel, then ran. The rain was cool; it washed away the dirt and soot. She fell to her knees beside him and pulled his head to her breast. He clutched at her.

After a moment he looked up at her, the rain matting his white hair. "Am I different than he was?" he said, not moving his lips.

"Yes," she said. "Very different."

"I've done nothing but kill since I learned to use the gift. Kill and act like an irresponsible child. Haverstock and poor Henry and Tim . . . " He stopped. "We have to find Tim. He's out in the dark all alone."

"We'll find him; then we'll go home. My parents . . . " A lump of pain caught in her throat. "My parents will be worried about me."

She helped him to his feet and they started toward town.

32.

The black Model-T Ford sat beside the painted circus wagon in the still heat of late August. The mess of the burned-out tent show had been cleaned up, but the grass hadn't grown back yet. The people of Hawley scarcely noticed the wagon and the car anymore. They had become a part of the landscape, curiosities grown common.

Phineas Bowen and Jack Spain quickly crossed the street, using only the sides of their bare feet on the blistering pavement. They hopped with relief onto Old Miss Sullivan's Bermuda grass and peered pensively back across the street.

"Wonder what they're gonna do with 'em," Finney mused.

"I heard my pa say the sheriff was gonna put 'em up for auction," Jack said. "He said the wagon had a lotta valuable old books in it."

"Yeah?" Finney said with perking interest. "Wonder why Angel didn't want 'em?"

"Guess a circus wagon isn't much good on a farm."

"Hey!" Finney piped. "Maybe I could get my pop to buy it for me."

Jack frowned. "What do you want it for? School starts next week and the summer's over. Circus wagons are part of the summer. They're no good after school starts."

"Yeah, I guess you're right," Finney sighed. "It was a good summer, though, wasn't it?"

Jack grinned. "Sure was."

They ran toward Crooked Creek, laughing and shoving, hopping quickly over the hot spots.

"The best summer I've ever had," Finney yelled. "A phantasmagorical summer. Something happening all the time."

A truck passed them and stopped at the depot. A woman dressed in dark traveling clothes got out. She put on her hat and pinned it, then took a straw valise from the back of the truck. She said something to the driver and went into the depot. The truck turned around and went back the way it had come.

"There goes Miz Gardner," Jack said, "off to Kansas City again. Ma says Miz Gardner's sister is lingering."

"What does that mean?"

Jack shrugged, then he stopped. "Look, there's Rosie and her mama. Where they going?"

Finney stuck his nose in the air. "You know Mamzelle Willet don't like to be called 'Rosie.'"

Jack sniggered.

"Mom said Rose is going to St. Louis to visit the judge's sister. Said she won't be comin' back till next year," Finney said.

"Who cares?"

"Why'd you ask?" Finney gave Jack a shove and grinned suddenly. "Wait'll next summer. There'll be something even better than Haverstock's old Wonder Show."

253

"Of course," Jack laughed. "Every summer's better than the last one."

They ran on across the bridge and down the bank. They shucked their clothes and jumped in the water, splashing and laughing.